SWEET GERANIUMS,
AND SODA BREAD, TOO

Also by Elizabeth Nielsen

Soda Bread on Sunday

SWEET GERANIUMS
AND SODA BREAD, TOO

by

Elizabeth Nielsen

RIVERCROSS PUBLISHING, INC.
Orlando

ISBN: 1-58141-033-6

Library of Congress Catalog Card Number: 99-23222

First Printing

Library of Congress Cataloging-in-Publication Data
Nielsen, Elizabeth, 1933-
    Sweet geraniums and soda bread too / by Elizabeth Nielsen.
        p.   cm.
    ISBN 1-58141-033-6 (hc)
    1. Irish Americans—History Fiction.   I.   Title.
PS3564.I3493S94   1999
813'.54—dc21   99-23222
                                                                CIP

For my Uncle Vincent John Nielsen,
Annie's little boy.

SWEET GERANIUMS,
and Soda Bread, Too

CHAPTER 1

Annie Enright couldn't believe over a year had passed since she first set foot in America. She was happy to be living in New York City, a place she'd heard about all her life. Things were strange to her at first, but she soon got used to it. Annie was eighteen years old and considered herself very grown up. She'd be an American if she had anything to say about it. Annie was a warm and friendly girl and made friends easily.

It was 1901 when she'd left her home in the Craggs, a section of Askeaton in Ireland. Many years before, her father Cornelius had come to America and earned enough money to return to Ireland and buy the ten-acre farm in the Craggs. He'd married Annie's mother, Anne Fitzgerald, and raised a family. He'd promised his sons, young Cornelius, William, Michael, and Jack, they could go to America someday if they wanted to. That had been Annie's dream since she was a little girl and she convinced her father that she should go, too.

"Old Da," as the children called their father, filled their heads with tales of his great adventure. He told them they'd have to work hard, and warned them of the pitfalls. The children would sit around the long wooden table in the little cottage and listen to his stories. Annie was sure he was making half of them up.

"It's a grand place," Old Da would say. "A place of opportunity to be sure. Living in Ireland when I was a boy was hard, but not as hard as me dear old father had it."

Cornelius Enright had been born several years after the potato famine. His father told him of the terrible starvation of the Irish people.

"He told me they were mostly tenant farmers, and when the crops failed they were thrown out of their cottages. It was a terrible sight to see families walking the roads begging for a crust of bread for their wee ones," Cornelius said. "He told me the only way to survive is to own me own land. If your crop failed, you still had a roof over your head. Land is more important than bread."

Anne Fitzgerald Enright died in 1893 when Annie was only ten years old. She was buried in the graveyard of the Robertstown Church in Askeaton. Annie was lost without her, but knew it was now her job to care for the family and run the little cottage. The boys worked the farm with their father.

After a proper time of mourning, Cornelius married the widow Rose Maloney, a woman of means. At first, Annie didn't care for her and resented her taking her mother's place. In time, Annie grew to love Rose and knew she'd take care of her father.

Annie's oldest brother, young Cornelius, decided to stay in Ireland and run the farm. He married Nellie Sullivan, a local farm girl, and they had a child. William, Michael, and Jack, Annie's other brothers went to America a few months

10

before Annie. Each boy was given money, but warned to find work as soon as possible.

Old Da was sure his children would do well, but he did worry about Jack, who was always getting into mischief. Old Da had broken many a switch on Jack's backside when he was a little boy. Jack had bright red hair and green eyes. He was the best looking of the boys, and knew it. William and Michael were much alike. They were the same size and had light brown hair and blue eyes. They were hard-working and most reliable young men.

The boys had been advised to learn how to drive automobiles. That was the coming thing in America and many of the wealthy were looking for chauffeurs. So that is what they did, and Michael and William soon found good jobs. Michael worked for a family in New York City, while William got a position in Greenwich, Connecticut, a small town just twenty miles away.

Jack wasn't doing as well. He'd been fired from two jobs in a short time. He drank too much and liked nothing better than a good fight. He'd been arrested for brawling, which was an embarrassment to his brothers. They hoped Annie would straighten him out.

When Annie first arrived, she rented a room in a boarding house in a section of New York City called Red Hook. Jack had a room there as well. It wasn't the way she'd planned to start her life in America, but she was satisfied. The boarding house was run by Mrs. O'Brien, who catered to Irish immigrants. She knew how hard it was to come to a new place, and wanted to make her boarders feel at home. The boarding house was three stories and made of brick. On the window sills were pots of red geraniums, Annie's favorite flowers.

From the minute Annie met Mrs. O'Brien she liked her. Mrs. O'Brien was a large woman with red cheeks and snow white hair. She pinned her hair at the back of her head and always wore bright print dresses. She would be a good friend to Annie.

Annie worked in a factory sewing pieces of shirtwaists together, but she didn't care for it. "If you don't die of boredom, you'll die of heat prostration," she'd say. "Then in winter, they freeze the backside off you."

The money wasn't good, so Annie decided to look for a position in one of the fine homes in the city. She was a good housekeeper and cook, and felt sure she could learn to be a ladies' maid. Annie was attractive, well mannered, and knew how a proper young lady should act. She had long, light brown hair with streaks of gold running through it, braided neatly and pinned at the back of her head. Her eyes were blue and her cheeks would turn pink at the slightest embarrassment. She didn't want to leave the boarding house, but knew she could always visit on her days off.

Annie talked it over with Mrs. O'Brien, and decided to give notice at the factory. She said good-bye to the other workers and was out the door. Even though her salary at the factory was small, she had managed it well and had put a little aside. She was looking forward to spending time with Mrs. O'Brien while she looked for a new job.

"Yoo hoo, I'm back!" Annie called as she entered the boarding house.

"Hello, deary," Mrs. O'Brien said. "Are you finished with the factory?"

"Yes, I am. Thank the good Lord," Annie said.

"It'll be lovely having you home for a while. Would you be liking a nice cup of tea?" Mrs. O'Brien said as she got out the cups.

"That'd be lovely," Annie said.

"Are you sure you're wanting to work private?" Mrs. O'Brien said. "Some of those swells aren't very nice."

"Well, I won't know until I try," Annie said.

"Very true, very true. I'll be sending out the word you're looking."

"You know more people than God," Annie laughed. "If anyone can help, it will be you."

"Come along, deary, and give me a hand with the evening meal," Mrs. O'Brien said.

By six o'clock, the other boarders were arriving home from work. Annie knew all of them and greeted them as they took their places at the big table. Mrs. O'Brien had invited William and Michael to dinner as a little surprise for Annie.

"It's lovely to see you," Annie said to William. "How's your darling wife?"

"Just fine, to be sure," William answered.

"Yeah, she's fine all right," Jack teased. "Still bossing the bejesus out of him."

"Never you mind," William said. "You should be so lucky to find a girl like me Alexandra."

Much to Annie's surprise, William had met and married Alexandra only a month after he'd arrived in America. She was the chambermaid on the estate in Greenwich where he'd gotten his job. Alexandra was half Irish and half Polish, a thing that Jack took great delight in teasing his big brother about.

"We all know which is the good half," Jack laughed.

William would pretend not to hear him, knowing he was only trying to get a rise out of him. Annie liked Alexandra right off, and they became good friends. William would bring his new wife to visit his sister, but Annie'd never been to Greenwich to visit them. On her days off, William and Alexandra always seemed to have to work.

Mrs. O'Brien was a devout Catholic and insisted grace be said before every meal. That always made Annie feel good as it was something her mother had done back home in the Craggs. As children, they didn't dare put one morsel of food in their mouths until grace was said. Everyone bowed his head as Mrs. O'Brien chose a boarder to say it.

"Annie dear, I believe it's your turn," Mrs. O'Brien said.

"Yes, it is," Annie replied.

She said the prayer softly and made the sign of the cross. She was seated next to Jack, who nudged her.

"Good thing she doesn't ask me," Jack whispered.

"Why? Mother taught you your prayers, too," Annie said.

"I don't remember half of them," Jack laughed.

"If you said them more often you wouldn't be forgetting. You should be ashamed of yourself," Annie scolded. "What would our dear mother be saying, God rest her soul?"

Mrs. O'Brien passed the food around the table. Annie laughed watching Jack clean his plate. He was always hungry and never seemed to get his fill. Annie finished her meal and sat back as Mrs. O'Brien passed soda bread around. Annie knew it wasn't as good as her own, and would have given her recipe to Mrs. O'Brien, but her mother had made her swear she'd never give it away. It was a family secret. Only her sisters-in-law were to be given it, and that was only for the sake of her brothers.

Michael finished his meal and stood up, saying it was time to leave. William had to catch the train to Greenwich as he'd be on call first thing in the morning. Jack was staying at Mrs. O'Brien's for the time being, when Michael and William were paying his rent since he'd lost his job. They told him they couldn't support him much longer, and he better stay out of the bars. Jack promised to behave and try to find work.

When the meal was finished, Mrs. O'Brien's roomers said good night and left. Jack walked Annie to her room. It was on the third floor and faced the street. Jack's was on the third floor, too, but was at the back and overlooked an alley. Annie's room was small, but it suited her. It had lovely wallpaper with cornflowers and pale green leaves. It was much like the paper on the walls in her room at her stepmother's cottage. She'd only lived there a short time, but would never forget it. Only people of means could afford wallpaper in the Craggs.

There were blue drapes on the one window. It was a lovely summer evening, so the drapes were open to let in air. Annie looked out of the window and watched the people down below. The street was lit, and would be busy until late at night. Jack said good night and left. Annie took off her dress and hung it up for the next day. She brushed her hair and stood in front of the mirror. She always thought herself as a plain girl. She looked at the china Madonna that her mother had given to her. It sat on the nightstand. She lit a candle and said her prayers. She lay back on the clean white sheets and watched the lights that danced on the ceiling. Within minutes, she was fast asleep.

The next morning, Annie woke with a start. She could hear a trolley passing in the distance and the calls of the peddlers starting the day. She looked out the window at the street below. It seemed to be fresh and clean in the morning sun. It'd rained the night before and washed away the grime. She dressed as fast as she could, not wanting to be late for breakfast. Annie was washing her face in the china basin when she heard a knock on the door.

"Are you up yet?" Jack called, as he stuck his head in the door. "Hurry up! I'm starving. Mrs. O'Brien is cooking up something awful good by the smell of it."

Annie fixed her hair and went down with Jack. She laughed to herself thinking nothing ever changed. Jack was always hungry. As a little boy he could eat more than his older brothers put together.

Mrs. O'Brien sat next to Annie and poured a cup of tea. Most of the boarders had gone to work, so the house was quiet. Many of the young girls worked in the dress factories, and Annie was glad she didn't have to go with them. That was one place she wouldn't miss.

"Hope you slept well, deary," Mrs. O'Brien said.

15

"Just fine, thank you," Annie said.

Jack ate with gusto as the ladies watched. Annie scolded him, saying he'd choke putting too much food in him mouth. He finished before Annie'd taken a bite, and was out the door.

"See you tonight," Jack called as he left.

"Have you ever seen the likes of him?" Annie laughed.

Mrs. O'Brien sat stirring her tea, making a clinking sound on the side of the cup. Annie could see she was a million miles away.

"A penny for your thoughts," Annie said.

"I was just thinking about me darling husband, Patrick. This is the tenth anniversary of his death, and I'm feeling a bit blue," Mrs. O'Brien said. "Would you be going to church with me? I'd like to light a candle for him."

"Of course I'll go. I'll be lighting one for me husband, too," Annie said.

"Jack told me you'd been married in the old country, but you've never said anything about it. Jack got very upset when I asked him," Mrs. O'Brien said. "What was his name?"

"Robert Gilmour. He was Jack's best friend," Annie said.

"Why aren't you using his name?" Mrs. O'Brien asked.

"It got mixed up when I came through Ellis Island. They used me name from me birth papers. I tried to straighten it out, but they wouldn't listen, so I have to use Enright," Annie said.

"Well, that's a fine name, to be sure," Mrs. O'Brien said. "I've wanted to ask you about your husband, but thought you'd tell me when you were ready."

"He died on the way over, poor thing," Annie said. "He was ill before we left, but never let on. We'd planned to come to America for ever so long, and he didn't want his illness to stop us. I should have known, but I was so full of meself coming here I didn't think about anything else. We had wonderful plans. He was of the gentry, but loved farming. We were going to buy a lovely farm and raise a big family. The blame is on me."

"It wasn't your fault, deary," Mrs. O'Brien said.

"He'd contracted typhus on a trip to Dublin. He died only five days out to sea. The doctor could do nothing for him," Annie said, as a tear rolled down her cheek. "They buried him at sea. It was awful seeing his poor body slip into the black water. They did it at night so that no one would know. They swore me to secrecy. If the authorities here in America knew there was typhus on the ship, they would have sent it back."

"That's so sad," Mrs. O'Brien said. "Me Patrick died of the fever. He's buried here in the city."

"At least you can visit his grave," Annie said.

"Oh well, this is no way to be starting a lovely day," Mrs. O'Brien said as she wiped away the tears. "Look at the pair of us. Two old widows crying in our tea."

Mrs. O'Brien gave Annie a hug and started to clear the table.

"What are your plans this fine day," Mrs. O'Brien asked.

"I don't have any," Annie said.

"Well, then get your hat, deary. I'll be taking you to market with me," Mrs. O'Brien said.

"I'd like that," Annie said, as she got up to get ready.

Mrs. O'Brien took Annie's arm as they walked down the crowded street. They passed a bakery, a fish market and a fruit store. The aroma from the different shops reminded Annie of market day in Askeaton. There were brightly colored awnings shading the lovely food from the sun. On the sidewalk were pushcarts. Some had clothing for sale, while others sold household goods. There even was a flower cart with every kind of flower to be had. Some children were playing hopscotch on the sidewalk, and Annie had all she could do not to join them. Ladies gathered in small groups passing the time of day. As they made their way through a crowd, Mrs. O'Brien stopped to introduce Annie to a woman who was haggling over the price of a pot.

"What are you doing, Mrs. Flanagan? Trying to get a bargain?" Mrs. O'Brien laughed.

"To be sure. I love a good bargain," she said.

"I want you to be meeting one of my boarders. This is Annie Enright," she said.

"How do you do?" Mrs. Flanagan.

"Pleased to meet you," Annie said.

"Annie's looking for a position as a domestic. If you hear of anything, will you let me know?" Mrs. O'Brien said.

"Be glad to, deary," Mrs. Flanagan said. "Where are you off to?"

"We're off to church, then to do a bit of shopping," Mrs. O'Brien said.

"Say a prayer for me," Mrs. Flanagan called after them.

The church was dark. Annie dipped her fingers into the holy water and made the sign of the cross. They lit candles and said a prayer. Going to church always made Annie feel good. They dropped a few coins in the collection box and left. There would be no more sad thoughts that day.

They went to Delaney's Butcher Shop down the street. After Mrs. O'Brien made her purchases, they sat in the park for a time. It was as lovely as the park in Askeaton, and brought back sweet memories for Annie.

"It's getting late. If I don't get me meat home, it'll be going bad. I wouldn't want to be poisoning me boarders," Mrs. O'Brien laughed.

Annie carried Mrs. O'Brien's basket as they strolled back to the house. The sun was shining and the sky was clear. Annie loved living in New York, but did miss the Craggs and her Old Da. She did enjoy being with Mrs. O'Brien, however, it was almost like having a mother again.

A month passed before Mrs. O'Brien heard of a position for Annie. A chambermaid was needed at the home of the Thomson family. Mrs. O'Brien got the "lowdown" on the family, as she put it.

There were two old sisters that lived in a brownstone in Benedict Court. Their father had immigrated from Scotland and made a fortune in coal. Mr. and Mrs. Thomson died many years ago and left their children very well off, but with all their wealth, the sisters weren't known for their generosity or kindness. They were spoiled and demanded a great deal of attention. Some of the household help didn't stay long. Annie thought about it and decided to apply for the job.

"I'll do me best, and if it isn't good enough they can throw me out," Annie giggled.

They better be good to you, or they'll be hearing from me," Mrs. O'Brien said as she put up her fists and laughed.

CHAPTER 2

The day of the interview arrived. Annie pressed her black dress and attached a clean white collar. She brushed her hair and put on her best straw bonnet. Jack offered to walk Annie to the Thomson house and wait for her.

Down the street they walked, Jack tipping his hat to all the ladies. He'd made many friends in a short time, most of them girls. Annie noticed that his red hair was curling over his collar.

"You're needing a haircut," Annie said.

"Yeah, I know. How about giving me a trim? I haven't got the price of a cut," Jack said.

"You've got to get a job and keep it," Annie said.

"Don't start nagging. You sound like William."

As they walked, Annie could see the neighborhood change from small tenement houses and noisy streets to big

20

brownstones and quiet. There were a few carriages and automobiles driven up and down the street by men in black suits
and hats that had a shiny peak. There wasn't any pushcarts
on these streets, and the few children they saw walked with
nannies who were wearing white dresses, stiff white caps and
navy blue capes.

As they passed an expensive-looking china shop, Annie saw a sign on the door. It read, "Help Wanted. No Irish
Need Apply."

" 'No Irish need apply,' " Annie said. "What the
bejesus does that mean?"

"Just what it says," Jack said. "They don't hire Irish."

"Why not?"

"They think we're ignorant and dirty," Jack said.

"The nerve of them! Who the bleeding Hell do they
think they are?"

"There's a lot of prejudice in this country. Them used
to be fighting words for me, but now I don't pay any attention
to it," Jack laughed. "You better watch your swearing. It
isn't very ladylike."

"Look who's telling me not to swear!" Annie said as
she punched his arm.

Jack read the house numbers as they walked along
Benedict Court.

"Number nine. This is the one," Jack said.

Annie looked up at the big house. It had three floors
with long windows, and a fourth with small windows which
she guessed to be the attic. The front door was painted black
and had a brass kickplate and bellpull. There was a wrought
iron fence in front with two gates. One went to the front
door, and the other led to a walk that went to the back. On
the bigger gates was a brass plate that read "Thomson, 9
Benedict Court."

"I'm so nervous. Come with me," Annie said.

"I can't do that. What'll they be thinking? Go around
to the kitchen door. Somebody will come," Jack ordered.

Annie did as Jack said and walked down the alley between the houses. In the back of the house was a lovely flower garden surrounded by a brick wall. She saw steps leading down to what looked to be the basement.

"That must be the kitchen," Annie said out loud, then she thought, "I must stop talking to meself. They'll be thinking me daft."

Annie rang the bell, and the door was opened by a smiling woman wearing a white dress and a cap that covered her hair. Her hands were big and red, much like her face. The kitchen behind her was filled with steam from pots cooking on the stove.

"What can I be doing for you, deary?"

"I've come about the position as chambermaid," Annie said shyly.

"Come in, miss. Have a seat and I'll be letting me ladies know you're here."

The cook told the scullery maid, who told the butler, who told the Thomson sisters that a young lady was there to see about the position. Annie sat there shaking. She'd never applied for a job before, but knew she was a hard worker and learned fast. The butler returned and told Annie to follow him. He was tall and thin, and wore a black suit and stiff white shirt. His nose was stuck in the air as if smelling something bad. Annie wanted to laugh, but knew better to.

The house had large rooms with high ceilings. There was a center stairway that rose to the top floor. Annie followed the butler up the stairs from the kitchen into the main foyer. There was a chandelier hanging from the second floor ceiling. It was the biggest she'd ever seen, and she hoped they wouldn't ask her to clean it. The floor was laid with black and white tile in a lovely pattern. Annie admired the grandfather clock that stood near the front door. It was beautifully carved mahogany, and almost reached the ceiling. The sound of ticking echoed through the foyer.

Annie was ushered into a large room. Seated at a small tea table were the Thomson sisters. She curtsied and waited to be spoken to. The sisters didn't say a word as they looked her up and down. Annie felt like a prize cow at a county fair.

"Do you have papers?"

"Yes, madam," Annie said.

She handed her papers over. As they studied them, Annie looked around the room. It had windows from floor to ceiling covered in lace curtains and dark brown velvet drapes. The furniture was carved and heavy-looking. In the center of the ceiling was another chandelier, and there were lamps on every table. The floors were highly polished, and the carpets were thick, and done in a floral design. In the corners were potted ferns. There were many fine figurines on the tables, along with family photos in silver frames and bowls of flowers. A portrait of a stern-looking man hung over a huge fireplace. She thought he must be their father. Annie didn't imagine there was a houseboy for the dirty work. She guessed she'd be the one to clean out the ashes.

"You understand that you will have to clean and help wait table?" Miss Thomson said.

"Yes, madam."

"You must be very careful with the figurines when you dust them. They are very valuable, and the silver frames must be polished once a week. Of course you will also be expected to tend to our personal needs."

"Yes, Miss Thomson," Annie said.

"I prefer to be called Miss Jemima, and my sister is to be called Miss Lizzie. It creates less confusion since we're both Miss Thomson. Your name is Annie Enright?"

"Yes, madam," Annie said.

Miss Jemima was short and thin. She had gray hair that was braided and wound tightly around her head. On her nose were spectacles with gold rims. They were very thick, and she squinted as she peered at Annie. She wore a navy blue dress with a high white lace collar and cuffs. Annie could see the whale bones outlined under her dress, and saw that her corset was laced very tightly. Annie wondered how the old lady could breath.

Miss Lizzie sat quietly doing needlepoint, dropping the clipped threads on the floor. She motioned to Annie to pick them up.

"Well, what do you think? Should we hire her?" Miss Jemima asked.

"She'll do. Looks strong enough," Miss Lizzie said.

"You're hired. Bring your things this weekend and start Monday morning," Miss Jemima said.

"Thank you, ladies. I'll be working hard for you."

"You will, or you won't be here for long. We pay eight dollars a month, room and board. You'll have Thursday and every other Sunday off."

"I'd like to be going to Mass on Sunday mornings, if that's all right," Annie said.

"Yes, but you'll have to go to six o'clock Mass and be back to serve breakfast at seven."

The butler arrived to escort Annie out. Miss Lizzie called her back.

"Hand me the scissors, girl," she said.

Annie walked back across the big room and handed Miss Lizzie the scissors that were three inches within reach. She took a closer look at the second Miss Thomson.

Miss Lizzie was better looking than Miss Jemima. She had dark curly hair and brown eyes. She was a bit over-weight, and Annie knew she liked her sweets by the pile of candy wrappers that lay on the table. Miss Lizzie wore a pink dress and a woolen shawl. It was a hot day, and Annie wondered why she needed a shawl. She'd learn that Miss Lizzie was always cold no matter what the temperature was. Annie curtsied and left the room. She followed the butler down the stairs to the kitchen.

The cook was waiting to see if she'd gotten the job. Annie said she had, and would be starting Monday morning.

The cook invited Annie to sit, and poured her a cup of tea. Annie looked around the spotless kitchen and admired the huge black coal stove. There was a black cast-iron skillet sitting on the back burner. It had a glass lid, and Annie could see a lovely stew simmering in it. Against the other wall was a double porcelain sink. The floor was wood, and in one corner was a large icebox. In the center of the room was a worktable with a marble top. In another corner were a table and chairs where the servants took their meals. Hanging from the ceiling were rows and rows of shining copper pots.

"Me name's Mary. I'm the one that runs the show down here," she laughed. "It'll be nice having you with us."

"Where are you from," Annie asked, noting the strong Irish accent.

"I'm from County Cook. Me husband and I came here twenty years ago, but he was killed in an accident soon after we came. God rest his soul!" Mary said as she made the sign of the cross.

"That's a shame," Annie said.

"They say men are the strong ones, but we women seem to last longer."

"It seems that way," Annie said.

Annie had a sadness of her own, but felt she didn't know this woman well enough to tell her. Maybe some day she would.

"What do you think of the two old biddies?" Mary said.

"I haven't formed an opinion yet. What are they like?"

"Work hard and stay out of their way. Never speak unless spoken to. They're very demanding and expect to be waited on hand and foot. Old Mr. Thomson spoiled them rotten. Miss Jemima is more persnickety, and runs things. Miss Lizzie wants her own way and has a royal fit if she doesn't get it. They're usually pretty quiet, unless they have a fight. Then the roof comes off the house and they can be heard for miles around," Mary laughed. "Don't worry, deary. You'll do fine to be sure."

"They told me what was expected of me, but they never mentioned the floors and windows," Annie said. "They didn't say anything about taking out the ashes, either."

"That's not your job, deary," Mary said. "We have a girl to do that."

As they sat there, the scullery maid entered. She was very thin and had wisps of graying hair falling from her dust cap. Annie noticed she had a limp and dragged one foot a bit.

"This is Nancy," Mary said. "She does the jobs you were talking about."

"Nice to meet you," Annie said.

"How do you do," Nancy said as she disappeared into a back room.

"What's the butler's name?" Annie asked.

"Charles Powers. He's as Irish as Paddy's pig, but lets on he's English. He thinks it makes him high class," Mary laughed.

The clock struck eleven, and Annie realized Jack's been waiting a long time.

"I must be leaving. Me poor brother's outside and will be thinking I got lost," Annie laughed.

"He could have come in. This is me kitchen, and I do as I please. I was hired by old Mr. Thomson, and they wouldn't dare mess with me. I know too much," Mary said. Besides the two old ladies never come to the kitchen. "Bring him with you when you move in.

Annie thanked her and was out the door. Jack was standing across the street flirting with one of the housemaids, so he hadn't minded waiting.

"How'd you do?" he asked.

"Just fine. I got the job," Annie said. "The cook said you can come with me on Monday if you want, but you'd better behave."

"Good. I'd like to get a look in one of these swell houses," Jack said.

"I hope I'll like working for these people," Annie said.

"You're an official pot wrestler now," Jack laughed.

"Whatever do you mean?" Annie asked.

"That's what they call girls who work as domestics," Jack said.

"Away with you! Stop teasing me," Annie said.

"I'm not joking. You're a pot wrestler."

"No one better be calling me that, or they'll get a good smack for their trouble," Annie said.

"You get Thursday off, don't you?" Jack said.

"What of it?" Annie replied.

"They call that 'pot's day out,' " Jack laughed.

"Away with you! I'll not be believing a word of it," Annie said, as she punched him in the arm with all her might.

"Stop that!" Jack yelled as if she'd killed him.

They walked home slowly, talking about the future. Annie was glad she had work. She would write to her father and Rose tonight and tell them about her job. Her father'd think it fine, but Rose would be horrified, thinking it was beneath her.

Monday morning arrived. Annie was happy about her new job, but a bit nervous. It didn't take her long to settle in at the Thomson house. Her room was on the top floor. Mary and Charles had rooms next to hers. Nancy's room was off the kitchen and was the warmest in winter, but the hottest in summer. No one was ever invited into her room. The door was always closed and locked.

Annie's room was small and painted white. The bed frame was iron and had a well-worn mattress on it. There was a badly scratched chiffonier in the corner, and one bare light bulb hanging from the ceiling. It couldn't compare to the bright room she had at home in the Craggs, but she'd make do. Annie knew she could fix it up if she stayed. She'd get a flowered bed cover and hang her family pictures on the wall. A pot of sweet geraniums on the window sill would brighten it up.

The butler's room had a fireplace and lovely dark furniture. Heavy drapes hung on the windows, and there was a thick carpet on the floor. Being a butler in New York City was a most prestigious position. They ran the entire households and were treated with respect. He was called Charles by the Thomson sisters, but the staff was ordered to call him Mr. Charles. Annie stayed out of his way as much as possible. He only socialized with butlers who worked for other wealthy families. He'd meet them at one of the "better bars," —those that weren't frequented by any ruffians, as he would say—for an afternoon of cards and drinks. Annie was surprised to learn that there was class distinction even among the working people. She'd been told that in America everyone was equal, but found that not to be true.

It was Annie's job to help the ladies dress in the morning. They'd fight if one thought the other got more attention.

Being Scottish, the sisters held the purse strings tightly. "They'll be no waste in this house," Miss Jemima would say. She did the household accounts every Friday afternoon. Little did she know the cook was padding the food bill.

"I'm in cahoots with the butcher and the grocer," Mary laughed. "The old ladies can squeeze a nickel until it screams, but I'll be getting it back in me kitchen."

"Sweet Jesus! What if they find out?" Annie said.

"Don't you be worrying. Even old Charles does his share of skimming," Mary said. "We put it in that old salt box on the top shelf. Then at Christmas we divide it up."

"Aren't you afraid someone will steal it?" Annie said.

"No. Didn't you ever hear there's honor among thieves? Well, we're the thieves," Mary laughed.

Eight months passed as Annie busied herself tending the old ladies. It was now 1903, and she couldn't believe how fast the year had flown up. The Thomson ladies didn't entertain often, thinking it was a waste of good money, but Annie noticed that they never refused a dinner invitation to one of the other fine homes in the city. "A free meal is a free meal," Miss Jemima was heard to say.

Annie managed to go to Mass every Sunday. She returned one morning and saw that Mary had sacks of flour and sugar sitting on the marble worktable.

"What are you making?" Annie asked.

"I'm going to make soda bread," Mary said, as she put a tin of caraway seed next to the flour.

"Could I be making it for you?" Annie said.

"Of course, deary. I didn't know you knew how."

"I've been making soda bread since I was ten years old," Annie laughed.

Mary sat back and sipped a cup of tea as Annie set to work. Mary watched as Annie put four cups of flour into a big bowl, along with some baking soda and sugar. In went the butter and buttermilk. Mary saw Annie dump raisins and caraway seeds into the mixture without measuring. Next, Annie dropped an egg into the mixture and started to beat it.

"Are you sure you know what you're doing, deary?" Mary asked. "I've never put an egg in mine."

"Of course I know what I'm doing," Annie said. "I could make it in me sleep."

"I don't put as much sugar or caraway in mine, either," Mary said.

"Just wait and see," Annie said. "You'll love it."

As Annie put the bread in the oven, Charles appeared. He told Mary and Annie that the ladies wanted to see them.

Miss Jemima and Miss Lizzie were in the sitting room having tea when they entered.

"Our brother, Campbell, is coming for a visit, and I want to go over the menu. You're to have all his favorites on hand," Miss Jemima said.

"Yes, lots of lovely desserts," Miss Lizzie added.

29

"There'll be no desserts except fruit compote," Miss Jemima said. "You're too fat."

"I am not," Miss Lizzie said. "Besides, it's better to be pleasingly plump than an emaciated old witch."

"Be quiet!" Miss Jemima yelled. "I've had all I'm going to take from you this morning."

"You be quiet yourself!" Miss Lizzie yelled back.

"Mary, I'll leave it in your hands," Miss Jemima said, as she tried to ignore her sister.

"Yes, madam," Mary said. "I know what Mr. Campbell likes."

"Annie, get the guest room ready. Put fresh flowers in there and make up the bed with our best linen."

"Yes, Miss Jemima."

Mary and Annie left the sitting room and returned to the kitchen. Annie took the soda bread out of the oven and placed it on the marble table. Mary admired the lovely bread as she cut a slice. She blew on it as she took a bite.

"You're right, deary. I hate to admit it, but it is better than mine," Mary laughed.

"Thank you," Annie said. "Now, tell me about this brother. I didn't even know they had one."

"I thought I told you. He's a lot younger, and as wild as they come. He's a handsome devil, and can spend money like it's going out of style. His sisters adore him and overlook his wastefulness. He's the only one who can get away with it. He shows up every time he needs money, and knows how to get it out of the old battle-axes," the cook said.

"Is he nice?" Annie asked.

"He's a charmer, but watch out for him. Don't get caught in a dark hall with him. We've lost other girls because of him and his carry on."

"He'd better not be trying anything with me, or he'll get a taste of me Irish temper," Annie said as she put up her fists.

"You look like you can take care of yourself, but he can get you fired if he chooses."

Annie decided to be careful and steer clear of Mr. Campbell. She was saving her money and didn't want to lose her job. Other than putting a few coins in the collection box in church, her expenses were small.

Miss Jemima and Miss Lizzie continued to fight all morning. At last, their brother arrived. Charles opened the door as Annie waited in attendance. Miss Jemima and Miss Lizzie came running. Annie laughed, seeing the mood of the ladies change upon the arrival. He was tall and had sandy-colored hair and a pencil-thin mustache. He swooped into the foyer wearing a brown tweed cape and a hat to match. The sisters giggled as he kissed them. Even the sour-faced Miss Jemima acted like a schoolgirl.

"Annie, this is Mr. Campbell. Take good care of him," Miss Lizzie said.

"Yes, madam."

"I'm sure she will," Mr. Campbell said, as he pinched Annie's cheek and winked at her.

Annie was dismissed and flew down the back stairs. The cook could see her face was red, and knew she'd met the charming, Mr. Campbell.

The next morning was Sunday. It was Annie's day off, and she was glad to be away from the big brownstone. She went to early Mass, then off to meet Jack at Mrs. O'Brien's boardinghouse. It was a lovely day, and she enjoyed the walk. Jack was waiting for her on the front stoop. He was all dressed up, and she wondered what the occasion was. Surely he hadn't gone to Mass. His shoes needed a polish, but other than that he looked presentable.

"Top of the morning. How have you been keeping?" Jack said.

"I'm just fine. Did you go to Mass, and did you get a job yet?"

31

"No, I didn't go to Mass and I haven't found a job. Jesus, Joseph and Mary! Don't start on me this morning," Jack said.

"I'm sorry, but you practically promised Mother on her deathbed you'd go to Mass, and you can't be living off your brothers forever."

"Don't be worrying about me," Jack said.

"I've been worrying about you all me life," Annie replied. "Why are you all dressed up?"

"We're going to visit William and Alexandra."

"That'll be lovely. I've been here for so long and haven't even been to their home yet," Annie said. "Every time they're off, I'm not. How are we going to get there?"

"We'll take the trolley to the railroad station, and get the ten o'clock to Greenwich. William will meet us when the train gets in."

"That sounds grand," Annie said. "I love riding the trolley, and I've only been on a train once before. This will be a day to remember, to be sure."

"How much money do you have?" Jack said.

"You're wanting me to pay for it?" Annie asked.

"Well, you know I don't have any."

"You're really something. You're lucky you have such a generous sister, smart enough to save her money," Annie laughed.

"I could always count on me darling sister," Jack laughed.

"Darling sister, me foot! You think you can charm the birds out of the trees, but you'd better watch out. Someday, the bird is going to be a hawk," Annie laughed, and gave Jack a punch in the arm.

"Don't be hitting me!" Jack yelled.

"There's a flower shop up the street. I want to get William's wife a little gift," Annie said.

They entered the shop and the owner greeted them. Annie looked around wondering what to buy when she spotted geraniums in lovely painted pots sitting on a shelf.

"I'll be taking one of those," Annie said, pointing to the plants.

"Sweet Jesus! Do you have to bring one of those smelly things?" Jack said. "She's probably got a garden full of nice flowers."

"Yes, I do have to bring her one of these, and if you don't like it you can lump it."

The shopkeeper wrapped it in white tissue paper and handed it to Annie. She paid him a few coins and left the store. She laughed as Jack walked ahead of her holding his nose and making an awful face.

The trolley came clanging down the street. Jack and Annie jumped on and took seats in the back. Annie had ridden the trolley before, but got a thrill each time she rode it. Her eyes were wide with excitement as the trolley sped down the road. Annie held onto the pole near her seat with one hand, and gripped the potted plant with the other. Jack laughed seeing her knuckles turn white.

They finally arrived at the railroad station. Annie gave Jack the money for the tickets and boarded the train. They took seats near the front. The windows had shades on them with pull cords that had tassels on the ends. Annie pulled it down, then up.

"Bejesus, Annie, stop playing with the damn thing! Do you want the conductor yelling at us?" Jack said. "Behave yourself."

"Look who's telling me to behave," Annie laughed.

It would take over an hour to reach Greenwich. Annie enjoyed the ride and looked forward to seeing William and Alexandra.

A conductor walked through the train announcing the stations. Annie thought this a lovely idea. At last he called, "Greenwich, Greenwich, next stop!" Annie was so excited she was sure her heart would pound right out of her chest.

William was waiting for them when they got off the train. He hugged Annie and helped her into the automobile.

He said that Alexandra was waiting at home, and the tea would be ready by the time they got there.

"It's about time I got to see your home," Annie said.

"I know, and I'm sure you'll be liking it," William said.

They drove up Greenwich Avenue. It was lined with elm trees that formed an arch over the cobblestone street. They passed several white houses as well as lovely shops. Some of the shops had front porches where the shopkeepers displayed their goods. Halfway up Greenwich Avenue, Annie saw a stone church. The sign said "Saint Mary's Roman Catholic Church."

"Is that where you and Alexandra go?" Annie asked.

"Yes, every Sunday, do or die," William said.

"Yeah, if he don't go, Alexandra will make him die," Jack laughed.

"It has the same name as our school back home," Annie said. "Isn't that lovely."

At the top of the avenue they turned right onto the Boston Post Road. William drove to North Street, passing a huge stone church.

"What kind of church is that?" Annie asked.

"That's the Second Congregational Church," William said.

"My, it certainly is big," Annie said.

"That's the church where all the swells go," William said.

It was a long ride, but most enjoyable. Annie saw one large mansion after another set back on great rolling lawns. Her brothers laughed as her mouth fell open.

William turned onto a blue stone driveway. It crunched under the weight of the automobile as William drove slowly past a huge brick house.

"Saints preserve us!" Annie said. "Look at the size of this place."

34

William stopped in front of a garage. He explained that he and Alexandra lived over it. Jack walked ahead since he'd been there before, and led them up an outside stairway.

Alexandra opened the door and welcomed them in. Annie thought she was a very attractive girl and her brother had made a good choice. She was short and thin, and had thick brown hair with streaks of red running through it. Her eyes were a greenish gray. She kissed Annie on both cheeks and offered her a seat.

Annie handed the geranium to Alexandra and said it was a housewarming gift. Alexandra thanked her, but Annie could see she wasn't thrilled with it. She did admire the painted pot, and said when the geranium died she could use it for something else.

"I told you she wouldn't like that stinking flower," Jack whispered. "She's already planning its death."

"Whist!" Annie said as she pinched his arm.

William beamed with pride as he showed off their rooms. They had a big kitchen with a coal stove, icebox and sink. Beyond that, was a small sitting room that was closed off with heavy drapes covering the door. Annie had never see this done before and asked why the drapes were there. Alexandra explained it was to protect the furniture from sunlight.

"We only use it when we have special company," Alexandra said.

"I guess we ain't special company," Jack whispered to Annie.

Annie stomped on Jack's foot, letting him know to be quiet. They walked down a hall to a bathroom. Next to it, was the bedroom. Over the bed hung a wooden cross with Jesus on it. On the bureau was a small altar with a statue of the Virgin Mary. It was clear to Annie that Alexandra was a good Catholic. She knew her mother would approve of her.

After the grand tour, everyone sat at the kitchen table waiting for Alexandra to serve the meal she'd prepared. She set a tureen down and ladled out some thick red soup.

"I'm starving," Jack said as he tucked his napkin in under his chin.

"Don't pay attention to him. He's always hungry," Annie laughed.

"I know, he's eaten here before," Alexandra laughed. "Hope you like this. It's beet soup. It's called borscht."

"I've never had beet soup before," Annie said.

"Put a dollop of sour cream on top. I'm sure you'll enjoy it."

Annie put a small teaspoon of sour cream on the soup and tasted it. Much to her surprise, it was very good. Next came a platter of sausage and boiled potatoes. Annie had never seen sausage like this and asked what kind it was.

"It's kielbasa, Polish sausage. Have some. I know you'll like it. You'd be surprised the things I've eaten since I married me darling," William said. "She makes a thing called pieroges. I'll have her make some the next time you're here."

"That'd be lovely. Will you teach me how to make some of these dishes?" Annie said.

"That I will," Alexandra said, "if you teach me how to make proper soda bread."

"You better teach her! I haven't had any good soda bread since I left home," William said.

"My Polish grandmother taught me how to cook her dishes, but my mother is a terrible cook. I'm afraid my Irish cooking has suffered."

The bargain was struck, and in a short time the recipe would be exchanged. Time seemed to fly. Before long, it was time to return to New York. Jack and Annie thanked Alexandra for the lovely meal, and hoped to visit again soon.

Alexandra waved goodbye and thanked Annie for the geranium.

"At least she's got good manners," Jack said. "I wouldn't be thanking you for that stinking thing."

"You think you're so smart. I knew a cook who used the leaves to flavor jelly, and a doctor told me that it's used

36

in medicine. So there, Mr. Smarty!" Annie said. "One of these days, I'm going to find the recipe for geranium jelly and make you eat it."

"Over me dead body will I be eating geranium jelly," Jack said.

The ride home was pleasant. Annie saw all the houses lit up that lined the railroad tracks. When the train slowed, she could look right in the windows and see people having their evening meals.

"I'd like to have a home someday and be able to cook for me own family," Annie said.

"You'll probably be cooking up a mess of geranium leaves," Jack laughed.

"You didn't do so bad, eating me food all those years," Annie replied.

It was eight o'clock by the time they got to the Thomson house. Jack left Annie at the kitchen door, said good night and was off down the street. Annie knew he was headed for the closest saloon. She climbed the stairs to her room. She could hear Mary and Charles snoring. She didn't know which one was louder, and laughed to herself. Annie was so tired she almost forgot to say her prayers before falling asleep.

CHAPTER 3

Monday morning Annie was up bright and early to start the day. She covered her dress with a fresh starched apron and put on the silly little cap that she was required to wear. She'd always worn her hair in one thick braid that hung down her back, but now she pinned it up, giving a neat appearance. She heard a bell ring and looked at the annunciator. Number three popped up. She knew it was Miss Jemima's room. Just then, the bell rang again, letting her know that Miss Lizzie was awake and demanding service, too.

"Sweet Jesus, I should cut meself in two," Annie said.

"Better see to Miss Jemima. She'll raise holy hell if you go to Miss Lizzie first," Mary said.

Annie ran up the two flights and knocked on Miss Jemima's door. She told Annie to enter, and gave her the orders for the day. Annie laid out Miss Jemima's clothes and hurried off to tend to Miss Lizzie, who was in a snit having to wait.

"What took you so long?"

"I had to take care of Miss Jemima," Annie said.

"You should take care of me first," Miss Lizzie pouted.

"I'm sorry, but Miss Jemima rang first."

"Well, I'll ring first next time. I'll show her," Miss Lizzie said.

Annie helped Miss Lizzie dress. She wanted to know what Miss Jemima was wearing so she could choose a nicer outfit. Annie couldn't believe how childish the two women were.

Miss Jemima's room was dark and plain. In the corner was a small writing desk where she did her correspondence every morning. There was a large carved dresser with a mirror that went to the ceiling. On the dresser was her silver comb and brush set, along with some bottles of toilet water. The bedcover was dark blue, and on the side table was a lamp and the small bell she used to summon the servants when she was in bed. Across the room, near the marble fireplace, was the pull cord for the annunciator.

In contrast, Miss Lizzie's room was pink. She had a collection of dolls and talked to them as if they were alive. Annie thought her a bit daft. There was a pile of satin pillows on the bed, and a dressing table with a satin skirt. In front of the dressing table was a small lace-covered stool. Annie wondered how Miss Lizzie's rather large bottom fit on it.

After finishing helping the ladies, Annie went back to the kitchen.

It was Nancy's job to put the breakfast trays on the dumbwaiter to be sent up to the dining room. Annie offered to do it for her, but got a look from Mary letting her know not to. Nancy knew her job, and didn't like anyone interfering. Annie raced up the stairs so she'd be there when the food arrived. Miss Jemima and Miss Lizzie were already sitting at the table. Charles was pouring tea when she entered.

"Will Mr. Campbell be joining you?" Charles asked.

"No, he likes to lie in, so he'll have breakfast later," Miss Jemima said.

"Yes, miss," Charles said.

"He'll be staying a while, so we want you to give him full attention," Miss Lizzie said.

"Tell cook there will be four at dinner this evening. Give her this menu," Miss Jemima said.

"I wanted to choose the menu! You always get to do it," Miss Lizzie sulked.

"Don't be silly. I know what Campbell likes," Miss Jemima snapped.

"You think you're so smart. Even when Mother was alive, she let you choose the menu," Miss Lizzie pouted.

"She trusted me with it," Miss Jemima said. "Mother knew I'd do it right"

"Well, Daddy liked me better. I was his favorite," Miss Lizzie bragged.

"You were not," Miss Jemima said.

"Well, I'm the prettiest. Daddy always said so," Miss Lizzie sneered.

After breakfast, Annie cleared the table and sent the dishes back to the kitchen. She spent the morning making up the ladies' bedrooms and dusting the sitting room. Fresh flowers were put in vases and placed throughout the house.

At twelve o'clock, lunch was served. Mr. Campbell finally had gotten out of bed and was sitting at the table chatting with his sisters. Annie watched as the ladies listened to every word. Charles served, as Annie stood at attention at the side of the room. She knew Mr. Campbell was watching her, and didn't like it. He was wearing a red satin dressing gown and looked very handsome.

He was telling his sisters that they were going to love the young lady he was bringing to dinner that night. They seemed pleased that he might be settling down. They'd never been asked to marry, which was a sorrow to them. They'd be happy if Campbell married and carried on the family name. Of course, they'd have to approve his choice.

Annie spent the rest of the afternoon setting the table and helping the cook prepare dinner. Charles checked the table to see that it was done correctly. Annie followed him around as he straightened a spoon and moved a plate a fraction of an inch. He looked down his long pointed nose at Annie, showing his disapproval.

She returned to the kitchen and saw Nancy washing the pots and pans as Mary finished using them. Annie scrubbed the potatoes and peeled a bunch of carrots while Mary rubbed a huge roast beef with salt and pepper.

"I wonder who the lady is," Annie said.

"I don't know, but they're really putting on the dog," Mary laughed. "Wait until Miss Jemima sees what this roast cost."

"I hope there's enough left so I can have a taste," Annie said.

"Don't worry, deary, we eat the same as them," Mary said. "We'll have a nice dinner after they're served. I always buy enough for us, too."

"Maybe you shouldn't do that," Annie said. "If you get caught, you could loose your job."

"I told you, I can handle them. I know where the bodies are buried," Mary laughed.

Annie liked Mary. She reminded her of her stepmother, Rose. She had the same sense of humor and was very good-hearted. She watched out for the other help in the house. Annie wasn't so sure of Nancy, who hardly spoke. She didn't dislike Charles as much now that she'd gotten to know him. He had an English accent which Annie knew was put on. Every once in a while, he'd slip and sound as Irish as Mary.

41

At seven o'clock that evening the doorbell rang. Charles was in the foyer and about to open the door when Mr. Campbell came running from the sitting room to greet his guest. Annie's mouth fell open seeing a tall blond woman dressed in red satin standing there. Her gown was very low cut and extremely tight. Annie wondered how she could sit down in it. Her face was painted and her eyebrows seemed to be two pencil lines. There was a black beauty mark on her cheek, and the aroma of her perfume was overwhelming. Mr. Campbell greeted her with a kiss and ushered her into the sitting room. Charles followed them in to serve drinks. Annie returned to the kitchen.

"Sweet Jesus," Annie told Mary, "you should see the lady friend! She looks like a trollop. She's got more paint on her face than me Old Da has on the barn."

"You don't say. I'll sneak up and take a peek."

Mary was gone a few minutes and returned laughing. She had to sit down to compose herself. Charles entered and asked what was so funny.

"I got a look at the girlfriend. Bejesus, the old ladies will be having the vapors," Mary laughed.

"They'll never let him marry the likes of her," Charles said, being the biggest snob of all.

"Don't be too sure. He usually gets what he wants," Mary said.

Dinner was served as Annie cleared each course. Annie watched the two sisters. It was clear they didn't approve. Their faces were white and pinched.

The woman's name was Miss Joan Lamonte. She was starring in a variety show in the city. Mr. Campbell said she was a dancer. She sat smoking a long thin cigar, shocking the two old ladies. They coughed and waved the smoke away. Ladies of class did not smoke. Annie watched as Mr. Campbell filled her glass with wine. The more Miss Lamonte drank, the more common she became.

"Bejesus," Annie giggled.

42

Charles shot her a look to be quiet. Annie stood there and looked at the ceiling, trying to keep a straight face. She couldn't wait to tell Mary. Annie couldn't help giggling again, and was ordered back to the kitchen by Charles. When she got there, Mary was setting the table so they could have dinner.

"Well, what's going on up there?" Mary asked.

"Mr. Campbell's lady friend's name is Joan Lamonte. Isn't that fancy? She's a dancer," Annie said. "Imagine that!"

"That's probably not her real name. I'll bet she's one of those dancers who take their clothes off and flits around the stage!" Mary roared with laughter as she danced around the kitchen pretending to take hers off.

"Sweet Jesus, you don't mean that!" Annie said. "There's no such thing!"

"Yes, there is. Music, jokes and naked ladies," Mary giggled. "The gentlemen love it, to be sure."

"Good Lord! Me sainted mother would be turning over in her grave if she knew of such things," Annie said in shock.

"I'll be sending out me spies and find out what her real name is," Mary said. "if her name is Lamonte, I'll be eating me hat."

Charles returned to the kitchen and put a silver tray down. Annie could see he was not pleased having to serve the likes of Miss Lamonte.

"Mr. Campbell would like us to call the lady, Miss Joan.' Says she'll be one of the family someday and wants her to feel welcome," Charles said.

"One big happy family," Mary giggled.

After dinner, Mr. Campbell and Miss Joan left. He said he would escort her home, so not to wait up. The sisters retired to their rooms as Annie raced between them helping each to get ready for bed. Neither said a word. Annie could see how upset they were.

The next afternoon, Annie went to dust the sitting room and take the dead flowers away. As she entered, she was told to do it later. Miss Jemima, Miss Lizzie and Mr. Campbell were in deep conversation. She knew it must be about Mr. Campbell's lady, and lingered outside hoping to hear what was being said. The voices got louder as Annie pressed her ear against the door. The sisters started screaming at their brother while he tried to calm them down. Miss Jemima threatened to cut him out of the will and Miss Lizzie added he'd be disowned.

"She's really a lovely girl," Campbell said. "You just have to get to know her."

"Never in a million years!" Miss Jemima said.

"I love her and want to marry her, and she's willing to give up the stage for me," Campbell pleaded.

"Is she willing to live on your allowance?" Miss Lizzie asked.

"I thought you'd increase it once I married," Campbell said. "I thought we could live here with you."

"Over my dead body! Have you lost your mind? What would our friends say, having that person living here?" Miss Jemima said.

Annie was surprised to hear the battling sisters join forces against their brother. They usually never agreed on anything.

Charles appeared and caught Annie eavesdropping. He sent her flying back to the kitchen. Mary was having a cup of tea, and poured one for Annie.

"What's going on up there?" Mary asked.

"You wouldn't believe the carry on! They're threatening to disown him if he marries that woman," Annie said. "You should hear him pleading with them!"

"Well, you can't blame them. She looks like a tart."

"How can they take him out of the will? Doesn't the son always inherit the family fortune?" Annie said. "That's

44

the way it is in Ireland. It doesn't matter how bad the son is, he still get's everything."

"Not in this country, and not in this house. Old Mr. Thomson knew his son was a rascal from the day he was born. He left everything to his daughters. He was as tight as they were. Mr. Campbell will have to do as they say, or he won't see a penny until they're both dead," Mary said.

It didn't take long for Mary to find out Miss Lamonte's real name. She'd passed the word over the back wall. The servants in the brownstones knew more about the people they worked for than they knew about themselves. An ear to the right door was all that was needed.

A few days later, Mary's friend Maggie appeared. She was the cook at the Elton house on the next street. Maggie was known to be the biggest gossip around. If you wanted to know anything, she was the one to ask. Annie was washing the dishes as Mary opened the door and invited Maggie in.

"Nice to see you," Mary said. "Will you be having a cup of tea?"

"That'd be lovely," Maggie said.

"What brings you here this fine morning?" Mary asked.

"I found out about that woman, and couldn't wait to tell you," Maggie said.

"I've been dying to know," Mary said.

"Her real name is Jeannie McGinty. Her parents are off-the-boat Irish like us. Her father works on the docks and her mother takes in laundry."

"Mr. Campbell said his lady is a dancer in a show," Mary said.

"That's true, but it's burlesque. The ladies aren't naked, as some would have you think, but damn near," Maggie laughed.

"Sweet Jesus! If the old ladies knew, they'd having a fit," Mary said. "I wonder what Mr. Campbell is thinking, getting mixed up with a woman like that!"

"Well, he's got money, but that doesn't make him quality," Maggie said. "He's no better than her."

"I guess they deserve each other," Mary said.

The ladies had a second cup of tea and enjoyed catching up on the latest "dirt," as Maggie called it.

Annie'd never been a gossip, but didn't mind listening. She thought it was all right as long as she didn't repeat it.

Weeks passed, and the arguing continued. The sisters would not budge an inch, and Campbell didn't want to give up his lady. One minute they were screaming at him, and the next trying to bribe him. Finally, they promised to buy him a new automobile and raise his allowance if he stopped his pursuit of the glamorous Miss Joan. The thought of more money and a new automobile was too much to refuse. Besides, he knew he could still see Miss Joan behind their backs. He'd fool them into thinking they'd gotten their way. The ladies talked him into giving up his rooms at the Dorset Hotel and coming back home. He agreed.

Mr. Campbell moved in, bringing all his possessions. He took a room on the third floor that faced the back of the house. He kept the door locked, and only allowed Annie to clean it when he was there.

Campbell had been living there for two weeks when Annie was sent to the third floor to put some linen away. She knew he was in there since he hadn't come down for breakfast. She tried to be quiet so as not to disturb him. She was humming softly when she heard a woman's voice coming from the room.

"Sweet Jesus, who can that be?" she said aloud.

The door opened, and there stood Mr. Campbell. When he saw Annie, he shut the door quickly and locked it. As he closed it, Annie got a whiff of perfume. She knew at once it was the same scent that Miss Joan was wearing the night of the dinner.

46

Annie finished and hurried to the kitchen. Mary was stirring a pot of soup and singing to herself when Annie entered. She sat down at the table and fanned herself.

"Are you warm, deary?" Mary said.

"Yes, but it's not the weather."

"Whatever do you mean?" Mary said.

"I was putting the linen away on the third floor near Mr. Campbell's room, and out he comes," Annie said.

"What's wrong with that?" Mary said. "He didn't take liberties with you, did he? I'll be speaking to Miss Jemima if he did!"

"No, no, nothing like that. He won't be bothering me. He's got that woman in his room," Annie said.

"Away with you! He wouldn't dare!"

"She's in there, I tell you! I heard her and smelled that god-awful perfume she wears," Annie said.

"Come to think of it, I've been hearing strange noises in the night. Like the front door opening and closing. I thought I was hearing things."

"What are you going to do?" Annie said.

"Not a thing. They'll catch him. You wait and see."

A few days later, Annie and Mary were having tea when they heard someone screaming. It was coming from the sitting room and sounded like Miss Lizzie.

"Jesus, Joseph and Mary! What's that all about?" Annie said.

"They're on the warpath with Nancy. Seems she didn't polish the brass on the front door to suit them. I knew she'd be hearing about it," Mary said.

"Why don't they just ask her to do it over?"

"They take great pleasure in tormenting the poor thing," Mary said.

"Well, if it were me, I'd leave."

"She can't. Nobody'll hire her with that bad leg. You can see how slow she moves," Mary said.

47

"I'd starve before I'd take their abuse," Annie said. "I've wondered what happened to her leg. Was she born that way?"

"No. When she came here, she was fit as a fiddle. A sweet young thing to be sure," Mary said. "She was at the top of the stairs when Miss Lizzie got in a snit over something Nancy hadn't done to suit her. She was screaming something awful, so I thought I'd better go and see what was going on. Nancy had her back to the steps when Miss Lizzie went after her. She slapped Nancy so hard across the face she fell backwards and down the full flight of stairs."

"That's terrible," Annie said.

"Nancy lay there with her poor leg twisted under her and screaming in pain. Miss Lizzie denied doing it, but I saw it. She did get her medical treatment, but told the doctor the girl was clumsy and that it was her own fault. Now you know what I mean when I say I know where the bodies are buried," Mary said.

"Miss Lizzie hasn't learned her lesson from what I can hear by the carry on up there."

"It was very sad. Poor Nancy was engaged to be married, but the young man broke the engagement after the fall. It's made her as mean as the sisters."

"It's clear she hates them, and you can't blame her," Annie said.

Nancy entered the kitchen and went straight to her room. They could hear her lock the door behind her. Annie'd never seen so many locked doors in a house before. She laughed thinking, at home in the Craggs they never locked anything.

As time passed, things quieted down in the Thomson house. Annie was happy with her work and enjoyed the company of Mary. She'd gotten used to Mr. Charles and his stiff ways, and could get him to laugh on occasion at one of her jokes. Nancy was another story. No matter how hard she tried, she couldn't get close to her.

Mr. Campbell stayed in most evenings and played cards with his sisters, or read to them. Some evenings, when he retired, he'd take a tray of cheese and fruit up to his room along with a bottle of whiskey. He said he liked to have a nibble before bedtime. His sisters thought this is a fine idea.

Campbell began serving wine to his sisters before the evening meal. Charles was miffed, as it had always been his job, but the sisters loved the attention and didn't refuse a second or third glass when he'd insist.

"Bejesus, they're getting drunk every night," Annie laughed.

"Might do them good," Mary said.

"Disgraceful!" Charles added.

"If they get drunk enough, they'll sleep like babies and not hear Mr. Campbell sneaking that trollop into his room," Annie said.

"I hope I'm here when they catch him," Mary added.

Weeks went by, and the ladies slept later and later each morning. Annie guessed it was because of the wine they were consuming each night. It was hard on her as the later breakfast was, the later the other meals were, too. She didn't get to bed until midnight on many nights.

One morning, Miss Jemima's bell rang. It was ten o'clock, and Annie ran up the stairs to her room. When she entered, Miss Jemima was still in bed and complaining that she didn't feel well. She complained of a headache and an upset stomach. Annie could see how ill she was. There were dark circles under her eyes, and she seemed very weak. Annie got her some head powders and a glass of water. She washed her face and straightened her bed. Miss Jemima sent her away, saying she wanted to sleep. Annie thought she'd check on Miss Lizzie, and went to her room. Miss Lizzie was sitting on the side of the bed moaning. She looked much the same

49

as Miss Jemima, but her face looked almost green. Her eyes had the same dark circles. Annie tried to make her comfortable, and said she would bring her some hot tea and dry toast. As she left Miss Lizzie's room, she was met by Mr. Campbell.

"Good morning," Mr. Campbell said.

"Good morning, sir," Annie said. "I'm afraid your sisters are under the weather this morning. I think we should be calling a doctor."

"Nonsense. They just overindulged last night. They'll be fine."

Annie went back to the kitchen and told Mary about the condition of the sisters. Nancy offered to make the tea and toast for Miss Lizzie. Annie thanked her as Nancy fixed a tray and put it on the dumbwaiter.

"Those two need a doctor," Annie said.

"Well, it's not for us to say," Mary said.

Charles entered the kitchen and sat down at the end of the table. Mary could see he was troubled, and asked what the problem was.

"Mr. Campbell is doing the accounts for Miss Jemima. I never thought I'd live to see the day," Charles said. "I hope he's not helping himself."

"The butcher told me his bill hasn't been paid. I thought it was because Miss Jemima was ill," Mary said.

"She said Mr. Campbell would pay the bills until she was well. Doesn't look like he's doing a very good job," Charles said.

"I hope we'll be getting our wages at the end of the month," Annie said.

The dinners continued and the wine flowed. Mr. Campbell insisted that he select the wine and do the serving. Annie noticed that the sisters drank wine, while Mr. Campbell only drank whiskey and never got sick. She also saw that Mr. Campbell cleaned his plate every night, but the sisters ate very little. This was strange, as they usually had good appetites.

50

"This can't be good for them," Annie said to Mary.

"I think you're right. Mr. Campbell is pouring wine down them, and they're going along with it. Charles said Mr. Campbell gave Miss Jemima some in the morning. Said it would make her feel better. I'm afraid they'll be getting the habit," Mary said.

"I still think they need a doctor," Annie said.

"If they want a doctor, they'll let us know," Mary said. "They'd rather die than spend money on a doctor, and Mr. Campbell knows how they feel about it."

"I hope they die," Nancy said in a little voice.

"Don't be saying that! God will punish you," Annie said, making the sign of the cross.

Months passed as the ladies got more sick. Annie could see how weak they were, and she worried. She wasn't fond of them, but hated to see anyone suffer. They stayed in bed and had their meals served in their rooms. Mr. Campbell was at their beck and call. He took the trays from the dumb-waiter and carried them up to his sisters. He'd leave the dishes in the hall so Nancy could return them to the kitchen.

One night, Annie was asleep when she woke with a start. She sat up in bed and listened. She thought she heard Miss Lizzie call out. She slipped into her robe and tiptoed down the back stairs. Annie stood on the landing to the second floor and listened. She could hear voices coming from Miss Lizzie's room. She crept over to the door and put her ear against it. She could hear Mr. Campbell and Miss Lizzie.

"Drink this, Lizzie. It'll make you feel better," Mr. Campbell said.

"I don't want it," Miss Lizzie said.

"I'm not going to take no for an answer. Drink this or I'll force it down your throat," Mr. Campbell demanded.

"How can you be so mean to me?" Miss Lizzie cried.

Annie could hear Miss Lizzie choking and Mr. Campbell telling her she was a good girl for doing as she was told. With that, Annie ran back to her room. She could hear the

51

grandfather clock strike four, and knew she wouldn't be able to go back to sleep. She dressed and went down to the kitchen. She made a pot of tea and sat waiting for Mary to make an appearance.

"Good morning, deary," Mary said as she entered the kitchen. "You're up bright and early."

"I've been up for hours," Annie said.

"Couldn't sleep?" Mary asked.

Annie told Mary what had happened during the night. She couldn't imagine what Mr. Campbell was giving her sister.

"I think he's trying to kill her," Annie said.

"That's a terrible thing to say. Don't let him hear you say that," Mary warned.

"Well, it seems awful funny—Miss Lizzie and Miss Jemima getting sick at the same time."

"That could happen," Mary said.

"How come it started when Mr. Campbell came to stay?" Annie said.

"Don't be a silly girl. Your imagination is running away with you," Mary said.

"Maybe so, but I'm going to keep an eye on him," Annie said.

One afternoon, Mrs. Elton came to call. She'd been a friend and neighbor of the Thomsons for years and hadn't seen them for a long time. Mr. Campbell greeted her in the foyer and explained that his sisters were under the weather. He didn't invite her in, and acted as if he couldn't get rid of her fast enough. Mrs. Elton would say later there was something suspicious about his behavior, not to mention his rudeness.

Maggie reported Mrs. Elton's concern to Mary, who thought it strange behavior for the very charming Mr. Campbell.

Now that Miss Jemima and Miss Lizzie stayed in their rooms, Mr. Campbell started bringing Miss Joan openly to the house. After the sisters went to sleep, Mr. Campbell and Miss Joan would sit in the sitting room and drink. They were getting very brave, and made a great deal of noise. Annie would sneak up the stairs and listen at the door, hoping to hear what was being said. She knew this wasn't a nice thing to do, but curiosity got the better of her. One night, she heard a loud crash and Mr. Campbell and Miss Joan laughing.

The next morning, she went to clean the sitting room and found several figurines broken. There were empty bottles and glasses everywhere. Just then, Charles walked in. He was shocked at the condition of the room.

"Annie, best get this cleaned up before our ladies see it," he said.

"Yes, sir," Annie said. "I hope we don't get blamed when they see the broken china."

Nancy entered and grinned when she saw the fine figurines smashed to pieces. Every morning she'd wash the large silver tray that held the wine and whiskey decanters, and water the plants if needed. She had a routine and no one dared upset it. Annie wanted to be her friend, but Nancy would have none of it.

One evening, Mr. Campbell went out. He was dressed in a black evening suit and told Charles he'd be very late. He also told him not to disturb his sisters as they were asleep.

Mr. Campbell stayed away all night. The next morning, Mary was worried. She didn't want Miss Jemima and Miss Lizzie to know he'd not returned, as it would upset them.

"Annie, check on the ladies," Mary said. "They haven't rung yet, and it's getting late."

Annie did as she was told and went to Miss Jemima's room. As she opened the door, she detected a terrible odor. Annie put her hand over her nose. The room was dark and humid. She walked quietly over to the window and opened the heavy drapes, letting the light in. She lifted the window to air the room. As she turned, she could see Miss Jemima curled up in bed. The quilt was over her head. Annie pulled it down gently and looked at her mistress. Much to Annie's horror, Miss Jemima was staring up at her and didn't seem to be breathing. There were brown stains around her mouth, which hung open. Annie called her name and touched her face. It was cold. Clutched in her hand was the little silver bell she used to summon the servants at night. Annie gasped, knowing the old woman was dead.

"Holy Mother of God!" Annie said as she made the sign of the cross.

She ran to the back stairs screamed for the others to come.

"What's all the noise about?" Charles demanded.

"Take a look at Miss Jemima," Annie said.

Mary and Nancy arrived with Charles, and saw the look of horror on Annie's face. They went to the bed where Miss Jemima lay.

"Dear God! What's wrong with her?" Mary said.

"I think she's dead," Annie said.

Annie looked at Nancy and could swear she saw a smile come over her face.

"She must have been ringing for us during the night and we didn't hear her," Charles said when he saw the bell.

"I heard her, but I wasn't about to get out of me bed for the likes of her," Nancy said.

"Sweet Jesus, I must be seeing to Miss Lizzie!" Annie cried.

She ran to Miss Lizzie's room. It was as dark as Miss Jemima's. Annie walked carefully, not wanting to bump into the furniture. There was that same sickening odor. She opened the drapes and windows, then turned hearing Miss Lizzie moan. Annie ran to the bed and saw the old lady gasping for air. There was vomit down the side of the bed, staining Miss Lizzie's favorite pink linen.

"Get a doctor! Miss Lizzie's awful sick!" she screamed.

Charles didn't question Annie, and was out the door as fast as his legs could carry him. He knew the sisters were attended by Dr. Marshall, who lived nearby. It seemed to Annie an eternity until he returned.

The doctor was a dapper-looking fellow with white hair and mustache. He wore a dark suit with a red carnation in his lapel, and carried a black bag. He went straight to Miss Lizzie, who lay very still. He took out his stethoscope and listened to her heart. He turned to the waiting servants and shook his head.

"I'm afraid I'm too late," Dr. Marshall said.

"Saints preserve us!" Annie said.

"Why wasn't I called sooner?" Dr. Marshall asked.

"Mr. Campbell wouldn't let us. He said they'd be all right," Annie said.

"That's right. Mr. Campbell was adamant about it," Charles said.

"Miss Jemima's dead, too," Mary said.

"Good Lord, where is she?" Dr. Marshall asked.

"Follow me," Charles said.

The doctor entered Miss Jemima's room and examined the body. Annie, Nancy and Mary waited in the hall. The doctor came out, followed by Charles.

"Both of them dead at the same time! This is very strange," Dr. Marshall said. "I'm not sure what they died of. I'll have to get another opinion. Where is Mr. Campbell?"

"We don't know. He didn't come home last night," Charles said.

"I hope he's all right," Dr. Marshall said. "It could be some kind of food poisoning."

"Surely not from me cooking!" Mary said indignantly.

"We all ate the same thing, and we're not sick," Annie said.

"Since when do the servants eat the same thing?" Dr. Marshall asked.

"We do in this house," Mary said.

"There has to be another explanation. Or else it's something they ate that you didn't," Dr. Marshall said.

"Should I call the police?" Charles said.

"No, wait until I find out what they died of," Dr. Marshall said. "I'll be back with my associate. Don't touch a thing!"

Dr. Marshall returned within the hour with Dr. Lennon, who examined the bodies and said that he was sure they'd died of food poisoning. Dr. Marshall didn't agree, since no one else in the house was ill. The second opinion didn't settle his mind, but he had no other answer.

"I'm going to have more tests taken, to be sure. Do any of you have any idea where Mr. Campbell is?" Dr. Marshall asked. "He could be ill, or even dead."

"He might be with his friend, Miss Lamonte, but I have no idea where she lives," Charles said.

"We'll have to call the police now, even though I'm not sure of the cause of death. Mr. Campbell must be found, and they're the ones to do it. I'll have to remove the bodies as soon as possible," Dr. Marshall said.

"In this heat, the old ladies will be getting ripe," Mary giggled.

"Be quiet!" Charles glared at her.

"Her language may be crude, but it's the truth," Dr. Marshall said. "Best go to the police first, then to Mr. Hillis, the undertaker."

Charles didn't waste any time and was off to do as the doctor suggested. Dr. Marshall said he would wait in the sitting room. Annie, Nancy and Mary returned to the kitchen.

"I think the good doctor could use a cup of tea," Mary said.

"I'll take it up to him," Annie said.

Annie served Dr. Marshall and returned to the kitchen. She realized she hadn't had anything to eat, so she helped herself to a slice of bread and a cup of the freshly brewed tea. As she sat at the kitchen table, there was a knock on the back door. She opened it, and there stood Jack.

"What the bloody hell's keeping you?" Jack said.

"Holy mother of God! I forgot it's me day off!"

"What's going on?" Jack asked.

"Oh, it's terrible! The two old ladies are dead, and we don't know where Mr. Campbell is," Annie said.

"Sweet Jesus, did they eat your soda bread, or did you finally find the recipe for geranium jelly?" Jack laughed.

"That's not funny! The doctor says they could have died of food poisoning."

"I'm sorry. I'm always putting me foot in me big mouth," Jack said.

"It'll be a cold day in hell before I make you soda bread again!" Annie snapped.

"Don't be mad," Jack said. "I'm only kidding."

"I'll forgive you this time," Annie said. "If you've made plans, don't be waiting for me. I'll have to be staying here."

"I didn't make any plans. Besides, I don't have any money."

Annie didn't want Jack hanging around, so she gave him a dollar and sent him on his way.

"Now don't be spending it in a bar," Annie called after him.

But that was exactly what he *was* going to do. He'd be the center of attraction with the story he had to tell.

The bell rang from the sitting room. Mary, Nancy and Annie went to see what was wanted. When they entered, two policemen had arrived as well as Mr. Hillis, the undertaker.

Mary knew one of the policemen. His name was Joseph Murphy, and he'd walked the beat in the area for many years. He nodded to Mary and told them to sit down. He stood back as the other policemen, Officer Stuart, started questioning them. He couldn't make any sense of it either.

"I'll have to see the bodies," Officer Stuart said.

Dr. Marshall led the policeman and the undertaker to Miss Jemima's room. He closed the door, leaving the servants to wonder what was being said.

Charles returned with Mr. Campbell, whom he had found walking toward the house on his way home. He still had on his evening suit and looked as if he hadn't slept. He didn't seem to be ill. Charles had told him what had happened, and he seemed clearly upset. He went to the sitting room and poured himself a large whiskey.

Officer Stuart, Dr. Marshall and Mr. Hillis entered and sat down at the tea table. Officer Murphy, being of lower rank, stood quietly taking notes.

"You seem well enough," Dr. Marshall said. "Have you been taking your meals with your sisters?"

"Yes, last night is the first time I've been away in weeks."

"Annie says they've been ill for weeks. Didn't you notice?" Officer Stuart said.

"They were always pretending to be ill. They did it for attention," Campbell said.

"So you ignored their complaints?"

"Yes," Campbell said, "I'm afraid I did."

"I wanted to call a doctor," Annie blurted.

"Quiet!" Mr. Campbell said. "You keep your place, young lady!"

"I'm sorry, Mr. Campbell," Annie said softly.

The undertaker removed the bodies. Annie turned away, not wanting to see them being taken out like sacks of potatoes.

Dr. Marshall asked Mary to list all the food that had been eaten in the house for the past two weeks, and told Charles to bring the list to him the next day. He left, telling them to call him at the slightest sign of illness.

Officer Stuart asked Mr. Campbell to accompany him to the police station to fill out a report. Campbell changed into day clothes and went off with the policeman. Annie and Mary opened the windows in the two bedrooms and stripped the beds. They knew Mr. Campbell would be gone most of the day, so they didn't worry about the evening meal. Maybe he wouldn't come back at all. They all returned to the kitchen. The stove had been banked, and only glowed under one lid. It was enough to boil water for tea. The windows and door were opened, hoping to catch a breeze. It was a hot day, so Annie and Mary took off their heavy starched aprons and caps.

"Loosen your collar. You'll be dying of the heat, Mr. Charles," Mary said.

"No, thank you, it wouldn't be proper. What if someone calls?" Charles said.

"Suit yourself."

"Best get started on the list," Mary said, "Annie, come and help me."

Annie sat with Mary as she tried to remember what food had been eaten. Breakfast was the easiest since it was always the same. The ladies didn't have lunch during that time, so that left only the evening meal to remember. Mary checked the bills from the grocer and butcher that hadn't been paid by Mr. Campbell. Mary read the list over and was satisfied that it was complete.

"How about the chocolates the ladies kept in the sitting room?" Charles asked.

"It couldn't be the chocolates. I've been helping myself to them when I clean the room. I figured Miss Jemima would be blaming Miss Lizzie if she was counting them," Annie giggled.

"It's a good thing they didn't catch you. They'd fire you for less than that," Charles said.

"You're a bad girl," Mary laughed.

59

"What about the wine? They were the only ones who drank it," Annie said.

"Could be. I'll add it to me list," Mary said.

The food list was taken to Dr. Marshall's office by Charles. The doctor looked it over. When he saw that wine was listed at the bottom, he asked Charles to bring the wine bottles so that he could have them tested.

"I don't know anything about scientific methods, but the bottles have been washed," Charles said.

"Well, then it's too late to test them," Dr. Marshall said. "Don't bother to bring them."

Mr. Campbell returned at five o'clock. He rang for Charles and told him he was having a guest for dinner. He said the wake would begin the next evening and continue through the following afternoon and evening. The funeral would take place on Wednesday morning. Charles went to the kitchen and gave Mr. Campbell's instructions to Mary.

"Who can he be inviting, with his sisters not yet cold?" Annie asked.

"Probably that trollop, what's-her-name," Mary said.

"Now, don't be disrespectful. This is his house now, and we'd better please him or we'll be looking for new positions," Charles said.

Mary prepared a cold supper and put it in the icebox so it would be ready when Mr. Campbell rang. Annie washed up the few dishes and straightened the kitchen. Charles always had a glass of wine in the evenings before serving dinner, and was enjoying it when the front door bell rang. Up the stairs he ran to open it. Annie followed, knowing it was her place to stand in attendance.

The door opened, and there stood Miss Joan. She was wearing a large black hat with a veil that covered her eyes, but Annie could see that she had on even more makeup this night than the time before. Her gown was black, but had sequins sewn all over it. The dress was cut very low, revealing

60

her fine figure. Charles was so tall, Annie knew he was looking down her dress. She giggled. Charles heard her and knew
she'd seen him. His face turned a bright red. With that, he
told Annie to take the lady's wrap and get back to the kitchen.
Miss Joan floated into the sitting room and closed the door.

Charles, Mary, Nancy and Annie sat at the kitchen
table and ate supper. Mary had made a lovely meal of cold
salmon and salad, with chilled fruit and cheese for dessert.
Annie hadn't realized how hungry she was. She cleaned her
plate. After supper, she sat back and yawned.

"I know you're tired, deary," Mary said.

"You must be, too."

"That I am. Let's hope he sleeps late tomorrow morning," Mary added.

By twelve o'clock, Mr. Campbell rang. He told
Charles to clear the dishes and go to bed. His guest would
be spending the night.

The next morning, the servants were up early as usual.
Mr. Campbell and his guest were still asleep, but the servants
knew they could be called at any time. They wanted to be
ready. They were just finishing their breakfast when Officer
Murphy appeared at the back door. Opening it, Mary welcomed him in.

"Top of the morning," Officer Murphy said.

"Top of the morning to you. Come in, the tea's still
hot," Mary said.

"I could be doing with a cup, but I'm here on official
business," he said.

"You can be official and still have a cup," Mary
teased.

She poured him tea as he sat down. He took out a
notebook and started to ask questions. Annie sat there listening to every word.

"When did the ladies start getting sick?" he asked.

"A couple of months ago," Mary said.

"Come to think of it, right after Mr. Campbell came back. He could tell you the exact date," Charles said.

"He was questioned for hours and says they were sick only a few days," Officer Murphy said.

"Not true," Annie said.

"The girl's right. They were ill for a long time. Got so bad they didn't get out of bed for days," Charles said.

"At the end, they didn't eat very much, but they did drink a lot of that damn wine Mr. Campbell was giving them," Mary said.

"Please, watch your language!" Charles snapped.

"I heard Mr. Campbell forcing Miss Lizzie to drink something she didn't want. It was in the wee hours of the morning and it sounded like he was pouring it down her throat," Annie said. "She was choking something awful."

"I'll pass it along to Chief Logan. Might be something to it," Officer Murphy said.

"He probably gave her something bad," Annie said.

"Don't accuse anybody unless you can prove it," Charles said.

"Was he taking his meals here?" the policeman asked.

"Yes, all of them. We did, too," Charles said. "In fact, Mr. Campbell served the ladies himself when they were too ill to come to the table."

"He never drank wine," Annie said. "He only drank whiskey, and a lot of it."

"How do you know?" Officer Murphy asked.

"Because I clean the rooms. There was always two wine glasses and one whiskey glass used. I could tell by the amount of whiskey gone each day," Annie said. "I have to report to Mr. Charles, and he fills the decanters if need be. Ask him."

"Annie's right," Charles said. "I wash the decanters every morning and fill them up again ready for the evening."

"Have any of you been drinking the wine?" Officer Murphy asked. "If you have, I won't be telling on you."

Annie and Mary hadn't had any, but knew Charles had a glass every evening. He saw their eyes turn to him and became very indignant.

"Certainly not! I buy my own wine. I don't like the kind they drink. You can ask at Dunlap's Spirit Shop a few blocks away. I have my own account there."

"That will be checked," Officer Murphy said.

"What are they saying down at the police station?" Mary asked. "Do they have any idea what the ladies died of?"

"They're pretty sure it's poison. Off the record, it looks very suspicious, but to accuse anyone they'll need more than that," Officer Murphy said.

He took a few more notes, thanked them and left. Annie helped Mary clean up, then got out the dusting rags and mop. Mr. Campbell and his houseguest were still asleep, so she thought she'd get started in the sitting room.

"Have another cup of tea, deary. There's no hurry about the cleaning. Those two will sleep until noon," Mary said.

"Mr. Campbell will be wanting the house looking nice for the wake, won't he?" Annie said.

"The wake? What are you talking about?" Charles asked.

"The ladies will be laid out in the sitting room, won't they?" Annie said.

"You're still a greenhorn, deary," Mary laughed. "The wealthy don't hold wakes at home anymore. They have them in funeral homes."

"What do you mean?" Annie said.

"They have special places for wakes. The undertaker takes the deceased and lays them out in coffins in rooms at the funeral home," Charles said.

"They get them all dolled up and put a pound of paint on their faces. If you ever saw the likes of it, you'd swear they could sit up and talk," Mary laughed.

"Sweet Jesus! I never heard of such a thing," Annie said.

"You know how the dead were laid out at home and dressed in a long gown? Do you remember how their faces took on a gray look? Well, the swells here do them up," Mary explained.

"Will wonders ever cease?" Annie said.

"The only day we have to worry about is the day of the funeral. It's the custom to bring everyone home after the cemetery service for food and drink. I'll be asking Mr. Campbell how many he's expecting," Mary said.

Annie busied herself getting the house in order. Nancy worked with her, so it was finished in no time. Charles followed them, making sure everything was just so. Mr. Campbell and Miss Joan came down and asked that coffee be served in the sitting room. Annie and Nancy went off to fix a tray. Annie sent it up on the dumbwaiter, then took it into the sitting room. She was leaving when the door bell rang. Charles came running to answer it. Annie hung back, wanting to know who it was.

"Good morning Dr. Marshall," Charles said as he opened the door.

"Good morning. Is Mr. Campbell about?" Dr. Marshall asked.

"Yes, sir, he is."

The doctor entered the sitting room. Charles returned to the kitchen and told Mary who had arrived. She sent Annie to the sitting room to retrieve the coffee tray. As Annie entered, they stopped talking. When she left the room, she stood just outside listening and hoping that Charles wouldn't catch her.

"I've called a specialist on food poisoning to examine your sisters," Dr. Marshall said.

"Did you think that necessary?" Mr. Campbell said.

"Yes. Their deaths seemed very strange. Two in one house, and no others affected."

"What did you find out?" Mr. Campbell asked.

"They died of arsenic poisoning. This was no accident. They've been poisoned over a long period of time."

"That's insane. Who'd do such a terrible thing?" Mr. Campbell said.

"That's for the police to determine. I've turned my reports over to them,"

"Good God!" Miss Joan gasped.

"Calm yourself, my dear. They'll find out who did this," Mr. Campbell said.

"The police will be in touch," Dr. Marshall said as he left.

Annie was down the stairs as fast as her legs could take her. Charles, Nancy and Mary were sitting at the table. They could see how excited she was.

"What's the matter?" Mary said.

"You'll never guess! Not in a million years!" Annie blurted. "I heard Dr. Marshall tell Mr. Campbell his sisters were murdered."

"Away with you!" Mary said.

"You must have heard wrong," Charles added.

"No, I didn't. He said they died of arsenic poisoning, and somebody's been giving it to them for a long time," Annie said.

"Saints preserve us!" Mary said making the sign of the cross.

"They deserved to be murdered," Nancy said. "I hope they burn in hell."

Nancy got up from the table and went to her room, locking the door behind her. Annie was shocked hearing her say such a thing.

"The doctor said the police will be investigating. The ladies never went out after Mr. Campbell came here to live, and none of us would do it," Annie said. "I bet *he* did it."

"Mr. Campbell wouldn't be doing such a thing," Mary said. "I know he isn't much, but he's not a bad person."

"Well, he wanted to marry that woman, and they threatened to cut him out of the will if he did," Annie said. "I'll never forget the night he was making Miss Lizzie drink whatever that stuff was."

"Come to think of it, he was taking them their trays at the end," Mary said.

"Maybe he was putting something in the wine. You know very well they hardly drank a drop until he came," Annie said. "He never drank wine, only whiskey."

"I've known him since he was a boy," Mary said. "He was a lovely child."

"Either it was in the wine, or it was put in their meals," Charles said.

"Let's try to figure this out," Annie said. "Mary put the food on their plates, and each plate was different. You know Miss Lizzie wouldn't eat carrots, and Miss Jemima wouldn't eat green beans, so it was like putting a name on their plates. Every night there was always something one of them wouldn't eat that the other would. We all know their tastes."

"You're right, but maybe the poison was sprinkled on top of the food. I wonder if it has any taste."

"I wouldn't want to taste it to find out," Charles said.

"We must think like the authorities," Annie said, playing the detective.

"Once Mr. Campbell came, he started serving them himself. He'd dismiss me like a common servant," Charles said. "Then he started taking the trays to their rooms. He had the opportunity, and the most to gain."

"How about Nancy?" Annie whispered. "She insisted on putting the trays on the dumbwaiter. If I offered to do it, she'd have a royal fit. She could have put the arsenic in the food. No one watched her once she took the trays away."

"What about you?" Charles asked Mary.

"Don't be looking at me! What would I be gaining if they died?" Mary said indignantly. "I'm too old to be getting another job."

"I don't have anything to gain either," Charles said. "I've been here for years, and serving two old ladies is a good position. No rowdy children running about upsetting my routine, and no dinner parties to worry about."

"Well, we can't sit here all day. Best get our work done. Mr. Campbell is the new owner, and we don't want to make him angry. Maybe he'll be keeping us on," Mary said.

"It will seem strange just working for one gentleman. I got used to the two old ladies, even if they weren't the most pleasant people to serve," Annie said.

The morning of the funeral arrived. Mr. Campbell had breakfast and told Charles he'd be expecting twenty for a light lunch. He left with Miss Joan for the funeral home and said they'd return around twelve.

Mary sent Nancy to the market, and Annie off to dust the sitting room. Mary busied herself slicing ham and roast beef for small sandwiches. Annie returned and helped Mary set them on a silver tray. Charles polished stemmed glasses for the drinks and filled the decanters.

"Remember the wakes at home?" Annie said.

"Indeed I do," Mary laughed.

"Three days of singing, drinking and praying. A grand time was had by all. It was only sad when it was one of your own," Annie said, remembering her own mother's wake.

"How true, deary, how true," Mary said. "I still remember the day me darling husband died," Mary said as she wiped away a tear. "It was awful. I thought I'd die, too."

Annie thought about Robert as the tears ran down her face. She decided not to tell Mary about him dying. There was enough death in the house without bringing up more sad memories.

Nancy returned carrying two large cakes which would be served with tea and coffee. She could see that Annie had been crying.

"What are you crying for?" Nancy said. "Surely not for those two old witches."

Annie didn't answer and turned back to her work. No matter what, she never spoke ill of the dead and wasn't about to now.

As the food was prepared, it was covered with linen cloths and sent up to the dining room. Annie laid the table as Charles watched, making sure she'd done it properly.

It was only eleven o'clock, so there was time for the staff to have a cup of tea. Annie sat down and slipped her shoes off under the table. Sometimes, she missed being able to run about barefoot as she did in the Craggs.

"I'm fair tired out with all the excitement around here," Mary said.

"Yes, indeed," Charles said.

"What do you think will happen now that the ladies are gone?" Annie said.

"I haven't got a clue," Mary answered.

"I don't care what happens. The happiest day of me life was the day they died. I hope they suffered," Nancy said.

"Sweet Jesus, that's a terrible thing to say!" Annie said.

"Good riddance to them," Nancy said.

The door bell rang. Charles raced up the stairs to answer it. Annie ran behind, knowing she'd have to take the wraps. Mr. Campbell and Miss Joan were the first to get back from the cemetery. They were followed by friends and relatives of the family. Everyone was dressed in black. As they entered, they kept hitting the big black wreath that hung on the front door. The dried leaves fluttered to the floor, making a mess.

Annie took the coats, then went to the dining room to help Charles. Everyone was extending sympathy to Mr. Campbell.

"What will I do without my dear sisters?" he said. "This house won't be the same."

"No, it won't be the same. He'll be having a party every night," Annie giggled.

"Be quiet!" Charles ordered.

The bell rang again, and in walked a large man wearing a navy blue uniform. It had gold braid on it as well as gold buttons. Annie asked Charles who he was.

"He's the chief of police, the high and mighty Dennis Logan. He runs the city and has more clout than the mayor," Charles said. "Better to have him as a friend than an enemy."

"Why is he here?" Annie asked.

"He's a good friend of Mr. Campbell. Now hush, and put some more plates on the table," Charles ordered.

The luncheon ended by two o'clock. Mr. Campbell and Miss Joan thanked their guests and went to the sitting room. Annie set about putting the rooms back in order as Charles returned to the kitchen. Annie tried to be quiet as she straightened the room. She was hoping to hear what was being said.

"Darling, that was a lovely funeral," Miss Joan said.

"Yes, it's what my sisters would have wanted. Quiet and dignified."

"What are your plans now?"

"I think I'll close up the house and take a suite at one of the hotels for the time being. This place is too big and gloomy for my taste. I'll have to let the staff go. It'll be hard sending Mary away. She's been with us since I was a boy, but I'll not be needing her anymore."

"What about the police? They're still investigating your sisters' deaths," Miss Joan said.

"That they are, but so far they don't have a clue as to who did it," Mr. Campbell said.

"I heard Chief Logan say it had to be someone in the house. That means you or one of the servants. You're the only one to gain by their deaths," Miss Joan said. "I certainly don't think you did it, but it does look bad."

"They don't know where the arsenic came from, and I most certainly didn't purchase it," Campbell said.

"What about the servants?" Miss Joan asked.

"Mary and Charles wouldn't have done it. I don't know much about the new girl, what's her name? Annie? She's just off the boat. She could be some loony they let loose in Ireland for all I know," Mr. Campbell said.

"Surely you don't believe that," Miss Joan laughed. "Now, if there's a loony in the house, it's Nancy. I don't know her very well, but you have to admit she's a strange one, always creeping about the house."

"She hated my sisters. They were very mean to her over the years," Mr. Campbell said. "I must mention her to Chief Logan when he starts on me again."

"Maybe you should have them check Annie's background. You never know," Miss Joan said.

"Good idea. If they're investigating the others, they just might leave me alone."

That was all Annie needed to hear. She was off down the back stairs taking two steps at a time. Charles, Mary and Nancy were in the kitchen.

"Holy mother of God! You look like the Devil's after you," Mary said.

"What's the matter?" Charles said, seeing how upset Annie was.

"Mr. Campbell and that woman are saying Nancy or me might have killed the sisters. Says he's going to have the police check up on us. He said I might be a loony let loose from Ireland. The nerve of him!"

"Saints preserve us! What a terrible thing to say!" Mary said.

"He's only doing that because they suspect him," Nancy said.

"I don't like this. I don't like this one bit," Charles said. "I think I'll look for a new position. I don't want to work for the likes of him, and besides, that woman is too common for my taste. I'm used to people of quality."

"You don't have to worry about leaving. I heard him say he's going to sack the lot of us," Annie said.

"Me too?" Mary asked.

"Yes, all of us."

"I've been here since he was a boy. That's gratitude for you!" Mary said. "Well, I'll just go live with me sister. Her children are grown, so she'll like having the company. While we're still here, they won't be getting the fine meals I usually cook. I'll fix them!"

"I'd burn everything if I were you," Annie laughed.

"That wouldn't be proper," Charles said, always being a stickler for the rules.

"To hell with him and his trollop! Maybe they'll be finding some arsenic in their food, too," Mary giggled.

"Don't make jokes about such things," Charles said.

"What will you be doing, Nancy?" Annie asked.

"I've saved most of me money for years, so I'll be going back to Ireland. I still have relatives there."

"That'd be lovely," Annie said. "Sometimes I think I should never have come here. It's not the grand place me dear Old Da said it was. If I didn't have me brothers, I might be doing the same."

That evening, they were called to the sitting room. Mr. Campbell was at the desk going through a pile of papers. Miss Joan had Miss Jemima's and Miss Lizzie's jewelry boxes, and was looking through them. She'd changed out of the black dress and was sitting in the blue velvet chair near the window. She was dressed in a dark green dressing gown that had red roses surrounding a very low neckline. There was a front slit in the skirt that was very revealing. Annie giggled, watching the very proper Charles stare at her long, crossed legs. Hearing Annie, he cleared his throat and looked away.

"I'm sorry to say that I'll be closing the house and you will no longer be needed. I want you to get the house in order. I'll give you a letter of recommendation and two weeks severance pay when the time comes," Mr. Campbell said.

As he was giving them their orders, the door bell rang. Charles went to answer it and found Police Chief Logan standing there. Charles ushered him into the sitting room.

"Good evening," Mr. Campbell said. "What brings you here? Have you found out anything?"

"Not yet, but we're checking all the shops for sales of arsenic. It may take time, but we'll get whoever did this," Chief Logan said.

"I've been telling my staff that I'm closing the house and letting them go."

"That may be, but I want to know where everyone can be reached. No one is to leave the city without telling me. Is that understood?" the chief said. "I have to do this."

The servants were dismissed and went back to the kitchen. Mary put the kettle on and made a pot of tea.

"Better make it strong," Annie said. "We'll be needing it."

"I'll not be staying around here cleaning up the house for the likes of them," Nancy said. "I'm leaving as soon as I'm packed."

"If you do, you won't get your severance pay or a reference letter. How will you ever get a job without it?" Charles said.

"They can stick their severance pay where Nora stuck the rent!" Nancy snapped.

"I haven't heard that expression since I was home in Ireland," Annie laughed. "Me sainted mother, God rest her soul, would wash our mouths out with soap if we said that. As a child, I never did know where Nora stuck the rent."

"You're too much, deary!" Mary said, as she burst into laughter.

It was late so Annie said good night and climbed the stairs to her room. She said her prayers and lay down thinking about Robert. The tears ran down her face as she thought how different her life would have been in America if only he hadn't died. She pictured the farm they were to buy, and the seven children they planned to have. Annie turned out the light and fell asleep.

The next morning, Mary had breakfast on the table when Annie entered the kitchen. The bacon smelled delicious as she filled her plate. Charles was on his second cup of tea and reading the newspaper.

"Are the trays ready to send up to the dining room?" Annie asked.

"Mr. Campbell said they wouldn't be up until noon and didn't want a meal, so we have plenty of time to enjoy ours," Mary said.

"That's lovely," Annie said. "Where's Nancy this morning?"

"Her door is closed. I guess she's still asleep. Let her be a while longer. I've put a plate in the warming oven for her," Mary said.

"When you're finished, we'd better get started covering the furniture with the dust sheets. Mr. Campbell said they would be leaving today, but will be back to check on us," Charles said.

Annie followed Charles up the stairs into the sitting room. The plants were removed and the fireplace dampers closed. Annie was thankful it was summer so there weren't any ashes to be taken away, even if it was Nancy's job. She got tissue paper and boxes for the many figurines and photos that cluttered the room. She wrapped them carefully and marked each box. Charles locked the windows and closed the heavy drapes. Each room would be done the same. Annie looked around when they finished. The room had an eerie look. It was dark, but the white sheets draping the furniture could be seen, and looked like ghosts. Annie shivered as they returned to the kitchen.

"Isn't Nancy up yet?" Annie asked.

"No. I've been so busy I forgot about her," Mary said. "Best be waking her."

Just then, there was a knock at the kitchen door. Opening it, there stood Jack. Annie was glad to see him, as she hadn't in over a week. He'd gotten a job, which he knew would please her. Mary was glad to see him, and welcomed him in for a cup of tea. Jack was a charmer and could get on the best side of anyone he had a mind to.

"Have the police found out who did it?" Jack asked.

"No, but they're telling us not to leave town. I heard that woman, Miss Joan, say I could be some loony escaped from Ireland. Imagine the cheek of her!" Annie said indignantly.

Jack started to laugh. Annie gave him a swat on the head. She said it wasn't funny, but ended up laughing with him.

Nancy was still nowhere to be found. Mary knocked softly on the door. She waited a bit, then knocked louder. There wasn't a sound coming from the room. She turned the knob and found it locked.

"Jack, me darling, would you be a dear and go outside and knock on the window? Maybe she's sick and can't answer," Mary said.

Jack did as he was asked, and returned shortly. Her room was on the ground floor. The windows were narrow, but big enough to see in.

"She's not in there," Jack said.

"That's strange. Maybe she got up early and went to Mass. We'll wait and see if she comes back," Mary said. "She has a friend a few blocks over. She could be there."

"This isn't her day off," Annie said.

"Well, she was pretty upset last night, and from what she said, she doesn't care about her job. She'll be back."

Jack left, saying he had to go to work, but would stop stop in again. Annie told him she'd be leaving the employ of the Thomson family, and to see if he could get her a room at the boardinghouse. He said he was sure there was a vacancy, and would arrange it. She'd saved most of her money, so would be in no hurry to find a new job. She planned to take time to see the sights of New York and visit her brother in Greenwich.

The bell rang on the annunciator, letting Charles know that Mr. Campbell needed him. He was gone for an hour and returned saying that he'd packed Mr. Campbell's bags. Mr. Campbell and Miss Joan had then left, saying they'd be back to check on the house.

"I don't know about you, but I'm taking the day off," Mary laughed.

"Me, too," Charles said, as he took out his bottle of wine. "I'm going to drink the whole damn thing and sleep it off."

"Mr. Charles, you shock me with your bad language!" Mary laughed. "I do believe you're human after all."

Annie took pen and paper and went out to the garden to write to her father. She could smell the lovely roses, and it reminded her of home. As young as she was when her mother died, she could still remember the roses her mother grew in front of their cottage. She was so homesick, she wanted to pack her bags and sail back to the Craggs.

That evening, Annie climbed the stairs to her room. A cool bath would be most enjoyable, and the breeze coming through her window on the third floor was lovely. Charles went to his room and wouldn't reappear until the next morning. Annie passed Mary's room and could hear her snoring. The house was still as she climbed into bed. The only sounds came from the street below. She said her prayers and fell asleep.

The next morning, Mary and Charles were in the kitchen when Annie came down. They looked worried. Annie asked what the matter was.

"Nancy didn't come home last night. I hope nothing's happened to her," Mary said.

"Sweet Jesus, has she ever done this before?" Annie asked.

"Never in all the years she's been here. I'm really worried. Best open her bedroom door and see if she's left a clue to where she is," Mary said.

Charles got the key ring from the top shelf in the pantry and unlocked Nancy's door. It was humid in the small room, so Charles opened the windows. Everything was neat, and the bed was made. Mary opened the closet and saw that Nancy's clothes were gone. The dresser drawers were empty as well. The cross and holy pictures had been taken down and the dresser top was bare. Her brush and hairpin dish were gone.

"Well, I'll be," Mary said, as she stood with her hands on her hips.

"Looks like she's flown the coop," Charles said.

"She said to hell with them. Guess she meant it," Mary said.

"I don't think we should say anything about this. Maybe she'll change her mind and come back," Charles said.

Nancy never did come back, and they guessed she'd gone to relatives. Mary was hurt that she didn't say goodbye. It was agreed not to tell Mr. Campbell about Nancy leaving. Besides, he was gone, too, and probably wouldn't notice the little lame girl was missing. Each day, another room was closed up. Annie helped Mary pack the kitchen. They kept out just enough utensils and dishes for them to use for their meals.

Several months passed as the servants remained in the big house. They had their bags packed and piled at the door, wondering when they would be told to leave. They'd packed their winter clothes, and weren't happy about unpacking them. The leaves were turning and it was getting cold. Mr.

Campbell sent their wages by messenger each month. Mary put Nancy's aside, thinking she might return.

At last, Mr. Campbell sent a note saying he would be arriving to give them their severance pay and letters of recommendation. Nancy hadn't come back, and it worried Charles how to explain it to Mr. Campbell. Charles planned to take a short holiday, then look for a new position. Mary was going to live with his sister. She'd been a cook for forty years, and it was time to retire. Jack would book a room at Mrs. O'Brien's boardinghouse for Annie when the time came.

Mr. Campbell arrived and called everyone to the foyer. Mary and Annie waited as Charles took Mr. Campbell from room to room making sure everything was done. It was cold in the foyer with most of the house closed up. Mary kept the kitchen stove burning to keep them warm during the day. Annie called her room the icebox, and piled every blanket she could find on her bed. She'd be glad to be away from the gloomy house.

Mr. Campbell and Charles returned to the foyer. From his pocket, Mr. Campbell pulled four white envelopes and handed them out. He looked around and saw that Nancy wasn't there.

"Where's that scullery maid, what's-her-name?" Mr. Campbell asked.

"She's not here," Charles said.

"I can see that, you fool!" Mr. Campbell said.

"She decided to leave early," Mary said, without saying *how* early.

"Write down your addresses for me. The police want them in case they have any more questions. Put Nancy's down, too."

"We can't. We don't know where she's staying," Annie said.

"I'll let the police know when I give them your addresses," Mr. Campbell said. "They'll find her."

He shook their hands, wished them well and was out the door. Mary expected a warmer good-bye since she'd taken care of him for so long, but none was forthcoming. They returned to the kitchen for one last cup of tea before locking up and leaving.

"Many a year I spent in this house," Mary said. "I wonder if we'll ever find out who killed the ladies."

"At least, the three of us seem to be in the clear," Charles said. "I guess they'll direct their inquiry towards Mr. Campbell, and yet, I can't see him as a murderer."

"They'll probably be looking for Nancy, too. Everyone knows how terrible they treated the poor soul," Mary said.

"It seemed the older they got, the meaner they were," Charles said. "I must say, they always treated me with respect."

"They yelled at me a few times, but I held me tongue and did what I was told," Annie added.

Annie looked at the clock and knew it was time to go. She thanked Mary and Charles, then left. She liked Mary very much, and would miss her. She hoped they'd see each other over the years. Now that she was leaving, Charles didn't seem so bad, but she wouldn't miss him. Down the street she walked heading for the boardinghouse. It was a nice day, and she was looking forward to going back to Mrs. O'Brien's.

CHAPTER 4

Annie was welcomed in by Mrs. O'Brien and shown to the same room she had when she first came to America. Annie stood there admiring the lovely cornflower paper, and felt right at home. Jack still had the room next to hers. He was working at a brewery, and delivered barrels of beer all over the city. He'd be home soon, and Annie was anxious to see him.

Before long, Annie heard Jack coming through the door making more noise than a herd of cows. He came flying into the room where she was waiting.

"Bejesus, Jack, slow down!" Annie said.

"Wait until I tell you what I heard!" Jack gasped.

"What is it?" Annie asked.

It's about Nancy, that scullery maid at the Thomson's. She's been arrested for killing the two old ladies. I just saw Officer Murphy. He told me."

"Holy mother of God!" Annie said. "When did this happen? I just left there, and no one knew where she was."

"They just nabbed her," Jack said.

"Dear God in heaven! The poor thing!" Annie said.

"The police checked the shops near the Thomson's place to see if anyone had bought arsenic. They said Nancy did, but Nancy says Mr. Campbell told her to. Said he saw rats in the garden. You know, you have to sign for that stuff when you buy it," Jack said.

"I never saw rats in the garden, and I used to sit out there all the time. And that still doesn't mean she gave it to them," Annie said.

"Murphy said she was screaming her head off," Jack said, "swearing on everything that's holy that Mr. Campbell told her to buy it."

"Are they questioning him?" Annie asked.

"Yeah, but he denies it, and he's a good friend of Chief Logan, so they let him go."

"That's terrible! I guess it's all in who you know that counts. I bet *he* did it," Annie said.

"They searched her room and found a box of arsenic on the closet shelf," Jack said.

"There's something not right here," Annie said. "When Nancy went missing, Mary and me checked her room trying to find out where she could have gone. There was no box of arsenic in her room. I'd swear to that on me mother's grave!"

"Maybe old Campbell put it there after you all left," Jack said.

"I'll bet he did. Where did they find her?" Annie asked.

"She bought passage on a ship. They were on the lookout for her since she said she wanted to go back to Ireland."

"Poor thing! She must be scared out of her mind," Annie said.

"Well, they've pinned it on her. Murphy said it'll be a quick trial," Jack said.

"I best be going to the police station and tell them what I know," Annie said.

"You better tell them how Mr. Campbell forced the old lady to drink something whatever it was," Jack said.

"I'll go there right now. I'll ask Mrs. O'Brien to go with me," Annie said.

Annie told Mrs. O'Brien what she knew, and without a second though, Mrs. O'Brien was out the door with Annie. Mrs. O'Brien marched down the street like a general leading her troops. Annie had to run to keep up with her. Up the stairs and through the door of the police station she stormed.

"Hello, Mrs. O'Brien. What can I be doing for you this fine day?" the policeman behind the desk said.

"You can be getting Chief Logan, that's what you can be doing for me," Mrs. O'Brien demanded.

"I'll see if he has time to see you."

"He'd better be seeing me. I have important information about the Thomson murders."

The ladies waited a few minutes, then were ushered into Chief Logan's office. Annie was a bit frightened by it all. Mrs. O'Brien took a seat across from the chief, as Annie stood by. She remembered him well. He looked like a very important man in his handsome uniform.

"Now what's this about the Thomson murders?" Chief Logan said.

"This is me friend, Miss Enright. She worked for the Thomson's for a long time and has something to tell you," Mrs. O'Brien said.

"Speak up, young lady," Chief Logan said.

"I was told you arrested Nancy, the maid from the Thomson's, because a shopkeeper said she bought a box of arsenic," Annie said. "Now, it seems that one of your men found a box of arsenic in her room. Well, I'm here to tell you that there was no arsenic in her room after she left. Someone must have put it there."

"Nonsense! You must have overlooked it," Chief Logan said. "Who in the world would put it there?"

"Mr. Campbell, that's who. I heard him making his sister drink something she didn't want. It was in the wee hours of the morning, and I think it was poison," Annie said.

"Never in a million years. He's broken-hearted over the death of his dear sisters. He's too fine a gentleman to do such a fiendish thing. His sisters were old. If it was for the money, all he had to do was wait. They weren't going to live forever," Chief Logan said.

"I know what I saw. There wasn't a thing left in Nancy's room. Ask Mary the cook, or better still, ask the butler. They were there, too," Annie said.

"I'll look into it, Miss Enright, but I'm sure you're mistaken," Chief Logan said. "Good day."

Mrs. O'Brien and Annie left, slamming the door behind them. Down the street they marched back to the house.

"He'll look into it, me foot!" Mrs. O'Brien said. "It'll all be swept under the carpet, if you ask me."

"You know, Mr. Campbell left the house before we did. Maybe he waited until we left and went back and put the arsenic in Nancy's room," Annie said.

"Of course he did. He wouldn't want you to be seeing him in Nancy's room," Mrs. O'Brien added. "You did the right thing telling Chief Logan."

"I don't think it'll do any good. He's got his mind made up," Annie said.

Annie left Mrs. O'Brien, saying she was going to church. She wanted to light a candle and pray for Nancy.

Weeks passed as Annie enjoyed her days of leisure. She went to Mass and visited William and Alexandra as often as she could. She'd learned to take the trolley and train to Greenwich and felt like an experienced traveler. On Michael's day off, he'd show up at the boardinghouse and take her to tea. He liked the people he worked for, and was happy he'd met a girl named Nora. Annie was happy that two of her brothers had found someone. Now if only Jack would.

Annie was content living at Mrs. O'Brien's, and glad to be away from the Thomson house. Mrs. O'Brien introduced Annie to several Irish girls that worked in a dress factory nearby. She'd go walking with them in the evening.

One afternoon, Kathleen Kiley appeared on Mrs. O'Brien's doorstep. She was one of the girls that Annie had met while working in the factory. Annie was delighted to see her. Kathleen had left the factory as well, and was working in Henkler's Food Shop. She shared a room with another Irish girl. Kathleen was happy, but was on the lookout for a husband.

"I'm so glad to see you. I've been wondering how you've been keeping," Annie said.

"I'm doing very well, thank you. The people I work for are Danish and a bit hard to understand at times, but I manage," Kathleen said.

"Are they nice to you?"

"Yes, they are. The only thing is that they have no sense of humor. If you tell a joke, they look at you as if you are daft," Kathleen laughed.

"I can't abide people like that," Annie said.

"It takes all kinds," Kathleen said, "especially here in America. I've never met so many different people in me life."

"I haven't met as many as I'd like, me being in service," Annie said. "I'm not too sure about the Danes. We learned in our history class how they invaded Ireland. They took over Limerick and the Shannon River. That's me part of Ireland, you know. We were taught that they were the devil's own, horns and all."

"Don't be worrying about that. I'm sure they're really nice people. I almost forgot what I've come for," Kathleen said. "The Henklers belong to a Danish club, and have invited me to a dance. Mrs. Henkler said I could bring a friend. Will you go with me?"

"It sounds lovely, but I haven't danced since I left home," Annie said.

"Please go! I don't want to be going alone," Kathleen begged.

"I suppose it'd be all right," Annie said.

"That's grand," Kathleen said. "It's tomorrow night. I'll walk by and get you. It's not far from here."

Kathleen said good-bye and left. Annie climbed the stairs to her room. Kathleen couldn't know the real reason Annie hesitated about the dance was because of Robert. She'd been in mourning for ever so long. She'd never told Kathleen about him, and besides, she didn't feel that close to her. She opened the trunk that sat in the corner and looked at all the lovely dresses that lay in it. She hadn't hung any, knowing she wouldn't be wearing them for a long time. As she looked through them, she came across the pale blue silk that Rose had made for her. It had white lace on the collar and cuffs. Annie eyed the dress and decided to wear it to the dance.

The next day, Annie put her hair in rag curls and pressed the dress. She ate a light supper, knowing there would be lots of food at the dance. Kathleen had told Annie about the delicious open-faced sandwiches and Danish pastries that would be served. Annie dressed, and admired herself in the mirror. She brushed her hair high on her head and let corkscrew curls fall down one side. Down the stairs she floated, allowing her full skirt to billow as she went. Jack was at the foot of the stairs and whistled when he saw her.

"I guess that's a compliment," Annie giggled.

"That it is," Jack said.

Just then, the door bell rang. Jack opened it and there stood Kathleen. Annie watched as Jack's eyes widened. Kathleen's dark red hair was pinned neatly with a gold clip, and fell in soft curls down her back. She was wearing a rust-colored dress that almost matched her hair.

"Hello, Kathleen," Annie said. "You're a good time-keeper."

"I try to be. My, you look lovely! The young men will be going crazy over you," Kathleen teased.

"Thank you, but I'm not looking for a fellow," Annie said.

"Who is this dashing lad?" Kathleen giggled.

"Oh, he's only me brother," Annie said. "This is Jack."

"How do you do," Jack said, as he bowed.

"Such a gentleman!" Kathleen said. "Nice to meet you."

The girls left, waving to Jack as they walked down the street. They took the trolley to Sullivan Avenue and walked the rest of the way to the Danish Club. Annie noticed the Danish flag hanging outside the building, and could hear the music as they entered. Mrs. Henkler called to them from across the room.

"I'm so happy you came," she said.

"Thank you," Kathleen said. "This is me friend, Annie Enright."

"How do you do," Mrs. Henkler said.

"You have a very nice club," Annie said politely.

"I'm glad you like it. Please make yourself at home. We're very informal here. Just a few homesick Danes having a good time."

Kathleen led Annie to a table and sat down. Two steins of beer were placed in front of them by a large woman wearing an apron. The girls giggled and sipped the beer. Across the room was a long table laden with all kinds of foods. Plates were stacked at one end and everyone helped himself. Kathleen got up and told Annie to come along.

"May as well have something to eat," Kathleen said.

"Looks lovely," Annie said.

The girls filled their plates with cheese, meats and some strange-looking fish. A second plate was taken for rye bread and butter. Kathleen dug right in as Annie examined the food.

"What's this god-awful stuff?" Annie said, as she poked at it.

"That's creamed herring," Kathleen said. "Surely you've had it before."

"Can't say that I have," Annie said.

"It's good. Raw fish in cream," Kathleen said.

"This isn't for me," Annie said, putting her hand over her mouth.

They sat there for a long time listening to the music and watching the dancers. Some of the men and women had on their native costumes. The ladies wore full skirts and peasant blouses, and had ribbons and flowers in their hair. The men wore pants held up by colorful suspenders. Some had felt hats with a feather sticking out of the band. The dancing wasn't much different than an Irish jig, and Annie was sure she could do it. She saw a large blond man dancing around and stomping his foot in time to the music. The floor shook as he whirled past them shouting, "Ooley, ooley!"

"Sweet Jesus, what is he saying?" Annie giggled.

"Who knows? But he sure is having a good time," Kathleen laughed. "I met a nice boy the last time I was here. His name is Ludde Dahlberg. I hope he's here again."

Just then the young man appeared and headed in their direction. He was with another man and waved to Kathleen. She beckoned them over.

"Good evening, Miss Kiley," Ludde Dahlberg said. "This is my friend, Nels Peter Nielsen."

"How do you do. This is me friend, Annie Enright," Kathleen said. "Would you like to join us?"

Ludde Dahlberg accepted and sat down next to Kathleen. Nels Peter seemed a bit awkward, but pulled a chair out and sat next to Annie. She peeked at him from the side, trying to get a good look at him without being too forward. Ludde Dahlberg was short and a bit overweight, and wore thick glasses. He was not handsome by any means, but had a beautiful smile. Nels Peter was tall and thin, and had the bluest eyes Annie had ever seen. He had dark blond hair and a deep tan. He seemed a great deal older than Ludde.

"Tell us about yourself," Kathleen said, looking at Nels. "Do you live here in the city?"

"No. I'm only here to wait for a ship to take me home," Nels said.

"You're going back to the old country?" Kathleen asked.

"Yah, I've had enough of this country. I've been here a long time. It's time to go home."

"Glory be," Annie said. "Why would you want to be going back?"

"I came when I was eighteen, and have been here thirteen years. I thought I'd have my own farm by now, but it hasn't worked out," Nels said.

"Sweet Jesus!" Annie whispered to Kathleen. "He's an old man."

"You must have made some money in all that time," Kathleen said.

"I had to send my earnings home to keep the farm in Denmark, so there's nothing left."

"That's too bad. To work hard all those years and have nothing to show it," Annie said. "Thank the Lord I get to keep me wages."

"It is my duty as oldest son to help the family, so it wasn't for nothing," Nels Peter said.

"I'm sorry. I didn't mean anything by it," Annie said.

They sat there all evening drinking beer, and talking about home and what they missed the most. Annie listened to Nels talk about his adventures in America. He'd worked his way all over the country, mostly going from farm to farm. She had to listen very carefully as he was hard to understand.

She liked him, and thought him very nice-looking, but he seemed too old.

The dance was over at eleven o'clock and everyone left the hall. Ludde and Nels said they would see the girls home. Kathleen and Annie protested, but they were gentlemen and insisted. Nels extended his arm to Annie. They walked down the street to the trolley. Much to her surprise, he boarded the trolley with her, saying he would take her to her door. Ludde and Kathleen decided to stop at a bar before going on. Annie didn't like the idea of going to a bar, and was glad Nels said he would escort her. When they arrived at Mrs. O'Brien's boardinghouse, Nels asked Annie if he could call on her the next day, Sunday, at two o'clock. She accepted without thinking. Nels thanked her and was off down the street. Annie climbed the stairs to her room and got ready for bed. She sat there thinking about Nels Peter, and wondered what had possessed her to say she would see him again. She had to admit, he was very nice, but so old. It kept going through her mind all night.

"Sweet Jesus, he's too old," Annie kept repeating.

Just then, Jack stuck his head in the door. She was surprised to see him home so early.

"Who the bleeding hell are you talking to?" Jack asked.

"I'm talking to meself."

"Better watch out. They lock people up for less than that," Jack laughed.

"Away with you! You should have been locked up years ago," Annie shot back.

"Did you have a good time with all those old square heads?" Jack laughed.

"Whatever do you mean, square heads?"

"That's what they call Scandinavians. It's like calling us Micks," Jack laughed.

"Well, I don't think that's very nice," Annie said. "Go to bed. I'll be seeing you in the morning."

The next afternoon, Annie sat in the sitting room dressed in her favorite green dress. Nels would be there soon. She was glad Jack was out, afraid he'd think it funny and call Nels Peter a square head. She could tell a sense of humor was something Nels Peter had little of. The door bell rang as the hall clock struck two. Annie opened the door, and there stood Nels holding a pot of red geraniums.

"Come in," Annie said.

"Good afternoon," Nels said, as he pushed the potted plant towards her. "This is for you, Miss Annie."

"Oh, thank you," Annie said.

"I wouldn't have brought you geraniums, but your friend said you like them," Nels said.

"I do. They're me favorite."

Mrs. O'Brien entered the sitting room and was introduced to Nels. Annie could see her eying the plant, and knew she was wondering why a gentleman caller would bring geraniums to a young lady.

"I do believe it needs a bit of water," Annie said.

"Yah. I had to bring it dry so it wouldn't spill on the trolley," Nels said.

Annie left the room as Mrs. O'Brien followed. Nels looked very uncomfortable as he sat down. He was holding his hat so tight he was crushing the brim.

"Good God, where did you get him?" Mrs. O'Brien giggled.

"I met him at the dance," Annie said.

"What's with the geranium?"

"He found out they're me favorite flower, so he got me one. Wasn't that nice of him?" Annie said, as she poured a little water into the pot.

"That was sweet he remembered, but you'll have to be upgrading your choice of flowers," Mrs. O'Brien giggled. "I'd be asking for roses. I guess he's nice enough, but he's too old for you," Mrs. O'Brien said.

"I know, but I don't want to hurt his feelings."

Nels and Annie left, and walked down the busy street. She had no idea where he was taking her. Before long, they arrived at a small park. Nels Peter motioned to Annie to sit on a bench. They sat there for a long time. Nels Peter never said a word. Annie felt awkward, and tried to make conversation. The most she could get out of him was an occasional "Yah."

After an hour of silence, Nels Peter said he would like to take her for Sunday dinner. Annie accepted, and was glad to leave the park. They walked down the street to a small restaurant. Nels Peter opened the door and found a table near the window. He pulled out her chair and waited for her to get settled.

The waiter came and handed them a menu. Annie looked at it and realized she had no idea what the strange-sounding dishes were.

"I'll read for you, Miss Annie," Nels Peter said.

"That'd be nice."

"I think maybe you like Danska Frikerdeller and red cabbage."

"What's that?" Annie said.

Nels Peter ordered beer to be served with the meal. Annie wasn't fond of beer, but would drink it to be polite. Two steaming plates were put down in front of them. Annie saw that there was a pile of meatballs drowned in a light brown gravy, along with red cabbage and new potatoes. The potatoes had the skins on, just the way she liked them. It was served on blue china and made a nice contrast with the red cabbage.

After the entree was finished, Nels Peter ordered apple cake and coffee. Annie enjoyed the meal, and decided she would taste all kinds of food in America. She'd already had Polish food, and now Danish. Her father'd told her how good Italian food was, so she wanted that to be the next on the list.

"Do you always use your first and middle names?" Annie asked.

"Yah, that's the way it is in Denmark," Nels Peter said. "You can call me Nels, if you want."

"I'd like that. Nels Peter sounds too formal," Annie said. "I don't have a middle name. It wasn't done back home. We took another name when we were confirmed."

After the meal, Nels walked her back to the boarding-house. He stood on the top step, thanked her and shook her head. Without another word, he was gone, leaving Annie standing there with her mouth hanging open.

Mrs. O'Brien heard Annie enter, and couldn't wait to hear about her day.

"Well, how was it?"

"I don't really know. We went to the park and stopped for a lovely meal. Then he brought me home. He hardly spoke a bleeding word. 'Yah, yah, yah' was all he said, Annie giggled.

"Stop teasing. He must have said more than that."

"Not really. I don't think I'll be seeing him again. He shook me hand and left. He's much too old. I felt like I was with me Old Da. He never smiled, but it was nice he brought me the geranium," Annie said.

"Did he tell you about himself?" Mrs. O'Brien said.

"Not very much. I know he's been here thirteen years, and sent all his money back to Denmark. He's supposed to be going back there, so I'll not be seeing him again. To tell you the truth, I couldn't care less."

Months passed and Annie didn't hear from Nels. She didn't give him much thought. She had agreed to work for Mrs. O'Brien, whose housemaid was leaving to get married. Annie needed a job, so a bargain was struck between the two ladies. Annie would work for Mrs. O'Brien in exchange for her room and board and a small wage. Annie felt very close to Mrs. O'Brien, and Mrs. O'Brien thought of Annie as her daughter. Working at the boardinghouse was easier than working for the Thomson family. She cleaned the house in the morning, which gave her most of the afternoon off, and after she helped with the dinner dishes she was free to do as she pleased in the evenings.

One afternoon Mrs. O'Brien came home from shopping. Annie went to the door and took the bundles from her. Annie could see she was out of breath and very excited. Mrs. O'Brien sat down and fanned her face.

"What's happened?" Annie asked. "You're all in a dither."

"I've just heard the most awful news about your little friend Nancy," Mrs. O'Brien said.

"What about her?" Annie said. "They should let her go!"

"She's been let go all right, but not the way you think. The poor thing's dead," Mrs. O'Brien said. "They found her stone cold, God rest her soul."

"Sweet Jesus," Annie said, making the sign of the cross.

"They say she hung herself in her cell," Mrs. O'Brien said. "People are saying it's because of a guilty conscience. Chief Logan said this finishes the case, and it saves the state a lot of money. I guess the high and mighty Mr. Campbell Thomson is glad. They won't be looking at him any more."

"I still don't think she did it, but for a Catholic to commit suicide is as bad as committing murder," Annie said. "She must have been out of her mind, poor soul."

Annie and Mrs. O'Brien went to Mass and prayed for Nancy. They dropped a few coins in the box and lit a candle for her.

Kathleen and Annie were becoming good friends, and spent their free time together. Kathleen wasn't seeing Ludde Dahlberg any more. She said he was boring. Annie knew what she meant. Jack would arrive home for the evening meal and escort Annie and Kathleen to the local bar. Annie could

92

see that Jack was smitten with Kathleen, and hoped Kathleen felt the same for Jack. Annie warned Jack that Kathleen was looking for a man of means, or at least, a man with a good job. Jack was neither of those. Annie didn't like going to bars, but it was the gathering place for all the young Irish immigrants. She did enjoy the fiddler, and it was nice to be with your own kind, Annie would say.

Annie enjoyed working and living at the boarding-house. One afternoon, she was busy cleaning the kitchen and when Mrs. O'Brien appeared, waving a letter in her hand.

"Annie, Annie! I've just gotten the grandest news," Mrs. O'Brien said.

"It must be good, by the way you're acting," Annie said.

"That it is. Me sister's girl is coming to America. I haven't seen her since she was a baby."

"That's lovely!" Annie said. "When is she coming?"

"She'll be here in three weeks. I can't wait to see her," Mrs. O'Brien said.

"To be sure," Annie said. "Will she be living here with us?"

"No, she's going to visit for a few days, then be off to Ohio. Her father has relatives there, and she'll be living with them," Mrs. O'Brien said.

"Well, at least you'll see her for a bit."

"Would you be doing me a favor and go with me to meet her?" Mrs. O'Brien asked.

"I've love to," Annie said. "I haven't been to the sea-port since I came meself."

"She'll be going through Ellis Island, like you did. I was never there since I immigrated before there was an Ellis Island," Mrs. O'Brien said.

"We can't go on the island, but you can see it from the dock," Annie said. "It's a lovely sight."

"I can't wait to see the darling girl!" Mrs. O'Brien said.

"What's her name, and how old is she?" Annie asked.

"Her name is Peggy McCray, and she's only sixteen."

"My, that is young to be leaving home," Annie said.

"I know, but me dear sister has twelve children and wants Peggy to have a better life. I imagine some of the rest will follow in time," Mrs. O'Brien said. "This way they can send a bit of money home to help out."

The three weeks flew by as Mrs. O'Brien scrubbed and cleaned for the arrival of her niece. She purchased some new clothes for Peggy, knowing she'd need some nice things to start her new life in America.

The morning of Peggy's arrival, Mrs. O'Brien and Annie left the house at eight o'clock and took a trolley to the seaport. Peggy's trunk would be sent on ahead to Ohio, so all she would have to carry was a small bag.

When they got off the trolley, Annie could smell the sea air. There was a strong wind and she had to hold onto her hat.

"Can you smell the salt?" Annie said.

"Yes, and some dead clams, too," Mrs. O'Brien laughed.

The ladies stood on the dock and watched the hustle and bustle about them. Annie remembered back to the day she had arrived.

"It's lovely here, isn't it?" Mrs. O'Brien said.

"That it is," Annie answered.

"What was it like on Ellis Island? Is it terrible?" Mrs. O'Brien asked.

"Needless to say, I was scared out of me wits, but it wasn't bad at all. The place is huge. Like a big hall, with red-tiled floor and big windows. They check your papers, then have a doctor look at you. You have to pass a health and mental test, and if you don't pass, God help you! They'll make you stay there or get shipped back to the old county.

You have to wear a name tag and carry processing papers. I couldn't believe all the stupid questions they asked," Annie said.

"Whatever do you mean?" Mrs. O'Brien said.

"They ask if you can read and write. The nerve of them, thinking we're ignorant! Then they ask if you've ever been in prison. To add insult to injury, they ask if you ever were locked away in the loony bin," Annie said.

"What did you say when they asked you about the loony bin? Did you tell them you were an inmate, and cross your eyes to prove it?" Mrs. O'Brien laughed.

"Now you sound like Jack," Annie giggled. "I did say something stupid when they asked me if I were a polygamist. Not knowing what it meant, I said, 'No, I'm not a polygamist. I'm a Catholic.' When the immigration officer laughed at me, I knew I'd shown my ignorance."

"You're a caution, deary," Mrs. O'Brien laughed.

At last, the small boat from Ellis Island arrived. Mrs. O'Brien saw Peggy as she walked down the gangplank. She had a picture of her and spotted her in a second. She ran to meet her, pushing others aside. Annie waited, not wanting to intrude on Mrs. O'Brien's special moment.

Annie was introduced to Peggy, and within minutes they were on the trolley going home. It was three o'clock, and the ladies were looking forward to a nice cup of tea. Mrs. O'Brien's niece hardly said a word, but had the same expression on her face that Annie had had when she arrived. Peggy was tall and thin. Annie knew Mrs. O'Brien would fatten her up in no time. Peggy had long dark hair that looked like it needed a good wash. Her eyes were dark brown and had a sadness about them. Annie guessed it was from having to leave home so young. Annie didn't think she looked Irish, but she surely sounded it when she spoke.

For the next few days, Mrs. O'Brien entertained her niece. Annie stayed out of the way, knowing Mrs. O'Brien only had her niece for a short time. Before she knew it, the young girl was gone. Mrs. O'Brien had a good cry as she sent her off on the train to Ohio.

On occasion, Annie would do the marketing for Mrs. O'Brien. She liked visiting the small shops and making the purchases. She especially liked the fruit shops with the barrels of apples and boxes of fresh grapes on display.

On the way home, she passed a paper boy. The headline on the paper screamed out at her. She stopped dead in her tracks and read it over and over again. She grabbed a copy, paid the boy and ran back to the boardinghouse.

"Mrs. O'Brien!" Annie screamed as she flew through the front door.

"What's going on? You're acting like the devil's after you," Mrs. O'Brien said.

"Read the paper! Read the paper!" Annie said breathlessly.

Mrs. O'Brien sat down and read the headline out loud: "Campbell Thomson Arrested In Sisters' Murders.

"I knew he did it!" Annie screamed. "Tell me what it says!"

"Seems his lady friend and him had a falling out. In a moment of remorse, he'd confessed to her that he'd murdered his sisters. After that, she didn't want any part of him, thinking she could be accused of conspiracy. She threatened to tell the authorities unless he gave her a lot of money. In other words, she was blackmailing him. He got drunk one night and almost beat her to death. The neighbors heard her screaming, and called the police. They rushed her to the hospital. Says she almost died. That's when she told them," Mrs. O'Brien said.

"I thought there was no justice in the world. I guess there is," Annie said.

"He'll be put to death, that's for sure," Mrs. O'Brien said.

"He deserves it," Annie said. "He really murdered three people. Poor little Nancy was another one of his victims."

The arrest was the talk of the neighborhood. Everyone praised Annie, since she'd said Campbell was the murderer all along. Even Officer Murphy tipped his hat to her as she passed by.

One morning, Annie went to the mailbox to collect the mail. Much to her surprise, there was a letter for her. The only letters she ever got were from Ireland, and this was not from there. She ripped it open and saw that it was a note from Nels. It was hard to read, as his writing was terrible and his spelling atrocious. Annie ran to the kitchen and asked Mrs. O'Brien to help read it.

"Glory be! He says he'd like to see you again. He'll be here come Sunday."

"Well, this is a surprise," Annie said. "I didn't think he liked me. I wasn't too thrilled with him, either. I thought he was going back to Denmark."

"He says he isn't leaving, so wants to visit you," Mrs. O'Brien said.

"I guess it'd be all right. I've nothing better to do," Annie said.

"At least you might get another free meal," Mrs. O'Brien giggled.

Sunday arrived, and Nels was right on time. Once again, they walked to the park and sat on the bench. Annie looked at him and still thought he was nice looking. She liked his clear blue eyes and tanned face. He was much taller than she, and very trim. She was determined to get him to talk, so she decided to ask questions. He'd be forced to answer her, if only to be polite.

"Tell me about your family and Denmark," Annie said.

"My father and mother are still alive and working the farm. My brother and sister came here and live in Racine,

Wisconsin. They're living on our uncle's farm. There's another sister and two brothers still at home," Nels said.

Annie tried to keep a straight face at the way he said "mother" and "father." She realized how easy it was for the Irish to come here, speaking the same language, and how hard it must be for those that didn't.

"What's the farm like in Denmark?" Annie said.

"It's pretty big for the island we live on. You know, Denmark is all islands," Nels said.

"I didn't know that."

"We have ninety acres, mostly wheat. I used to love playing in the windmill when I was a boy," Nels said. "The town is called Jorlouse, on the Isle of Fyn. It's been our family's farm since 1770. A lot of Nielsens have been born there."

"Our farm's only ten acres," Annie said. "We have milk cows and raise corn."

"I miss my family, but I miss my church the most. You should see it. It's white stucco with a red tile roof," Nels said. "I was in California for a while, and the churches are the same there."

"That sounds lovely. Our church is small, and made of stone with a slate roof. I miss going there and hearing the organ," Annie said.

"Yah, I know how you feel," said Nels.

"You said you were going back. Are you still planning that?"

"I don't know what I should do. I have passage on a ship, but that can be canceled if I decide to stay. This has not been the land of opportunity, as I expected. As you said, I've worked so hard and have nothing to show for it," Nels said. "I'm thirty-three years old. I guess you think I'm an old man?"

"Of course not," Annie lied.

Nels started to laugh at the face she made, knowing she'd lied. For the first time, Annie heard him laugh and saw his beautiful smile. She decided he was human after all. Annie looked at him and compared him to her poor dead husband. Robert had been of the gentry and was well educated. He could be quiet like Nels, but he had a great sense of humor. Annie knew it took a lot to make Nels laugh. She looked at his hands and saw they were tan and calloused from years of hard work. She was beginning to like him, even if he was an old man. Annie could see that he was spotless. His suit was a bit shiny and his collar frayed, but his shoes were highly polished. She remembered how she was always after her brothers to polish their shoes before going to Mass.

Nels took Annie to the same restaurant for afternoon coffee and cake. She enjoyed it, but it was getting late, and she had to get back to the boardinghouse to help with the evening meal.

Nels took Annie home and thanked her for going out with him. Annie said she had had a nice time, and extended her hand. Much to her surprise, Nels kissed her. She backed away in shock, hoping none of the neighbors saw it. She stood there and watched him go off down the street.

Annie opened the door as Mrs. O'Brien greeted her.

"Did you have a nice time, deary?"

"I can't believe it! He kissed me good-bye. Right on the lips!" Annie gasped.

"He didn't!" Mrs. O'Brien said. "You're teasing me."

"He did! I couldn't believe it! He's so shy."

"You know what they say about still waters," Mrs. O'Brien laughed.

"Yes, I do. They run deep and dirty, with a devil at the bottom," Annie giggled.

Mrs. O'Brien went to the kitchen as Annie headed for her room. She sat at the window and looked down at the busy street. The thought of the kiss made her heart pound. It had taken her by surprise, but she *did* like it. She hadn't felt like this since she'd first met Robert. She gave her geranium some water and turned it to the sun, still thinking about Nels and wondering if she'd ever see him again.

Annie didn't hear from Nels. She thought about him everyday, and wondered what he'd decided to do. It was strange he hadn't even called on her to say good-bye if he was still going back to Denmark.

It was winter now, and had snowed for days. Annie got up early to go to Mass. She tried to get Jack up, but he wouldn't move. She was upset with him as he'd lost his job again and had stayed out half the night drinking.

She put on a warm coat and high lace boots to keep out the chill. Her stepmother had sent her a lovely green and white scarf from Ireland. She put it over her head and wrapped it around her neck. In one of her frivolous moments, she'd bought a fur muff, and she felt grand as she walked down the street showing it off. She knew it was the sin of pride, but would say an extra prayer and hoped to be forgiven. It was still snowing, making the street look clean. She could see her breath in the cold air and hear the crunch of the snow under her feet. The church bells were ringing in the distance, making a lovely sound.

Going to Mass always made Annie feel good. The priest seemed nice enough, but she missed Father O'Leary, her parish priest in Askeaton. Her father called him an old flannel mouth, but he was loved by all. The priest here was Father Doyle, and she liked him well enough, but he was a bit aloof for her taste. People in America didn't seem to be as close to their parish priests as they were at home.

After Mass, Annie stopped to light a candle for Robert. She stood there looking at the little candle flickering in the dark church as tears ran down her face. She said a prayer for Nancy and hoped she'd be forgiven. She'd heard that Nancy's few relatives didn't attend her burial because she'd committed suicide. Annie wiped her tears away and left the church. As she started down the steps, she was surprised to see Nels waiting for her. He was smiling up at her as she came down.

"Good morning," Nels said.

"Good morning. This is a surprise," she said. "I thought you'd gone back to Denmark."

"I've decided to stay. I canceled my passage and found a new job," Nels said.

"That's wonderful," Annie said.

"Are you glad I'm staying?"

"Yes, I am."

"I wrote to my mother and father and told them. They're doing better now, so I can work for myself," Nels said.

"That's grand," Annie said.

"Would you like to go for coffee?" Nels asked.

"That'd be nice," Annie said.

Annie went to take Nels arm, but he took her hand instead. She was surprised, but had to admit she liked it.

They found a coffee shop not far from the church. Nels showed Annie to a table and ordered coffee and pastries. She'd had a big breakfast, but did enjoy the sweet pastry. It had almond filling, which was her favorite. A second cup of coffee was poured as they sat there.

"Why did you change your mind about going home?" Annie asked.

"Like I say, the farm is doing better. My younger brother, Peder, in Wisconsin, will help them for a while. I've been doing it for thirteen years, so now I start my life."

"That's only fair," Annie said.

"I have to tell you the rest," Nels said shyly. "I don't know what comes over me. I met you, and don't want to go back."

"My, I don't know what to say," Annie said, as Nels took her hand.

"I don't know you long, but I like you very much," Nels said.

"Holy mother of God," Annie said. "You're staying because of me?"

"Yah, I am. I was hoping you could get to know me and maybe like me, too."

"I already like you," Annie said.

"Good, then maybe I have a chance with you?"

"Yes, but there's something I must be telling you," Annie said. "I was married in the old country. Me husband, God rest his soul, died on the way over."

"Yah, that is a sad thing to happen, but that is in the past now," Nels said.

Annie couldn't believe how calmly he took it, not that there was anything to be ashamed of. She told him the whole story. He sat there listening and nodding his head. He never said a word, and acted as if it had never happened.

"Maybe I could court you, and see how you feel," Nels said. "Do you think that'd be all right?"

Annie didn't know what to say, but nodded her head in agreement. That was all Nels needed. He began to tell her his plans. He said he knew from the first night he met her that she was the one for him. He'd traveled all over the United States and had never met anyone he cared for. This surprised Annie, but she was flattered. He told her he'd gotten a position as head gardener on an estate on Long Island. They would supply a cottage for him to live in, along with his wages. His employers, Mr. and Mrs. Jensen, were Danish and preferred to have Danes work for them. Annie knew the Irish that had money always hired their own, so this seemed right. He told her he'd be able to come to the city often, as he had Thursday and every other Sunday off. This she knew from working private herself. Nels said he'd visit her on his days off, if it was all right with her. Annie agreed, thinking she hadn't made any promises, but this way she'd get to know him. Maybe something would come of it. Nels saw her to the door and kissed her once again. She was expecting him to do this, and decided it was very nice. Annie watched as Nels took two steps at a time down the stairs of the boarding-house. When he reached the bottom, he turned and smiled up at her.

"I think I love you, Miss Annie!" Nels shouted, as he went down the street waving to her.

Annie looked around, hoping none of the neighbors had heard. She was blushing as she opened the door. Mrs. O'Brien came running when she heard Annie.

"Well, how was your day?"

"Nels met me after Mass and took me for coffee," Annie replied.

"What did he say?" Mrs. O'Brien asked.

"I think he's going to propose. In fact, I know he's going to propose," Annie said.

"You don't mean it! Tell me what happened," Mrs. O'Brien said.

Annie told her about her time with Nels. Mrs. O'Brien sat there listening, not saying a word.

"He says he's going to court me for a year," Annie said.

"This isn't what I'd call a whirlwind courtship," Mrs. O'Brien laughed.

"What do you think?" Annie said.

"I don't know what I think. The question is, do you like him?"

"Yes, I do. He told me so much about himself today. I think he's an honest, hard-working man, and one of responsibility by the way he helps his family. He's nice looking and very clean. To tell you the truth, me heart did flips when he kissed me," Annie giggled.

"I do believe you're falling in love, but are you forgetting he isn't Catholic? You can't marry outside the church," Mrs. O'Brien warned.

"He hasn't asked me to marry him yet, but if he does, I'll worry about it then."

"This is very serious, deary. You'd better be worrying about it before you get in too deep," Mrs. O'Brien said. "This decision will be for the rest of your life."

Annie went to her room and lay on the bed. She stared at the ceiling and watched the sunlight dancing on it. She knew she really liked Nels, but he was so different from the people she was used to. What would her family say if she married him? She knew her father would have a royal fit if she married outside the church. Her brothers just might shoot him. Then, there was the age difference. Over thirteen years!

"I could be a young widow again," Annie said aloud as she dozed off.

She decided not to tell her brothers about Nels for a while, and knew Mrs. O'Brien would keep her secret.

CHAPTER 5

Six months passed. Annie worked for Mrs. O'Brien and saw Nels on his days off. It was a long trip from Long Island to the city, but Nels always arrived on time. Annie fussed with her hair and tried to look as nice as possible for him. Nels said she was the most beautiful girl in the world. It made Annie blush as she'd never thought of herself as being beautiful. With Nels, compliments were few and far between. Annie would remember his words for a long time.

Nels finally proposed. She could tell it took all his courage to ask. They walked to the park and sat on what was now their bench, and he blurted out the words. In a heartbeat, she accepted. She knew in that moment she loved Nels even more than she had loved Robert. If she'd had any doubts about him, they were gone.

"Annie, you make me so happy," Nels said. "I promise to be good to you."

"I know you will," she said shyly.

"I think you'll like the cottage I have for us. I've been fixing it up for you. We'll need more furniture, but I think it will be good," Nels said.

"I'm sure I will, but we're not thinking of all the problems that face us," Annie said.

"What do you mean?"

"I haven't told the family about you. Me brothers think I've only seen you a couple of times. Your not being Irish will be hard for them to handle, but not being Catholic will send them through the roof," Annie said.

"Don't worry. I will talk to them," Nels said.

"Sweet Jesus, they'll kill you. You realize, if I don't get married in the Catholic Church, I'll be living in sin?" Annie said.

"I'm Lutheran, and supposed to marry my own kind. My family won't approve either."

"Your family doesn't live here. Mine does. I've got three big brothers to contend with, plus me own conscience. I've been a good Catholic all me life, and will be going against everything I've been taught."

"I don't think God will disapprove. That's all that counts. A lot of people in America marry different nationalities and people of different faiths. I know an Italian man who married a Jewish girl, and they're doing fine," Nels said.

"What about their families? Are they accepted?"

"No, I guess not, but they're happy. That's what's important."

"Maybe so, but I'm very close to me brothers. It'd break me heart if they disowned me," Annie said.

"We'll work it out. You'll see," Nels said.

"I'll have me brothers come to Mrs. O'Brien's next Sunday, and we'll tell them. It'll be better to do it there. I doubt if they'd cause a ruckus in front of her."

"I'll do whatever you say," Nels said.

106

Annie wrote to William and Michael and told them she had something very important to tell them, and to be at Mrs. O'Brien's the following Sunday. She asked Jack that night so he wouldn't make any other plans. He begged her to tell him what was going on, but she said she'd wait until they were all together. Annie knew it best to talk to her brothers on Sunday morning. Jack would be sober, at least.

It was the longest week of her life as she practiced how she'd tell them. Nels insisted on being there. Annie wasn't sure it was a good idea, but agreed. She'd ask Mrs. O'Brien to be there, too.

Sunday morning, she was up early and went off to Mass. It was a gray day, and looked as if it would rain at any minute. She knelt in church and prayed that God would forgive her for what she was about to do, and prayed her family would understand. As she lit a candle, she heard a crash of thunder so loud it shook the walls of the church.

"Sweet Jesus, it's starting already," Annie said. "The wrath of God is upon me!"

The woman standing next to her heard what she said and moved away. Annie giggled, knowing she'd scared the poor thing. She left church and walked back to the boarding-house. Nels was already there and seemed as nervous as she. They sat in the sitting room not saying a word. Mrs. O'Brien entered and offered them something to eat. They refused, knowing they wouldn't be able to eat a thing. Jack came in and was startled to see Nels there.

"Top of the morning," Jack said. "What's going on?"

"You remember me friend, Mr. Nielsen, don't you?" Annie said.

"Yeah, but I still want to know what's going on," Jack said.

"Don't be so rude. I'll be telling you when the rest get here," Annie said.

The door bell rang. Annie looked at Nels and clenched her teeth as she opened it. In walked Michael and William, laughing at a joke they'd shared. When they saw Annie, they hugged and kissed her, lifting her off the floor.

"How you been keeping, Annie me darling?" Michael said.

"I've been well," Annie said.

"Now what's all this about?" William said. "What's so important?"

"Maybe she'll tell *you*." Jack asked. "She won't tell me a bleeding thing."

"I want you to meet me friend," Annie said. "This is Nels Nielsen."

Nels stood up and the boys shook his hand. Annie offered them tea, but was turned down. Mrs. O'Brien walked in and sat next to Annie.

"I have something to tell you, and I'm not sure how you're going to take it," Annie said.

"Get on with it," Jack said, knowing the bars would be opening soon.

"I've been seeing Nels for ten months now, and he's asked me to marry him."

The room fell silent as Annie's brothers stared at Nels. He stared back, holding his ground. Annie held her breath and waited for the explosion.

"What the bleeding hell are you saying?" Michael roared.

"Nels and I want to be married," Annie said.

"You're wanting to marry this, this *Dane*?" Jack said. "We don't even know him!"

"Well, I know him, and that's all that counts," Annie said.

"We don't know anything about him! There must be a reason you've been hiding this from us," William roared. "Are you in trouble?"

"Don't speak to your sister like that!" Nels roared back. "Annie's a good girl."

"Don't you be telling me how to talk!" William yelled. "I'll be talking any way I damn well please!"

"Now stop this!" Mrs. O'Brien ordered. "This isn't getting you anywhere."

"Annie, you're not serious, are you?" Michael said.

"Yes, I am. He's a fine man and I'm going to marry him," Annie said.

"Never on God's green earth will you be marrying a heathen!" William yelled.

"How dare you call me a heathen!" Nels yelled even louder.

"You're not a Catholic, are you?" Jack said.

"No, but I'm no heathen. I belong to the Lutheran Church and we're every bit as God-fearing as you!" Nels roared.

"If you're not Catholic, you're a heathen in my book!" Michael yelled.

"Stop this yelling!" Annie cried. "I love Nels, and I want to marry him, and I would like your blessing."

"You're not getting any blessing from us! Jesus, Joseph and Mary! Have you lost your senses?" Jack said.

"You're not marrying him, and that's final! End of discussion!" William said.

"I am marrying him, and it's just too bad," Annie said.

Annie's brothers could tell by her face she would do as she pleased, whether they liked it or not. They knew how stubborn she could be once she'd made up her mind.

"Why the hell did you bother to ask us here if your mind's already made up?" William asked.

"You're me family, and I was hoping you'd be happy for me," Annie said.

"How can we be happy with our sister living in sin? It's a disgrace to the Enright family," Jack said.

"Don't you be talking to me about disgrace! The life you lead is a disgrace!" Annie screamed.

Michael stood up and stepped towards Nels, who was already standing. Annie feared there'd be a trouble. She could see Jack clenching his fists and knew he'd like nothing better than a fight.

"Now, boys, we'll not be having any brawling in me house," Mrs. O'Brien said.

Michael stepped back and looked at Annie. He couldn't believe she'd turn her back on the church. He would try guilt.

"If you do this, you'll kill Old Da. How the hell will you tell him?" Michael said. "He'll die of a broken heart."

Annie felt terrible at the thought of hurting her father, but she loved Nels and wanted to spend the rest of her life with him. She could picture her father in Corbett's Pub getting very drunk. In fact, he'd probably be drunk for a week. William told her she should talk to a priest. He'd straighten her out. But that was one thing she didn't want to do.

"I'm sorry you don't approve of me, but I love your sister and I'll be good to her," Nels said.

"Don't even talk to me," Jack said.

"Maybe you could turn Catholic," Michael said, thinking this was a good solution. "Then you wouldn't be hurting our father, and Annie wouldn't be living in sin."

"Never," Nels said. "I'm as strong in my faith as you."

"Then there's nothing more to be said," William sighed. "You do this, and you'll no longer be our sister. As far as we're concerned, you're dead."

"I'll never speak to you again!" Jack yelled. "Come on, boys, we're needing a drink!"

They were terrible things to say, and Annie knew they meant them. They walked out the front door, slamming it so hard the whole house shook. Annie sobbed at the thought of never seeing her brothers again. Nels put his arms around her and tried to console her. Mrs. O'Brien made a pot of tea and returned to the sitting room. She handed Annie a steaming cup and told her to drink it, knowing it would make her feel better.

Annie and Nels stayed in the sitting room all afternoon and evening trying to find a solution for their problem. None was found. It was getting late, and Nels had to get the last train home. Annie walked him to the corner, kissed him good night and returned to the boardinghouse.

The following week was torment for Annie. Jack wouldn't speak to her. They had rooms next to each other and ate at the same table, but not one word came from his mouth. Nels sent her a letter asking her to come to Long Island the following Sunday. He'd planned to see her on Thursday, but had to work. He enclosed directions and a dollar to pay the fare. He'd meet her at the train.

Off she went on Sunday morning right after Mass. She had on her best blue dress and straw hat. She wanted to look extra nice since she'd be meeting some of the people Nels worked with.

Nels was waiting for her when her train arrived. He had come in a buggy to fetch her, and cracked the whip to get the horse moving. The countryside was lovely and reminded Annie of her home in Ireland. They rode through a village on a dirt road and headed out towards the coast. She could see the green fields and the ocean beyond. The wind was so strong it almost blew her away. They turned into a long drive that was lined with trees. On the edge of the cliffs was a huge mansion. It was stone, and trimmed in dark green. Annie's eyes widened at the sight.

"Saints be praised," Annie said. "This place is bigger that Desmond's Castle back home."

"I know what you mean. It's the biggest house I've ever seen. It took a while to get used to."

Nels turned the buggy into a side lane and pulled up in front of a small cottage. It was made of wood, and freshly painted grey. It had a front porch and shutters on the windows that were painted green. Much to Annie's delight, there was a window box filled with geraniums sitting on the railing of the porch. Nels knew how much she liked them, and thought it would please her. He helped Annie down, then stood back watching her face for a reaction.

"Is this your cottage?" Annie gasped.

"Yah, it's mine. Mr. Jensen said I can paint the rooms if I want. Do you like it?"

"I love it," Annie giggled. "It's beautiful, and with me sweet geraniums it looks lovely."

"I don't know why you like those things," Nels laughed. "They don't smell so good, and when the flowers drop off, all you have is thick green stems. Looks like tree stumps."

"Everybody teases me about them, but I've always loved them."

Nels opened the front door and led Annie into a small sitting room. Beyond that was a kitchen, which he showed her with great pride. He'd made a cabinet and put up shelves, showing off his carpentry skills. There was a black coal stove with a coffee pot sitting on it. Annie knew she'd have to learn how to make coffee. In the corner was a wooden icebox. The floor was laid with green and white tiles. There were a few dishes on the shelves, but no curtains on the windows. In the center of the room were a kitchen table with four chairs. Off the kitchen were two small bedrooms and a bathroom. In the back of the cottage there was room for a flower garden. Annie wouldn't have to have a vegetable garden, as the estate had a large one that supplied the big house and workers.

Nels made a pot of coffee and offered Annie a chair. She watched Nels filled the pot with cold water and counted out six tablespoons of coffee. It had a lovely aroma as it cooked away on the stove. When it was ready, he poured it into two white enamel mugs and handed one to Annie. She'd buy some china cups for her tea when they married. She could never drink tea from a tin cup!

"Well, what do you think? Could you be happy here?" Nels asked.

"To be sure. It's a lovely place."

"Then all you have to do is say you'll marry me," Nels said.

"It's not that easy. What am I to do about me church and me family?" Annie said. "I can't be married in your church. I don't think I could bring meself to be doing that."

"We can be married by a judge and if we're blessed with babies, you can have them christened Catholic. Would that help?"

"Yes, but I'd still be living in sin," Annie said.

"Do you really believe that? It's all nonsense to me. We have a loving God. He knows you're a good person. I doubt if you'd be punished," Nels said.

"When you say it like that, it seems right, but me family will never forgive me."

"Annie, you've always put your family first. From what you tell me, you took good care of them after your mother died. Isn't it time you did for yourself?" Nels said.

When Annie talked to Nels, everything seemed right. Without another thought, she said she would marry him. She wanted to have her family's blessing, but if it was not to be, then that was the way it was. She'd talk to her brothers one more time and hope for the best.

They spent the rest of the day making plans. Nels would find a judge that would marry them in a month's time. This would give them time to furnish the cottage, and time for Mrs. O'Brien to replace Annie.

Nels took Annie on a tour of the estate. It had huge gardens which Nels was in charge of. There were two greenhouses. One was filled with lovely cut flowers that Nels took to the main house every morning.

They walked around the big house to the kitchen door. Nels knocked softy. A blond woman in a white uniform opened it. Nels introduced her to Annie. She was Swedish and hard to understand, but she was pleasant enough. Her name was Ranghild, and she had worked there for years.

113

"I thought you said the Jensens only hire Danes?" Annie whispered.

"They usually do, but she's a good cook, so Swedish is close enough," Nels said.

Annie had enjoyed the day, but it was getting late. Nels drove her to the railroad station. He kissed her goodbye, and said he wouldn't be able to see her until the following Sunday. He was off on Thursday, but needed time to find a judge.

Annie sat on the train as it chugged through the countryside. She knew she'd have to face her brothers again and hoped they'd understand. She'd marry Nels no matter what they said. It was late when she returned to the boardinghouse. She'd hoped Jack would be around, but he was nowhere to be seen.

The next morning, Jack was having breakfast when Annie entered. She could tell he was still angry with her. He kept his eyes on his porridge and wouldn't look at her.

"Good morning, Jackie," Annie said, hoping to get a laugh out of him.

"Don't be calling me that," he snapped.

"You old grouch," Annie teased.

"Don't be talking to me," Jack said.

"I'm talking to you whether you like it or not. I've decided to marry Nels and I hope you'll be happy for me, but if you're not, I'm sorry."

"You're out of your mind. You marry that Dane, and I'll never speak to you again! How can you go against your family and church?" Jack said.

"If I want to marry him, then that's what I'll have to be doing."

Jack got up from the table, knocking over his chair, and stormed out of the room. Annie sat down and wrote to William and Michael, asking them to come on Thursday. She wanted to talk to them without Nels being present. She was afraid they'd have a few drinks in them and really cause trouble if Nels was there.

Thursday afternoon, Michael, William and Alexandra arrived. Jack was out, and wouldn't return. Annie was glad to see Alexandra. She served tea and cake to her guests, then told them about her plans. She waited for a reaction, but none was forthcoming. They sat there in silence.

"Say something," Annie said.

"What's to say? Looks like you've made up your mind," Michael said.

"I can't believe you're doing this," William said. "Mother will be turning over in her grave, and Old Da will never forgive you."

"It's bad enough he's not Irish, but not being a Catholic is going too far," Michael said.

"Now, just wait a minute!" Alexandra said. "You married me, and I'm only half Irish. I was born in this country. I'm an American. Can any of you say the same thing?"

"She's right," William said. "We are in America, you know. Everybody is mixed here, but at least you're a Catholic."

Alexandra seemed to be on Annie's side, and she was glad for the help. Annie went on and explained that they would be married by a judge and hoped they would attend.

"Never in a million years will I come!" Michael roared.

"Alexandra and I won't be a party to this, either," William added.

"I'd come, but I must do as my husband says," Alexandra whispered.

"I know, but thank you anyway."

"What about all the babies you wanted," Michael said. "What will they be if you're not married in the church?"

"I'll be having me babies, and Nels promised they'll be brought up Catholic," Annie said.

"That may be, but you still won't be married in the eyes of the church," Michael said.

"We won't be seeing you again. I hope you know what you're doing," William said.

With that, they left. Alexandra came back and kissed Annie on the cheek, letting her know she was still her friend.

Annie cried until Sunday, when Nels came. He could see how upset she was, and took her for a walk in the park. Nels told her he'd arranged to have a judge marry them on October 14th. It was 1903, over two years since she'd stepped off the boat. She felt better now that Nels was there. The next thing she'd have to do was write to her father. She knew he'd be very upset at her marrying a Dane, and a Lutheran would surely send him into a rage. She filled the letter with all the wonderful qualities Nels had, hoping that would help.

Mrs. O'Brien had a friend who owned a store that sold household goods. His name was Sidney Levine, and he'd had his eye on Mrs. O'Brien for years. Sometimes, she'd invite him to her home for tea. He was a widower and enjoyed her company.

One morning, she took Annie to his shop and introduced her. Annie couldn't believe all the wonderful things she saw on the shelves. Sidney seemed to be a nice man, and Annie could tell he liked Mrs. O'Brien.

"Good morning, Sidney," Mrs. O'Brien said. "I've brought a young lady to see you."

"What can I do for you this fine day?" Sidney said.

"I'll be needing a few things for me new home," Annie said shyly.

"Look around, deary, while I visit with Sidney," Mrs. O'Brien said.

Annie bought some pots and pans and, of course, a big tea pot. Next, she chose six tea cups and saucers. She would need sheets and a blanket. She had to guess about the size of the windows, but knew she could alter the curtains to fit. Sidney gave Annie his "special price," as he would say.

116

Annie knew it was because of Mrs. O'Brien. They left the shop and walked down the street. Annie was glad she'd saved her money when she'd worked for the Thompsons.

"Is Sidney your sweety?" Annie teased.

"Of course not," Mrs. O'Brien blushed. "I've known him for years. Knew his wife, too. She was a fine woman."

Annie packed here treasures in boxes to be taken to the cottage. Mrs. O'Brien asked her friend Sidney to take them. He said he'd be happy to. He owned an automobile with a large trunk, and all Annie's possessions could be taken in one trip. Annie was impressed that he had an automobile. Mrs. O'Brien said he bought it to drive to the cemetery every Saturday to visit his wife's grave, which was in the country.

"He's got nothing else to spend his money on," Mrs. O'Brien said. "He may as well enjoy himself. He's doesn't have any children to leave it to."

"Now I know where you go on Saturday," Annie giggled.

"Well, I have accompanied him on occasion," Mrs. O'Brien said. "Now stop your teasing!"

Annie had so many things to carry she was grateful for Sidney's help. They spent the day fixing up the cottage. Nels and Sidney sat on the porch as the ladies got to work. Annie was pleased to see that Nels had put up a shelf in the sitting room. It was a perfect place for her treasured china Madonna and the big gold cross she'd brought from Ireland.

After tea, Mrs. O'Brien and Sidney left for the city. Nels wanted Annie to stay. He would send her home on the late train.

October 14th arrived. Annie was up early, and dressed in a new green suit she'd purchased at a nearby dress shop. The suit cost eight dollars, making Annie feel like a spend-thrift. It was a month's wages at the Thomsons. She also bought a velvet picture hat with a fine green veil that covered her eyes. Around her neck she wore the gold cross her Aunt Eleanor had given her when she was confirmed. She looked at her left hand and could still see the mark from her first wedding ring. She'd taken it off when she'd met Nels. She put on little white gloves, and stood back and admired herself in the mirror.

She hoped her brothers would change their minds and show up. She knew that Jack was the angriest of all. He hadn't spoken to her since she first told him. Jack would walk past her acting as if she wasn't there. She felt worse about him than her other brothers as she'd always been so close to Jack.

Mrs. O'Brien agreed to be matron of honor. Ludde Dahlberg, Nels' friend, would be the best man. Nels arrived with Ludde Dahlberg right on time. Nels was carrying a bouquet of yellow and white daisies for Annie. She hadn't thought about a bouquet, and thought it so sweet that he'd remembered. He had on his best suit, which had been freshly pressed. His shoes were shined, and his stiff white shirt was starched like cardboard. Annie could see his suit was well-worn by the shine on the elbows and knees. His shirt collar was a bit frayed, but she thought he was very handsome.

Annie's heart was pounding as Nels took her arm and walked down the street to the trolley stop. Mrs. O'Brien and Ludde Dahlberg followed the bride and groom. They didn't have to wait long for the trolley, and were off in seconds. They got off several blocks away and walked towards a big house. Annie could see a sign hanging outside. It said "Judge Marcus J. Brown" in big gold letters. Annie was very impressed. In that one split second, she almost turned and ran. She knew she was doing a terrible thing by not getting married in a Catholic church. Nels seemed to read her mind, and squeezed her hand. One look at Nels put that thought out of her mind.

The ceremony was short and businesslike. It was nothing like the church wedding she'd had when she married Robert, but it counted, and that was all she cared about. Nels placed a small gold band on Annie's finger as Judge Brown pronounced them man and wife. Nels kissed her quickly. It would take Annie a long time to get used to Nels' serious nature.

After the wedding, they went to a fine restaurant. Nels ordered wine. Ludde Dahlberg stood up and toasted the newlyweds. Mrs. O'Brien always carried a huge pocketbook, and out from it came a gift for Nels and Annie.

"This is for you," Mrs. O'Brien said, as she handed Annie a lovely wrapped gift.

"How nice of you," Annie said.

"I hope you like it. Sidney gave me a good bargain," Mrs. O'Brien laughed.

Annie opened the package carefully so as not to rip the paper. She folded it and laid it on the table. In the box was a white lace tablecloth. It reminded Annie of the one her mother had many years ago, and she started to cry.

"Now, now, deary, don't be crying," Mrs. O'Brien. "This is a happy day."

"I wish me brothers were here to celebrate with us," Annie said.

"Nels doesn't have any family here, either. I'm sure he feels the same," Mrs. O'Brien said.

"You're right. As long as we have each other and dear friends like you," Annie said.

Mrs. O'Brien got Annie laughing, and before long she was having a lovely time. They ordered roast beef, a favorite of Annie's. The table looked lovely, with stemmed glasses and sparkling silverware. After the main course, a white cake with globs of icing was served. It was as close to a wedding cake as they could get. After dinner, Ludde Dahlberg paid the bill. It was his wedding gift to them. Nels and Annie thanked their friends for coming, and went off to catch the last train to Long Island. Ludde Dahlberg would see Mrs. O'Brien home.

It didn't take long for them to reach their station. Christian, the second gardener from the estate, was there to meet them. Nels had arranged it before he left. He nodded to Annie as she climbed into the carriage, but he never spoke.

When they reached the cottage, the lights were on and there were bowls of flowers in every room. The table was set, ready for a last cup of tea before bedtime. Annie was pleased to see how lovely everything was.

"This is wonderful," Annie said.

"I'll try to make you happy," Nels said.

"You've made me happy already," Annie said.

"I'll make some tea," Nels said.

"No, I'll be doing it. It's me job now," Annie said as she filled the kettle.

"I'll let you be the boss in the kitchen," Nels laughed.

"You're so good in the kitchen. Who taught you?"

"I had to teach myself. When you live alone as long as me, you have to learn to cook or go hungry," Nels said.

They spent their wedding night in the little cottage, and were up early the next morning to start their new life together. Nels left at the crack of dawn, but came home every day for lunch. Annie worried she'd be lonesome, but her days flew as she took care of her home and husband. She did miss her brothers and their great sense of humor. The other help on the estate were very reserved and rather unfriendly, or so Annie thought. It would take time to realize it was just their Scandinavian nature.

Mr. and Mrs. Jensen told Nels to bring Annie to the big house so that they could meet her. Annie dressed carefully so she'd make a good impression. Nels was a bit nervous, but was indeed proud of his new wife. They walked across the great rolling lawn to the kitchen door. Nels held it for Annie. Ranghild nodded to Annie as they entered, then turned back to her work. The houseman arrived and was introduced to Annie. His name was Frederick, and he was a bit more friendly than the other servants. He said he'd inform the Jensens that Nels and his wife were there.

Mr. and Mrs. Jensen entered the kitchen, and Nels introduced Annie to them. Annie curtsied and said good morning. They looked her up and down, smiled and shook her hand. The meeting didn't take long, which was a relief to Annie.

Nels and Annie settled into their new life on Long Island. Nels worked hard, but had time to spend with Annie. Sometimes he would take her to visit Mrs. O'Brien.

In 1905, Annie had her first child. Nels had ordered a boy, and a boy was what she'd delivered. They named him Niel Peter, Americanizing his name a bit.

Nels sent word to Mrs. O'Brien that the baby had arrived. She was delighted and decided to pay Annie a visit, but not before sending the good news to Annie's brothers. She hoped they'd be so pleased they would forget they'd been angry with her. She told Jack, but he walked away without saying a word.

Sunday afternoon after the baby was born, Nels and Annie were in the sitting room when they heard an automobile stop. Nels got up to see who it was. Much to his surprise, it was Mrs. O'Brien, Michael and William.

When Annie saw them, she began to cry. Tears of happiness streamed down her face.

"Look at the two scallywags I found by the wayside," Mrs. O'Brien laughed.

William and Michael hugged their sister. In that moment, they'd forgiven her. They decided that if Nels could make her happy, that was all that counted. Of course, they would expect Nels to keep his promise of having the baby christened Catholic.

"We missed you so much," Michael said.

"That we did," William added. "We missed you getting after us about our dirty shoes."

"I missed you, too, but where's Jack? Couldn't he come?" Annie asked.

"I'm sorry, deary, but he hasn't changed his mind," Mrs. O'Brien said.

"I'm afraid he's mad at us, too," William said. "He showed up at me place last night, and when I told him we were going to come and see you, he hit the roof. He was pretty drunk, and looked like he'd been in a fight. You know how he gets."

"That I do," Annie said.

"When I went to Mrs. O'Brien's this morning, he was pretty hung over and in a foul mood. I tried to talk some sense into him, but all he did was swear at me," Michael said. "I thought he was going to hit me, he was so mad."

"He swore on everything that's holy he'd never forgive you for going against the church, and for us siding with you," William said.

"Since when is he holier than thou?" Annie said. "Bejesus, he doesn't even go to Mass. He has a nerve, passing judgment on us!"

"He said if we made up with you, he was finished with us, too," Michael said. "Told me he never wants to see any of us."

"He'll come around. Just wait and see," William said. "It was the drink talking."

"I hope so," Annie said. "Try talking to him again."

That night, the Enrights' reunion turned into a wild Irish party. Nels wasn't a drinking man, but he had a good supply of Irish whiskey in case his rowdy brothers-in-law ever visited. Mrs. O'Brien brought a cake from the Irish bakery, reminding Annie of home.

By one in the morning, they decided to leave. They hugged and kissed all the way out the door. Blessings were given to the new baby by the very drunk uncles. Annie worried about them driving home, but Michael assured her he was fine.

"I'm so glad we've made up," Annie said.

"Yah, it's good," Nels replied.

"I hope Jack'll come around," Annie said.

"I'm sure he will," Nels said.

By 1908, Annie had two more babies. One was a girl named Anne for her mother. But her name would soon be changed to Sis, since little Niel couldn't say "sister." The name would stick. Another boy was born, and was named William. He'd be called Billy. Annie was well on the way to having the seven children she'd always wanted. Nels would throw up his hands and say, "Three is enough!" but Annie had other plans.

Annie's family came to welcome each new arrival, but Jack, that is. She knew he'd like Nels if he got to know him, and that he'd have great fun with her children. After all, he still acted like a child himself.

Taking care of the children, Nels and the cottage was a great deal of work, but Annie still managed to cook wonderful meals and make soda bread on Sunday. It was a thing her mother had done when Annie was a girl, and Annie wanted her children to have the same tradition. She learned to make Danska Frikerdeller, red cabbage and Danish apple cake. However, her housekeeping was not up to Nels' standard, and he *would* let her know.

One day, Nels came home for his noon meal and found Annie in the front yard playing with the children.

"Is my lunch ready?" Nels asked.

"Yes, I've got the soup heating," Annie said.

Nels entered the cottage, followed by Annie. Black smoke was coming from the kitchen. Nels ran to the stove and pulled the burning pot off the fire.

"Damn it, what are you doing?" Nels roared. "Are you trying to burn the place down?"

123

"I'm sorry, I didn't think the fire was so high," Annie said.

"No, you don't think! I don't know what's the matter with you. All you want to do is play with the children."

"This is the first time I've ever burned anything," Annie explained.

"Well, it better be the last," Nels added.

"Who do you think you are? Don't talk to me like that!" Annie yelled.

"I'll talk anyway I want! Look at this place! It's a mess! If you spent more time cleaning and less time playing with the children, you'd be better off," Nels yelled back.

Annie was furious, but she knew he was right. If she had the choice of washing the floors or taking the children for a walk, she'd choose walking.

"I've been cleaning house all me life," Annie said. "First for me father, then for the Thomsons and now you."

"You got to do better!" Nels demanded as he left, slamming the door behind him.

Annie cleaned up the kitchen, all the while doing some slamming of her own. She was angry, and would be all afternoon.

"Who does he think he is? Mr. Perfect?" she said, as she threw the burnt pot out the back door. She would retrieve it later and spend an hour trying to get it clean.

Annie decided to keep the peace and clean the cottage. She put the children down for a nap and got started. By the time Nels got home, it was shining. A stew was simmering on the stove along with some new potatoes.

It was almost dark when Nels arrived. He washed up and sat down at the kitchen table. Annie told him what was for dinner, but he never said a word. She put the food on the table and waited for Nels to notice how nice everything looked. The meal was eaten in silence. Even the children were quiet, knowing that Dad was still angry. After dinner, Nels took his coffee into the sitting room. Annie was sure he'd

124

notice how neat and clean it was. She waited, but he said nothing.

"Well, aren't you going to say anything?"Annie said.

"About what?" Nels said.

"I broke me back cleaning and scrubbing the house to please you, and you don't even notice," Annie said.

"I noticed," Nels said. "It should be like this all the time. If my mother could do it with six children, you can do it with three. She didn't waste time playing silly games with us," Nels said.

"Playing with the children is good for them. It helps them learn, and at least they have a sense of humor, a thing you're missing!" Annie yelled.

"Don't need humor. Life is hard. Working is all that counts," Nels said. "My mother knew what was important."

"Why don't you go back to your mother! You won't be missed!" Annie screamed.

Annie was furious as she went to put the children to bed. She listened to their prayers, then returned to the sitting room. She sat there glaring at Nels. Within minutes, he got up and went to bed without saying good night.

Annie put on her shawl and went out onto the porch. She stood there looking up at the stars. There was a full moon. The shadows of the trees on the ground looked like monsters with outstretched arms. She could hear the ocean crashing on the rocks at the front of the main house. She was still angry, and thought a walk would make her feel better. Down the gravel path she went towards the sound of the water. She stood on the edge and looked out on the waves.

"I wish I could fly. Fly away back to me Craggs," Annie said, as she started to cry.

The wind blew, making Annie shiver. She pulled her shawl around her shoulders.

Huge waves were rolling in and causing a fine spray to make the grass wet under her feet. Annie turned to go back when the earth beneath her gave way. Down she went, hitting the rocks as she tried to stop herself. The cliff edge ended as Annie fell to the bottom, striking her head on a rock that was buried in the sand. Everything went black.

Nels woke up at five o'clock. He washed and dressed and went to the kitchen for his morning coffee. Much to his surprise, the coal stove was out and the coffee hadn't been made. Billy was crying in his crib, and he wondered where Annie was. Nels went outside and called her. Getting no answer, he began to get angry again. He saw Christian arriving for work and asked him to send a girl from the big house to sit with the children until he found his wife.

The sky was gray and Nels knew there'd be a cloudburst at any minute. He walked down the path to the barn and toolshed. He walked around the main house, and on out the main gate. Annie was nowhere to be seen. He was beginning to worry. They'd had arguments before, but she'd never left the house. It wasn't like Annie to leave the children. Nels went to the kitchen door of the main house and asked Ranghild if she'd seen his wife. Ranghild looked at him as if he'd lost his mind.

"What in the world would she be doing here at this time of the morning?" Ranghild asked.

"I can't find her, and I'm beginning to worry," Nels said.

"What happened? You have a fight?" Ranghild said.

"Yah, but nothing serious," Nels said.

"I'll send Frederick to help look for her," Ranghild said.

Nels went outside as Frederick joined him. Nels explained that Annie had disappeared. Frederick went ahead of Nels and started towards the cliffs. Nels followed him, but didn't think she'd go there. As they walked along, they kept trying to see down below. Nels' heart was pounding. He feared she had been foolish enough to go there, and might have fallen. Frederick suddenly stopped short and called to Nels to come.

A short way down, they saw Annie's shawl blowing in the wind as it hung from a small limb that jutted out from the rocks. Nels started down all the while calling to Annie, as Frederick followed. It was slippery, and the earth gave way underfoot. As Nels reached the bottom, he saw her lying on the sand. The tide was coming in and her feet were in the water. Nels got to Annie and turned her over. There was blood on her forehead. Her hair was matted with sand, and she was wet and cold. Nels' heart almost stopped, thinking she was dead. He started to shake her and call her name. Annie moaned and opened her eyes.

"Annie, are you all right?" Nels cried. "Talk to me!"

"Nels, what happened?' Annie said.

"I don't know," Nels said, as he wiped the blood away from her forehead. He could see she had a deep cut.

"I remember," Annie said, "I went for a walk and must have gone too close to the edge. I remember falling. Have I been here all night?"

"Yah, it's a wonder you weren't killed," Nels said. "I'd never forgive myself if anything happened to you. What would I do without my sweet little geranium?"

As much as Annie ached, she smiled. He'd never called her that, and would never again. Annie wouldn't forget that moment for a long time.

Nels and Frederick helped Annie climb the cliffs. When they got to the top, Nels told Frederick to send for the doctor. With that, he swooped Annie up in his arms and carried her home. He laid her on the bed and washed her face with warm water.

Doctor Whitcomb arrived a short time later and examined Annie.

"Nothing seems to be broken," Doctor Whitcomb said. "You're a lucky young lady. It's a good thing you landed on the sand, and not on the rocks. You could have been killed."

"Thank the good Lord," Nels said.

"She's very bruised, and should rest for a few days," Doctor Whitcomb said. "She'll probably have a small scar on her forehead, but nothing to worry about."

"I'll take good care of her," Nels said.

"Just keep an eye on her. She lay on that cold beach all night, and it could turn into pneumonia. If her condition changes, call me at once," Doctor Whitcomb ordered.

"I'm a strong girl," Annie said. "Raised with me four brothers, I had to be."

"Yah, I got good strong farm girl," Nels said.

It would take a week to recover. Nels waited on her hand and foot, a thing he'd never done before, even when she was expecting a baby. He said he was sorry for getting after her about the house, and knew she was doing the best she could.

Mrs. Jensen heard about Annie's accident and insisted that her girl stay and help with the children. Annie stayed in bed for a few days and enjoyed every minute, even if she ached from head to foot.

A month after Annie's accident, Nels came home with bad news. The Jensens had decided to sell the estate and move into the city. Nels would not only have to look for a new job, but a place to live as well.

Nels wrote to his old friend, Ludde Dahlberg, who lived in Newburgh, New York, and asked him if he could help him find a job. Nels said to let him know as soon as possible since they would have to leave soon.

It only took a few weeks to hear from Ludde. He'd arranged to rent a house for them in Balmville, a part of Newburgh. He said that Nels could work on an estate with him. He would only be second gardener, and no cottage went with the job, but that was the best he could do.

Nels was grateful for the help. The Jensens gave him two weeks severance pay, and Annie still had a small nest egg to see them through. It didn't take her long to pack. Nels hired a wagon to take their furniture to Balmville. Annie and the children went to Mrs. O'Brien's for a couple of days until Nels could get things ready in the new house. She would follow on the train with the children. Annie was sad to leave Long Island, but thought of going to Balmville as a great adventure.

Mrs. O'Brien was delighted to see her, and fussed over the children. It was most pleasant staying at the boarding-house. Annie was hoping to see Jack, who still hadn't spoken to her or her brothers since she'd married Nels. He'd never seen the children, and she was sure once he saw them his heart would melt.

"When does Jack get home?" Annie asked.

"I'm sorry to tell you, but he left the day he knew you were coming," Mrs. O'Brien said. "He wouldn't tell me where he was going."

"Maybe William or Michael will know," Annie said.

"I don't think so, deary," Mrs. O'Brien said. "But I've invited them for supper tomorrow night, so we'll soon find out."

"That's lovely. I haven't seen them in some time," Annie said.

Michael, William and Alexandra arrived the next evening. There was a great deal of news to catch up on.

The good news of the evening was that Alexandra was expecting her first child. That called for a toast. The other good news was that Michael was going to marry Nora, the girl he'd been keeping company with.

"At least Old Da will be pleased with *your* choice. Irish *and* Catholic," Annie said.

"Has he written to you?" Michael asked.

"No, he's disowned me," Annie said.

"He's written to me, but I'm sorry to say he never mentions your name," Michael said.

"I write to him all the time and tell him how good Nels is to me, and how I've had the children christened Catholic," Annie said. "I guess it doesn't make any difference."

"I knows he loves you and is just being stubborn. He'll come around," William said.

"Have you found out where Jack is?" Annie asked.

"No. He just cleared out," William said.

"He's been drinking a lot lately," Michael said. "Been in some bad fights, too."

"I think when you left and married Nels, he felt abandoned. He's so thick, he'd never admit he was wrong. You know, you were the one he always depended on," Michael said.

"Yes, I know. If only he'd talk to me," Annie said.

"He went bag and baggage when he left. Hardly said a word to me," Mrs. O'Brien said.

"I'm really worried about him. God only knows what could happen to him," Annie said.

"You know, the city's building a new-fangled train underground and they've been hiring laborers. Maybe he's working down there," Michael said.

"What are you meaning, a train underground?" Annie asked.

"It's a tunnel under the city that trains go through. Got stations and all. They're calling it the subway," Michael said. "Of course, it will take years to finish."

"My, my, won't that be grand," Annie said. "I'd like to ride on one someday."

The evening passed quickly. Everyone left, but promised to visit when Annie was settled in Balmville. Mrs. O'Brien gave Annie her old room on the third floor. It was a reminder of days past. The three children were fast asleep when she climbed into bed. She missed Nels. He'd been so nice to her since her accident, and she liked the attention.

Two days later, Mrs. O'Brien's friend, Sidney, drove Annie and the children to the railroad station. It was the first

130

time the children had ridden on a train, and they were very excited. Annie laughed as they pressed their faces against the glass. The tracks wound along the Hudson River. Ships sailed past bringing their cargo to the city.

The family arrived in Newburgh that afternoon. Nels was there to welcome them. He'd borrowed Ludde Dahlberg's wagon. The children thought this was great fun. They drove through the city and headed out on a narrow road. There were single-family houses on both sides. Annie noticed how poor-looking they were, and wondered what hers would be like. Nels pulled the wagon up in front of a small brown house. The shingles were in need of repair, and some of the paint was badly chipped. It was close to the road, but had a nice front porch. There was a white front door, and flower boxes under the two windows. In the boxes were red geraniums. Annie was delighted.

"Glory be, me sweet geraniums. How nice," Annie giggled. "You never forget."

"I hope you like it. I wanted to make it good for you," Nels said.

"It's grand, truly grand," Annie said, as she gave him a kiss on his cheek.

Nels looked around, hoping no one saw it. Even after living with the outgoing Annie, he still was as reserved as ever. Ludde Dahlberg arrived and helped Nels carry the furniture inside. There was a small sitting room and a good-sized kitchen on the first floor. Upstairs were two bedrooms and a small bathroom. Annie knew the children would fit nicely into one bedroom.

Nels and Ludde put their things in the rooms as Annie got a fire going in the coal stove. She looked around the kitchen and saw how shabby it was. It was in need of paint, and the floor was well-worn. There was a sink with rust spots from the dripping faucet. The icebox door was falling off, but Nels said not to worry. He'd repair it. Each room had one bare light bulb hanging from the middle of the ceiling.

Annie didn't care. She was happy, and knew she could fix it up. Annie thought of this as a new life and looked forward to making friends with the neighbors.

The next morning, Nels went off to work. She packed a lunch for him and watched him walk down the street. She came back inside and looked around the sitting room. Some of the plaster had fallen from a wall, but she thought she'd hang a picture to hide it.

After she tidied up, she put the little ones in the carriage, took Niel by the hand and was off down the street. She needed a few things at the market. Annie said hello to anyone that looked her way. She knew she'd have to make friends, or die of loneliness. The market was over a mile away, but Annie had walked the hills of Ireland and didn't think much of it. When she reached the store, she bought a roasting chicken, some potatoes, carrots and a bag of apples. She'd brought all her staples with her from the other house, so she was well supplied. When they got home, Annie fed the children and put them down for a nap. She'd planned a special meal for their first night in the new house, and hoped it would please Nels.

Nels arrived home after six. It was already dark, and Annie could see how tired he was. The children raced to the door, glad to see him. The house was filled with the aroma of the meal cooking on the coal stove. No matter how late Nels was, he'd always wash and change his clothes. He'd never come to the table without combing his hair. Annie would tease him, saying he should put on a tie. He'd tell her it was the way he was brought up, and he wanted his children to do the same. She remembered the meals at home in the Craggs. She'd fight with her brothers just to get them to wash their hands, let alone comb their hair.

After the meal, Annie and Nels sat at the table. She poured him a second cup of coffee, and a cup of tea for herself. She always saved the coffee for Nels, knowing how much he enjoyed it. Tea was cheaper, and she liked it better.

Nels noticed the bowl of apples. He knew they were expensive. He told Annie he'd bring any produce they needed from the estate he was working on. The day workers were allowed to take the leftover fruit and vegetables.

Months passed as Annie settled into her new life. It was hard, but she managed to make tasty meals with very little. She'd always made soda bread on Sunday, but that became a luxury.

Annie kept up with her correspondence. One letter to her Father and Rose, and one to young Cornelius. In every letter, she asked if they'd heard from Jack. Maybe he was writing to them and they knew where he was. They never answered, but the letters weren't returned, so she hoped someone was reading them.

Annie made friends with a woman that lived next door. Her name was Philomina Masi. She'd come from Italy with her husband, Danoto, and their daughter, Antoinette. Philomina wanted a big family, but it wasn't to be. Antoinette was a beautiful child with black curly hair and brown eyes. They'd only been in America a short time, but their English was very good. Philomina was ten years older than Annie. Her husband was a barber by trade and earned about the same as Nels. Philomina was as short of money as Annie, but knew ways to save a little that Annie hadn't even heard of. She taught Annie how to make pasta. Annie would pile cups of flour on the table, make a well in the middle, and put the eggs and salt in it. The children thought this was great fun. It was better than making mud pies. They'd never seen their mother mix flour without using a bowl. The children loved making pasta, and it made a good filler for three hungry children.

One morning, Annie checked the cupboard and saw that she needed some flour. It was a lovely morning, so decided to walk to the market. She changed her dress, washed the children's faces and was off down the street.

The market was busy as she made her purchase. She had a few coins left over, so she bought the children a treat. As they walked along, Annie spotted a large brown envelope lying in the gutter. It was partially hidden by leaves. Annie stooped over and picked it up. The envelope was sealed, and thick with its contents. There was a name written on it, but no address. The name was Ronald Sperling. Annie had no idea who he was. She had a great desire to open it, but knew she should turn it in at the police station. She thought it must be filled with hundreds of dollars. Annie laughed, thinking her imagination was running away with her.

The Balmville Police Station was only one street over, so she decided to go there before going home. She entered and gave the envelope to the desk sergeant, telling him where she'd found it. He took her name and address in case the owner wanted to get in touch with her. Off Annie went, feeling as though she'd done a good deed for the day.

The next morning, Annie heard someone knocking on the door. Opening it, she found a well-dressed gentleman standing there. She could see a long black automobile parked at the curb, with a chauffeur sitting behind the wheel.

"Can I be helping you?" Annie asked.

"Yes, are you Mrs. Nielsen?" the gentleman asked.

"That I am," Annie said.

"I'm Mr. Sperling, and I'm here to thank you for finding my envelope and turning it in."

"Think nothing of it," Annie said.

"May I come in?" Mr. Sperling asked.

Annie was surprised, but opened the door wider, allowing him to enter. He walked around the sitting room looking at the family pictures. He was tall and had black hair. His clothes were expensive-looking, and she could tell he was a man of means. He seemed to be about fifty years old.

"Will you be sitting down?" Annie asked, not knowing what else to say.

Mr. Sperling sat down and took an envelope from his breast pocket. He handed it to her and said it was a small reward. Annie refused it, saying honest didn't require a reward. He told her the envelope she'd found was very valuable to him, and he appreciated its return. He insisted she take it.

"Will you be having a cup of tea?" Annie said.

"That would be delightful," Mr. Sperling said.

Annie went to the kitchen and made the tea. All the while, she wondered whatever possessed her to invite him to tea. He wasn't a friend or family. She must be mad, she thought.

Annie picked up the tray and returned to the sitting room. She sat down on the sofa next to him and poured him a cup.

"Tell me about yourself," Mr. Sperling said.

Before she knew what she was doing, she was telling him her life story, and he was telling her his. As they talked, he kept his eyes on her and kept moving closer. She began to feel uncomfortable and thought it best he leave.

"Your husband is fortunate to have such a lovely wife," Mr. Sperling said as he patted her hand.

Annie pulled her hand away. Sweet Jesus, he's one of those my wife-doesn't-understand-me kind, she thought. Annie was an innocent, but wise enough to get his meaning.

"You'll have to excuse me. I have to be getting me children," she lied.

"You're a beautiful lady. It's hard to believe you're old enough to have children," Mr. Sperling said. "I've certainly enjoyed our conversation. May I visit you again sometime?"

"I think not, sir," Annie said. "My husband wouldn't appreciate that."

"We don't have to tell him, do we?" Mr. Sperling laughed.

"You'd better leave. I have things to do," Annie said.

Mr. Sperling bowed and kissed her hand, a very long kiss to Annie's mind. He said no more and left. Annie sat

135

there fanning herself. What in the world was she thinking, bringing a stranger into the house? She'd almost forgotten about the envelope that he'd left. She opened it and found twenty-five dollars, a small fortune in her eyes.

Annie told Nels about finding the envelope and getting a reward. She didn't mention that she'd been foolish enough to let Mr. Sperling into the house. She was sure she'd never hear from him again. Annie was annoyed, and yet flattered, thinking she could attract a man like Mr. Sperling. Nels was pleased with the much-needed money, and went on at great length to the children about honesty being the best policy.

The next morning, Mr. Sperling's chauffeur arrived at Annie's door carrying a bouquet of red roses. He said they were from Mr. Sperling. There was a card saying, "Until we meet again." Annie put the flowers on the table and ran to see Philomina.

Philomina opened the door and was surprised to see Annie standing there. She seemed upset.

"What's the matter?" Philomina said.

Annie told her about Mr. Sperling. She showed Philomina the card. Philomina said the card was a bit personal and she should throw it out.

"Nels might not like it, but you handled it very well," Philomina said.

Nels returned from work and saw the roses. He teased Annie about having a beau. He seemed to think it was all right, but Annie didn't tell him everything.

A week went by and Annie put the encounter in the back of her mind. When she thought of it, she'd giggle to think of herself as a femme fatale. She was still attractive and had kept her figure, even after three children. She'd stop and pose in front of the mirror, then laugh at herself.

One morning, Mr. Sperling's chauffeur appeared with another bouquet of roses and another card. It said, "I want very much to see you." Annie shoved the flowers back at him.

"Tell Mr. Sperling not to be bothering me again," Annie said.

Annie slammed the door in the man's face. She peeked out the window and saw him put the flowers on the porch. She rushed outside and put them in the trash, not wanting Nels to see them. He might think she'd encouraged Mr. Sperling.

Two weeks passed, and Annie was sure she wouldn't hear from Mr. Sperling again. Much to her surprise, he showed up on her doorstep again.

"What are you doing here?" Annie demanded.

"I just wanted to see you."

"Now you've seen me. Go away!" Annie said, as she tried to close the door.

He pushed his way in. Annie couldn't believe the cheek of him.

"Couldn't we just go to lunch? There isn't anything wrong with that, is there?" Mr. Sperling said.

"Should I see if your wife would like to join us?" Annie said.

Mr. Sperling didn't answer, but moved closer to Annie. She was shocked when he tried to put his arms around her. She slapped him with all her might across the face. Blood spurted in all directions, soaking his lovely silk shirt. He screamed in pain as Annie stood her ground, ready to hit him again. He glared at her as he put his handkerchief to his nose. Annie could see that's where the blood was coming from, and it was beginning to swell.

"You broke my nose," Mr. Sperling yelled.

"Good enough for you! Who the bleeding hell do you think you are, taking liberties with me!" Annie yelled, as she picked up the broom and threatened to hit him with it. "If you ever show your face around here, I'll be getting me three, big, Irish drunken brothers to beat the bejesus out of you, you old lech!"

Mr. Sperling turned on his heels and was gone. Annie collapsed into a chair and instead of being angry, she burst into laughter. The tears ran down her face as she thought about the look on Mr. Sperling's face as the blood poured from his nose. Annie wouldn't hear from him again! She was glad as a young girl she'd had so much practice punching Jack.

Nels came home that night and asked Annie how her day was. She told him it was the same as usual. Nels never did find out about Mr. Sperling.

In 1909, another son was born, child number four. They named him Cornelius, but called him Connie.

Nels worked hard, but the money he earned didn't go far. Annie cut corners as much as she could, but had to dip into the nest egg on occasion. Nels' pride was hurt knowing this, and thinking he wasn't providing for his family. They'd already used some of the money for the move to Newburgh, and they knew it wouldn't last forever.

It was getting cold and had snowed for days, making it hard for Nels to walk the long distance to his job. He'd spend days shoveling snow, and would come home and fall asleep before the evening meal.

Nels returned one evening and collapsed in front of the stove. Annie pulled his boots off and hung his wet coat. Then she called the children for supper. Sis and Billy sat in their chairs, while Niel put the baby in his. This was Annie's favorite time of day. She stood there admiring her handsome brood. Niel with his brown tosseled hair, and Sis chattering away, telling a story to baby Connie as Billy banged a spoon on his plate.

"Was it a hard day?" Annie said.

"Yah, very hard. I'm so tired I ache all over," Nels said.

Annie placed a bowl of hot soup and rye bread in front of him. She could see he had all he could do keeping his eyes open. Nels was getting older, and she worried that the job was too much for him. Being head gardener on a private estate was far easier because he had others to do much of the heavy work. Being second gardener meant *he* was the one who did those jobs.

It was almost Christmas, and Annie wanted to discuss her plans with him. She poured him a cup of strong coffee, hoping she'd keep him awake for a while longer.

She remembered their first Christmas together. His Danish customs were strange to her, but she went along with them. He'd walked in Christmas Eve and spread hay on her newly scrubbed kitchen floor. She screamed at him, asking him what in the world he was doing. He explained that the Danes celebrate Christmas on Christmas Eve, and it is the custom to put straw on the floor to symbolize the manger. Annie thought him daft, but allowed him to leave a bit under the stove. She knew he'd want to do it again this year.

"Now that we have four babies, I want it to be a real Danish Christmas," Nels said. "They should learn our customs."

"It's fine with me, but remember, only a little straw under the stove. The children will be tracking it all over me house," Annie said. "Don't you think I have enough to do?"

"Yah, but my mother always did it," Nels explained.

"Well, I'm not your mother," Annie snapped.

"We bring the animals in, too," Nels said and he put his hands up to protect himself, afraid Annie would hit him.

"Get out of here, you crazy old Dane," Annie laughed.

She was willing to go along with the straw, but put her foot down when it came to the animals. Candles were placed in every window, which was fine with her since it was also the custom in Ireland. Nels insisted on having roast pork on Christmas Eve. This shocked Annie, knowing you shouldn't eat meat on this holy night.

Nels put pine boughs around the house, giving off a lovely aroma. The children talked about the tree they would have, and started making ornaments for it.

"Nels, I'll have to be taking a bit of the nest egg for Christmas," Annie said.

"Yah, but be careful. We'll need that money for more important things," Nels said.

"When can you be getting the tree?"

"I'll cut one from the woods and bring it home," Nels said.

"That'll be lovely," Annie said.

"This has always been my favorite holiday," Nels said. "We'll have a good one."

Nels got his roast pork for Christmas Eve dinner, although they couldn't really afford it. Annie still wouldn't eat meat. He'd added a new tradition, now that their children were old enough. Nels said that this was what his mother did when he was a boy. He asked Annie to cook a big bowl of rice so he could put wrapped coins in it. The idea was to have the children eat the rice while trying to find the coins. This would fill them, so they wouldn't eat as much roast pork. There would be some left for the next day. Annie said this was another crazy Danish custom, and teased Nels about it. She knew she shouldn't make soda bread, but did anyway. It wouldn't be Christmas without it.

Annie had been busy before Christmas knitting sweaters and mittens for her children. She'd made a gray woolen vest for Nels. She would have made him a red one, but he was too conservative to wear red. Her Old Da would have worn it and showed it off to all his chums in Corbett's Pub in the Craggs. Nels made pull toys for Niel and Billy while Annie made dolls for Sis and the baby. With a decorated tree and a lovely meal, they had a fine Christmas.

New Year's Eve was spent at home. The children were allowed to stay up late to hear the church bells ring in the new year. Annie and Nels laughed watching each child fall asleep by ten o'clock. After they put the children to bed, they settled down in the sitting room. Just then, they heard a

140

knock on the door. Opening it, Annie was happy to see Philomina, Danoto and Antoinette.

"Happy New Year!" Philomina said, as she put a platter on the table.

"Happy New Year to you, too," Annie said. "I'm so glad to see you."

Nels stood up and shook Danoto's hand. Danoto was carrying a bottle of red wine and gave it to Nels.

"Get some glasses," Nels said. "We're going to do a little celebrating."

Annie got the glasses as Philomina uncovered the platter. On it were Italian cookies that were beautifully decorated and smelled delicious.

Annie watched as Nels poured the wine. Danoto gulped it down in one shot. Nels, seeing this, did the same. After three or four drinks, Nels was laughing and talking loudly. Annie couldn't believe this was her quiet Nels.

"I think I've found the secret to get me husband in a good mood," she said to Philomina.

"That wine is pretty strong," Philomina laughed. "He's not used to it."

It was twelve o'clock and the bells began to ring. Everyone toasted in the New Year. Nels grabbed Annie and kissed her right in front of their guests. It was one New Year's she wouldn't forget for a long time.

CHAPTER 6

The winter months seemed to last forever. It was a gray and gloomy time for Annie, who looked forward to spring. It was getting harder to make Nels' wages last the month. Annie was watering the soup more as the children grew. Nels was worried after hearing rumors that the estate he worked on was being sold. There was very little of the nest egg left.

Nels arrived home that night. Annie could see he was upset, and knew what she had to tell him would upset him even more. After he washed up, she poured him a cup of coffee.

"What's the matter?' Annie asked.

"My job is over," Nels said. "The place is sold. I was afraid this would happen."

"Sweet Jesus! What will we be doing now?" Annie asked.

"I'll look for another job. Ludde said he'd help if he could," Nels said. "I told him I'll take anything. Don't worry, we'll be able to feed all four children."

"You'd better be saying 'five children,' " Annie said quietly. She'd just discovered she was expecting again.

Nels sat there not saying a word. Annie started to cry, not knowing what they'd do. Seeing this, Nels put his arms around her and told her everything would be all right.

Nels left the house every morning looking for a job. He looked as if he was carrying the weight of the world on his shoulders. It was a week before he got a day's work. It was very little money, but it would help. Annie wrote to her brothers and asked for a small loan. She asked them not to tell Nels. He had too much pride to accept money from her family. The rent was due, and all they needed was to be put out of the house.

William was the first to answer, and was glad to help. There was a five dollar bill enclosed. Two days later, one came from Michael. It also had a five dollar bill in it. They said they would try to help them the next month, if needed, and not to worry about paying it back. They remembered how good she'd been to them as boys.

Nels took any kind of work that came along. He delivered coal, chopped wood, and worked in a mill for a time. He really wanted to get back to the work he liked best, but couldn't find a new position.

The summer came and went. Annie was glad to see the hot weather disappear. She didn't feel well, and snapped at the children at every turn. Nels wasn't in any better mood, and the two of them argued more and more. At times she wished she'd never left Ireland and the little cottage she grew up in.

Annie kept in touch with William and Michael. She'd write to them often and let on that things were all right. They could read between the lines and continued to send a little money. Annie would tell them it wasn't necessary, but in truth she didn't know what she'd do without it.

Their home was in sad shape, since Annie wasn't the best housekeeper. She'd let things go, but always took good care of the children. Now that she was having another baby, she just couldn't keep up. Nels would get after her, a thing he said he'd never do after her accident. He always compared Annie to his mother. She'd never met her, but disliked her intently because of this, which only caused more argument.

October arrived in all its glory. The leaves had turned to beautiful shades of red, yellow and orange. Annie swept the leaves from the front steps and walks. Her neighbors were burning them at the side of the road, giving off a lovely smell. Annie had taken the geraniums in for the winter and put them in the cellar. Sis wanted to know why she put them in that dark place. Annie explained she was putting them to sleep for the winter and would wake them up in the spring. Sis thought this a lovely idea.

It was 1911, and nearing Christmas. Annie wasn't feeling well, but it didn't stop her from making Christmas gifts for the children. Nels was working for a coal company, but wasn't happy about it. The work was hard, and wages were just enough to get by. Nels would return at night so tired he'd fall asleep before Annie could get the meal on the table. He was almost forty-two years old, and Annie worried about him.

She was glad everything was done for Christmas, knowing the baby would arrive at any minute. Nels didn't have to go to work Christmas Eve day, and was happy to be home with Annie and the children. The smell of pine boughs drifted through the house. Annie had been saving up for the traditional roast pork. She put it in the oven at three so it would be ready by six. Annie would never eat meat on Christmas Eve, but did admit it was a temptation she didn't think it was necessary for the children to fast, so allowed them to eat the lovely roast pork, thinking they needed the nourishment. Nels lit the candles on the tree and sat close by, making sure the children didn't touch them.

Annie finished up in the kitchen and sat down with Nels. The children were singing Christmas carols as Nels lit his cigar. He smoked one a week. He'd done that for years, and said that one cigar lasted a whole week. Annie was sure that wasn't so, thinking Nels didn't want to spend money on himself. They laughed watching two-year-old Connie trying to sneak a candy off the tree. He reminded Annie of her brother Jack, who would have done the same thing. He was like Jack in actions, but not in looks. Connie had blond hair, while Jack's was bright red. None of Annie's children had red hair, which was a surprise to her since it ran in her family.

At six o'clock the dinner was ready. Niel was allowed to light the candles on the table as Annie put the rice bowl out. Nels sat at the head of the table and said grace. The children were served the rice, and the race was on to find the coins. Nels had wrapped them earlier and buried them in the rice. Each child screamed in delight as he found a coin. Niel went back for more, but Annie told him there were only four. That was all that they could spare.

The roast pork and potatoes were delicious. Annie served apple sauce and creamed carrots with it. The children loved the meal, with the exception of the yucky creamed carrots. After dinner, the children were allowed to leave the table and sit in front of the tree, with the promise not to touch it. Annie said they'd have tea and cookies later.

Nels joined the children as Annie washed the dishes. She was drying them when the first pain came. A fifth child was born that night. He was named Albert John.

"This is the best Christmas present you could give me," Nels said as he kissed her.

"I think it's a good luck sign. Having a baby on Christmas Eve is special," Annie said.

The years passed as Annie and Nels struggled to feed their growing brood. Albert started school, although he'd rather stay home with his mother. Annie worried about him since he was such a shy little boy.

The house seemed to burst at the seams with children and activity. The clamor at the dinner table was defeating at times, each child wanting to tell about his day. It reminded Annie of the noise her brothers made at the evening meal back home in Ireland. After dinner, Annie would tell the children stories about her life in the Craggs. She had to admit she made half of them up, but she loved to watch their faces when she told them about Desmond's Castle and the ghosts that walked the halls when the moon was full.

The children loved Sunday morning. Not because they had to go to Mass, but because their mother made pancakes. She couldn't afford soda bread, with its raisins and caraway seeds and extra sugar. Pancakes only needed flour, baking powder and a little milk. She would stand at the coal stove making stack after stack, and the children would eat them as fast as she could make them. Sometimes Niel would get her a stool to keep her at her task. They didn't always have maple syrup, but they didn't care. Butter the grape jelly were just as good.

On Sunday afternoons, Annie would gather the children and tell them a story. They'd heard them all many times, but loved to hear them again.

"Tell us about the Fairy Folk," Sis would say.

"Yeah, I like that one," Connie would add.

Annie would tell them about the pot of gold and the little people with the pointed shoes and pointed ears. They never tired of hearing it.

Nels would hear the story and scold Annie for telling them such nonsense.

William and Michael visited as often as they could. When they'd leave, Annie would find a few dollars under the tea canister in the kitchen. She never told Nels.

146

Jack was still among the missing, and she worried that something had happened to him. Michael and William swore they didn't know where he was, either. It was a mystery to them all.

Annie continued to write to her Old Da and Rose in Ireland, but never received an answer. She missed her father and wished he'd answer her letters. She was sure he knew that all her children were christened Catholic, and hoped it would make a difference. They were learning their catechism and going to mass.

Annie couldn't believe how the years flew. Little Albert would be six years old soon, but he was still her baby and she felt very protective of him. He was left-handed, a thing that was frowned on. When he started school, his teacher tied his left hand behind him, forcing him to use his right hand. He would cry and say he couldn't do it. He'd get a crack on the knuckles for not trying harder. Annie didn't like this, but thought the teacher knew better. She did notice Albert was beginning to stutter, and it worried her. Nels said he'd grow out of it.

Albert's birthday was Christmas Eve, so Annie made a small cake and put candles on it. Albert was pleased, but what he really wanted was a wagon. It would be a sparse Christmas, but they were all well and together, thanks to the good Lord," Annie would say.

A few days after Christmas, the family had retired for the night when around two in the morning Nels woke hearing screams coming from the Masi house. He opened his eyes and saw a flickering light on the bedroom ceiling. Nels jumped out of bed and went to the window. He yelled to Annie, telling her that the Masi house was on fire and to wake the children. Nels put on his clothes and ran to the burning house. Antoinette was in the front yard screaming for her mother and father. They were nowhere in sight. The entire wood frame house was engulfed in flames. Nels could hear the fire wagon coming, but knew it was too late. Buckets of water were being passed by neighbors trying to keep the fire contained. Sparks flew in the air carried by the wind as thick black smoke billowed, making it hard to breath.

Annie threw on a robe and took Albert by the hand. He was screaming hysterically. Niel and Sis followed, dragging Billy and Connie behind them. Their eyes were wide with fright. She'd wrapped them in quilts and ordered them to stay on the porch. It was cold, and she worried they'd catch a chill, but she was more afraid that her house would catch fire, too. She left Niel and Sis in charge.

Antoinette was in a terrible state, knowing that her mother and father hadn't gotten out. Annie put her arms around her, but she broke away and ran into the blazing house. Annie screamed and ran after the hysterical girl. She managed to find her in the smoke-filled house and dragged her out. Nels roared at her for doing such a foolish thing.

The Balmville Fire Brigade pumped gallons of water on the house trying to put the fire out. At last, they got it under control.

Nels and Annie took the sobbing Antoinette to their house. Nels told her to sit by the kitchen stove. She was shivering from fright and cold. Annie's hair was singed around her forehead. She had a nasty burn on her arm that she hadn't felt until now. Nels slathered it with butter and wrapped it in a clean white cloth.

Nels, Annie and Antoinette stayed in the kitchen all night. Nels kept a sharp eye on the Masi house, knowing it could ignite again. By morning, there was nothing left but a black smoldering pile of timber. Icicles could be seen hanging from the burned rafters, and yet, in the freezing cold, steam was still coming from the ashes.

Annie made a pot of oatmeal and tried to coax the girl to eat a little. Annie's burned arm felt as if it was on fire again. She ran it under cold water hoping to cool it. This only got her a scolding from Nels, who insisted on putting more butter on it.

"Bejesus, Nels, it smells like frying bacon," Annie said.

"Just do as you're told," Nels ordered.

Nels asked Antoinette how the fire got started. She said one of the Christmas candles on the tree fell over and set it off. Her father tried to put it out, but the tree went up like a torch. All she remembered was her mother throwing her coat over her shoulders and pushing her out the door. With the door open, a gust of wind tore through the house, fueling the fire. She never saw her parents again.

Nels was covered with soot. He'd have to wash and dress for work if he didn't want to be late. He wanted to stay home, but they needed the money. Annie stood on the porch and watched him hurry off. She looked at her friends' house and started to cry. She'd miss Philomina, and swore she'd do everything she could to help Antoinette.

Annie decided to keep the children home from school. They'd been up half the night and were tired. Annie and Antoinette sat at the kitchen table. The young girl still had on her nightdress. Annie found a skirt and blouse that fit her. Luckily, Antoinette was wearing her shoes, and her coat was in good shape. As they sat there, someone knocked on the door. It was Father Guinan from St. Catherine's Church. He'd been the family priest since they'd moved there. He sat down with Antoinette and extended his sympathy. He bowed his head and said a prayer. Antoinette cried as Father Guinan tried to comfort her.

"Tell me, dear," Father Guinan said, "do you have any relatives?"

"Yes, I have an aunt," Antoinette cried.

"That's good," the priest said. "You're too young to be on your own."

"Father, I'd like to be talking in private," Annie whispered.

"Of course, Mrs. Nielsen," he said, and they went into the sitting room.

"What about a funeral?" Annie said.

"The fire chief said there wasn't much left of the bodies. We'll have to have closed coffins," Father Guinan said.

"Saints preserve us," Annie said, making the sign of the cross.

"We'll have a rosary and a Mass said for them," Father Guinan said.

The priest left, taking Antoinette with him. He would deliver her to her aunt that lived near by. Annie felt sorry for the young girl. She knew what it was like to lose your mother at a young age. Antoinette would visit Annie on occasion and make sure she was doing well.

In 1914, World War I broke out in Europe. Nels would bring the newspaper home each evening and read it to Annie. She wasn't too concerned as long as her Ireland was safe. Nels took it more seriously, worrying about Denmark being so close to Germany. He wrote to his parents often, but it was taking longer to get an answer. They wrote that they were well and he should not worry. Nels told Annie in great detail how Germany invaded Belgium, Hungary, and Russia. He'd say Great Britain was a strong county with a powerful navy, and they would beat the pants off Germany.

"America will have to go to war, too. Maybe not for a while, but it will," Nels said.

"Thank the good Lord you're too old, and our boys are too young," Annie said.

"So you're glad you married an old man?" Nels laughed.

"Yes and me brothers are too old, too. Saints be praised!"

By 1917, America joined in the fighting. Annie felt no more hardships during the Great War than she had before. She went to Mass and prayed for the young men's safe return.

Annie's friend Antoinette met a young man and they got married in Saint Catherine's Church on April 29, 1917. His name was Anthony Bruno, and he worked for his father in the family-owned bakery shop.

Annie and Nels were invited to the wedding. Annie looked forward to having a good time, since their outings were rare. It was a big wedding, attended by many friends and family. Annie couldn't believe how many relatives the Brunos had. There were first, second and third cousins, not to mention the aunts and uncles. Annie giggled to herself, wondering if half of Italy was there. Annie saw there were very few young men attending, since most of them were off fighting the war. Antoinette looked lovely in a satin gown. It had been Mrs. Bruno's, and she was pleased to have Antoinette wear it. Nels acted as father of the bride and walked down the aisle with her. Annie felt sad seeing how shabby his suit was, but he couldn't afford a new one. She assured herself no one would notice, since all eyes were on the bride.

The reception was held in the church hall, which was decorated with flowers and colored streamers. At the end of the room was a long table covered in a white linen cloth. On it were platters and bowls filled with all sorts of Italian foods. Mrs. Bruno and her daughters did the cooking and serving. The musicians sat at the side of the room playing a lovely tune.

"Isn't the music grand?" Annie said to Nels.

"Yah, sounds Danish."

"Danish, me foot!" Annie laughed. "Sounds more like an Irish jig."

Annie and Nels enjoyed the meal and sat back watching everyone dance. Niel was dancing with Sis, as Billy tried to drag Connie around the floor. Annie never allowed her children to act up in public, but there were so many little ones, it didn't matter. She tried to coax Nels to dance, but he refused, saying he was an old man.

"You're only old when it suits you," Annie said, as she gave him a playful slap.

Anthony's father appeared and asked Annie to dance. Nels nodded his permission, and away she went whirling around the floor. She hadn't danced in years, but managed very well. When the dance was over, Mr. Bruno returned her to Nels and thanked him.

Father Guinan arrived apologizing for being late. Annie liked him very much, and being Irish made him the perfect priest in her eyes. He took a glass of wine to toast the bride and groom and, another to bless the guests. He reminded Annie of her father, who could think of more toasts than anyone else. She laughed watching him to try to teach the Italian band an Irish jig. Under his direction, they played something that sounded like a jig, and yet had the beat of a Tarantella.

Father Guinan knew that Annie was the only Irish lady there, and he got her up to dance. She swirled around to the music, not missing a step. She could see her children laughing at her, and Nels clapping his hands in time to the music.

At the end of the reception, Antoinette and Anthony walked from table to table thanking their guests for coming. The bride carried a satin purse. Annie saw each guest put money in it. She'd never seen this done before, and guessed it was an Italian custom. She'd saved a brand new five dollar bill as a wedding gift, and put it in Antoinette's satin purse when she reached their table. Nels grumbled, saying it was half a month's rent. Annie knew Nels didn't begrudge Antoinette the money, but they had so little he did worry about paying the bills.

Antoinette went to live with Anthony's family and work in the family bakery. Annie would keep in touch with her.

Annie was sitting at the kitchen table one morning enjoying a cup of tea when she heard church bells ringing.

She wondered why? It wasn't Sunday. With that, the door burst open and, much to her surprise, it was her children.

"What in the world are you doing home from school?" Annie said. "What's all the excitement?"

"The war, Mom! The war is over!" Niel yelled.

"Thank the good Lord," Annie said, as she made the sign of the cross.

"You should see the people! They're going crazy, blowing horns and dancing in the street. One guy got a pot and is banging it with a big spoon," Billy laughed.

"Well, you can't blame them. Saints be praised, the boys will be coming home," Annie said.

Nels arrived. The day had been declared a holiday, and everyone was sent home. Annie could see the relief on his face. He'd been so worried about his family in Denmark, and now it was over. The children raided Annie's cupboard and took pots and pans outside to bang. Annie put her hands over her ears. The noise was deafening, but they were having a grand time.

"What day is this?" Annie asked.

"It's November third," Nels said.

"We won't be forgetting this day for a long time," Annie said.

Annie struggled to make ends meet with the little that Nels earned. It was 1920, and Annie had had two more babies: Grace, a most welcomed girl, and Vincent, Annie's seventh child. Her dream of coming to America and having seven children had come true. She remembered telling her father when she was a little girl that she'd go to America and be a grand lady. She'd have a fine house and lovely clothes to wear. She thought of how her Old Da had laughed at her. That dream hadn't come true, and she knew it never would be, but Annie felt blessed that her children were in good health and did well in school. Nels felt like a failure, not being able to provide a better life for his family. Annie tried to encourage him at every opportunity.

153

Connie was now eleven years old and considered himself a big boy. One day, after school, he took a bucket and went down to the railroad tracks that ran behind their house. He filled it with coal that had fallen off the coal cars that passed by. They needed a lot of coal to cook with and heat the house, and it was expensive for the struggling family. He dragged the bucket home, knowing his mother would be proud of him.

"Cornelius, me darling! I appreciate you trying to help, but you're not to go near the tracks again," Annie scolded. "You could be getting hurt."

"I know what I'm doing," Connie said.

"Cornelius, I've said me last word on the subject! Don't be going to the tracks again!"

Connie knew she meant business when she called him Cornelius. He sulked for a few days, thinking he was being treated like a baby.

One afternoon, Annie decided to bake soda bread. She'd been saving raisins and caraway seeds for months, and wanted to do something special. She had a lovely bottle of fresh buttermilk, and knew it would please the children when they got home from school. Annie put two loaves in the oven. Just then, Antoinette arrived. Annie was glad to see her and welcomed her in.

"Something smells good," Antoinette said, as she kissed Annie on the cheek.

"Making soda bread. Thought I'd give the family a treat tonight," Annie said.

Annie watched the clock, then opened the oven door and pulled out the loaves. She tapped the bottom of the pan to loosen the bread. Out it popped onto the table. She had to admit it looked nice with its golden brown crust and raisins peeking out. The aroma was heavenly.

"That's a picture to behold," Antoinette said.

"Thank you," Annie said. "It is lovely, if I do say so meself."

154

Antoinette examined the bread, turning it around so she could see all sides. Annie wondered what on earth she was doing. Antoinette had seen soda bread many times. What was the fascination today?

"If you'd like a slice, all you have to do is ask," Annie laughed.

"No, it's not that, but I think I have an idea," Antoinette said. "You know, we sell all kinds of bread in the shop, but we don't have soda bread. Maybe you could make some for the bakery. Nobody makes it better, and I'm sure a lot of people would buy it. What would you say to that?"

"I don't know. I'm very flattered, but I couldn't be leaving me children," Annie said.

"You wouldn't have to leave home. You could make it right here," Antoinette said. "I can have everything you need delivered."

"That sounds wonderful, but what would the Brunos be thinking?" Annie said.

"I'm sure they'd like the idea. This way, you can stay home and earn some money at the same time," Antoinette said.

Annie was thrilled at the idea of earning some much-needed money. Antoinette said she'd ask her father-in-law, and Annie would see what Nels had to say about it.

Antoinette left, saying she'd be back the next day for her answer. Annie sat down at the kitchen table and poured herself a cup of tea. She started making a list of all the things she'd need. Big bowls and lots of baking pans came first. The bread would have to be picked up, and, of course, they'd have to supply coal for the fire. She pictured her kitchen filled with lovely loaves of soda bread.

When Nels came home from work that night, Annie met him at the door. She didn't even give him a chance to take off his coat before she told him of Antoinette's offer. As usual, he didn't say a word. He washed up, and sat down at

155

the kitchen table. Annie crossed her fingers behind her back and said a prayer.

"Sweet Jesus, say something," Annie said.

"You know I don't want my wife working," Nels said. "You have enough to do with all these children, and you can hardly keep the house clean as it is."

"Now don't start on me about this damn house!" Annie yelled. "Nels, I want to do it! There's nothing I like to do better than bake, and I'm good at it!"

"I don't know. I'll have to think on it," Nels said.

"You'll not be thinking on it. I'm going to do it, and that's final! By the time you get home, all the baking will be done and you won't see a thing," Annie said.

Nels sat there in shock. It was the first time Annie had defied him. It even surprised her, but she would stick to her guns, no matter what.

"You're a crazy woman!" Nels yelled back. "You do what I say! My mother'd never disobey my father."

"You and your precious mother can go to blazes!" Annie screamed. "I will not be doing what you say! I'll be doing what I want for a change!"

Nels threw up his hands and left the room. Annie's heart was beating so fast she had to take a deep breath to calm down. Annie couldn't believe what she'd said.

The next morning, Nels ate his breakfast and left for work. He never spoke a word. Annie didn't care. She had a grand feeling of power, something she'd never felt before. She giggled to herself, thinking about the look on Nels' face.

Antoinette arrived by eight o'clock. She was as excited as Annie about their venture. Mr. Bruno thought it a fine idea and agreed to send everything Annie needed, if she accepted. Antoinette could tell by Annie's face that the bargain was set. Mr. Bruno would pay her eight cents a loaf and sell it for twenty cents. That was considered expensive bread, but the ingredients were expensive, and there had to be a profit.

156

That afternoon, a wagon arrived bringing bags of flour and sugar, and boxes of raisins and caraway seeds. Big bowls and tins arrived, along with bags of coal that were left at the back door. Antoinette even sent ice for the icebox, knowing the eggs and buttermilk had to be kept cold. Annie wouldn't have to spend any of her own money. She spent the day organizing her kitchen, as she didn't want to upset Nels any more than he already was.

That night, Annie lay in bed planning how she'd managed to bake bread and take care of her family at the same time. Dollar signs ran through her head as she counted loaves of bread at eight cents a loaf. She'd make ten the first day and see how well they sold.

"Ten loaves, at eight cents, is eighty cents a day. Five days a week is four dollars," Annie said aloud. "Sweet Jesus, it's a small fortune!"

Nels grunted and rolled over.

The next morning, Annie was up by five o'clock. She tended the coal stove so that the temperature would be just right. Next, she put out two huge bowls and measured the flour and sugar into each one. They would hold enough for five loaves each.

Nels entered the kitchen and poured himself a cup of coffee.

"Good morning," Annie said.

Nels didn't answer. He sat there stirring his coffee and looking out the window.

"Don't talk to me. See if I care," Annie said, as she turned back to her work. She couldn't believe the way she talked to him, but this was something she wanted to do, and do it she would.

Nels picked up his lunch pail and was out the door, slamming it behind him.

The children dressed for school, ate their breakfast and were off as well. Once she was alone, Annie got down to the business of baking. She mixed the ingredients, kneaded the dough and placed it in the pans. The oven would hold three at a time. It would take longer to bake than it took in the making. Annie sat down and poured herself a cup of tea. She felt very proud of herself.

"At least I can do *something* better than anyone else," she giggled.

Antoinette sent a man around to pick up the bread at nine o'clock. He carried a large basket. Annie arranged it nicely and covered it with a clean towel.

"Mrs. Bruno says to come by the shop later today," the man said.

"Tell her I'll be there," Annie said.

By twelve, the kitchen was clean, and the bowls and tins were ready for the next day. She checked the supplies and knew they would last a week.

Annie changed her dress, and combed her hair and was off down the street to see what Antoinette wanted. As she arrived at the shop, she stopped to look in the window. Much to her delight she saw her soda bread beautifully displayed. Over it was a sign, "Annie Enright's Home Made Soda Bread."

Annie thought she'd burst with pride. She'd never done anything special in her life, and couldn't wait to show Nels and the children. Antoinette waved to her to come into the shop.

"Well, what do you think?" Antoinette said.

"It's lovely," Annie said. "I've never had me name on a sign before."

"I was sure you'd be pleased. We want you to make ten loaves every day, and twenty on Friday for the weekend. Can you do it?"

"To be sure, I can," Annie said.

She walked home, feet hardly touching the ground. She couldn't remember when she'd been so happy.

Nels returned from work that evening. She heard him come in and go straight to the bathroom for the usual cleanup itual. When he finished, he entered the kitchen. She could tell by the look on his face he wasn't happy.

"What's troubling you, Nels?" Annie asked.

"You're troubling me!" Nels stormed. "What's the idea of that sign in the bakery shop?"

"What's wrong with it?" Annie said, forgetting he walked past the bakery on the way home.

"Annie Enright? Who is Annie Enright?" Nels yelled. "I thought there was a Mrs. Nels Peter Nielsen! No more Annie Enright! My name isn't good enough for you any more?"

"Nels, don't be silly. They used me maiden name because it's Irish," Annie explained. "They couldn't use a Danish name on the bread."

"I don't like it!" Nels roared. "Tell them to take it down!"

"I will not!" Annie said, as she planted her feet firmly and put her hands on her hips.

"I'm your husband! You do what I say!" Nels yelled.

"You can go straight to blazes if you don't like it!" Annie yelled back.

"What has come over you? You used to be such a good wife," Nels said.

"Maybe I've grown up," Annie said. "I want to do this, and it will help the family."

"I don't want your money. I earn the living for my family," Nels said. "I have my pride, you know."

"Pride be damned! I'm tired of pinching pennies," Annie said.

Nels glared at her. She knew that she shouldn't have said that. She tried to apologize, but he'd have none of it. She knew he was doing the best he could, and she'd hurt his feelings.

Annie continued making the bread, and loved the attention she got from doing it. Everyone said it was the best they'd ever tasted, and begged for the recipe. People were beginning to recognize her on the street as "the soda bread lady." Nels refused to take any of the money, so Annie used it to buy little treats for the children. She managed to save a bit, and bought herself a lovely green dress to wear to Mass. She loved being "in the bakery business," as she would say.

A whole year passed as Annie continued to make the bread for the Bruno Bakery. Nels seemed to get back to normal. He spoke to Annie as if her job didn't exist, but Annie didn't care. The children were proud of her, and that made her happy.

Annie had kept up her correspondence with her old friend, Mrs. O'Brien, and told her about her job. Mrs. O'Brien wrote back congratulating her, saying that Annie's soda bread was indeed the best she'd ever tasted. It was no wonder it was selling so well.

Mrs. O'Brien was a shrew businesswoman and had acquired a second boardinghouse. She was always on the lookout for a good investment. She decided if the Brunos could make money from Annie's talent, why couldn't she? Mrs. O'Brien would discuss it with her good friend, Sidney Levine. She knew that Annie and Nels hardly made ends meet, and her idea just might help Annie financially, *and* put a few dollars in *her* pocket as well.

Mrs. O'Brien went to see Mr. Levine to tell him about her idea. He was happy to see his old friend when she entered his shop.

"Top of the morning," Mrs. O'Brien said. "How have you been keeping?"

"Can't complain," Mr. Levine said. "What can I do for you?"

"I've had a wonderful idea, and want to run it past you and see what you think," Mrs. O'Brien said.

"I'm all ears," he said, as he offered her a chair.

"You remember me little friend, Annie Enright? The one who married that Dane?" Mrs. O'Brien said. "She's got seven children now, God bless her."

"Yes, I remember her."

"Well, she's a dear sweet soul, and hasn't had it easy. Her husband is a nice fellow, but hasn't been able to make a decent living. She's been baking bread at home for a local bakery in Balmville, where she lives. How she managed with seven children underfoot is a mystery to me! She bakes this wonderful soda bread, and it's sold out every day. The people just love it," Mrs. O'Brien said.

"Sounds like she's doing pretty well."

"She's working hard, but the money is small. I guess it helps," Mrs. O'Brien said.

"Well, then what's the problem?" Mr. Levine asked.

"I've been thinking, if she could get a bakery of her own, she'd make a lot more money. She's a marvelous cook, and soda bread isn't the only thing she makes."

"Can you get her own place?" Mr. Levine said.

"No, and that's where we come in," Mrs. O'Brien said.

"What do you mean?" Mr. Levine said, as he moved away a bit.

"Now don't get nervous," Mrs. O'Brien said. "I was thinking we could both get her started and have a share of the profit."

"I don't know," Mr. Levine said. "It's a big step to set someone up in business. I worked hard for the little I have and wouldn't want to lose it."

"Come on, Sidney, I've known you for thirty years, and you've got the first nickel you ever earned," Mrs. O'Brien laughed. "I'd be putting me money in, too. I know this girl, and I'm sure she could make a great success of it."

"What does she say about it?" Mr. Levine said.

"I haven't asked her yet. I didn't want to get her hopes up," Mrs. O'Brien said. "I wanted to talk to you first."

"I'll have to talk it over with my lawyer, and it'd have to be here in the city if you want me in on it. I'm not investing in any bakery in the woods," Mr. Levine said.

161

"That sounds good to me," Mrs. O'Brien said. "I'll be seeing you tomorrow."

Mrs. O'Brien left and went straight to church. She lit a candle and said a prayer. She hoped Mr. Levine would help Annie. He was a good businessman, and she knew he wouldn't pass up a good opportunity.

Mrs. O'Brien was at Mr. Levine's shop first thing in the morning. He was busy with a customer when she entered. At last, the lady made a purchase and left.

"Well, what did your lawyer say?" Mrs. O'Brien said.

"What's this? No 'good morning'?" Mr. Levine teased.

"Never mind 'good morning.' What did he say?"

"He thinks it's a good investment."

"Saints be praised, that's wonderful!" Mrs. O'Brien said. "When do we start?"

"Don't you think you should ask your friend first?" Mr. Levine laughed.

"I'll be taking a train this afternoon. I can't wait to tell her," Mrs. O'Brien said. "I'll see you first thing in the morning."

Mrs. O'Brien took the early train up along the Hudson River to Newburgh, then took the trolley to Balmville. She walked the last two blocks to Annie's house and knocked on the door. Annie opened it and screamed in delight at seeing her old friend standing there.

"Sweet Jesus, what in the world are you doing here?" Annie said, as she wiped her hands on her apron.

"I've come to see you with a business proposition," Mrs. O'Brien said.

"My, this sounds important! Come into the kitchen. I'll be making you a cup of tea," Annie said.

Mrs. O'Brien sat down and looked around the run-down kitchen. Piled in one corner were bags of flour and sacks of sugar. Boxes of raisins and caraway seeds were stacked on a small corner cabinet. Bowls and tin pans filled he sink, waiting to be washed. She could hear the children playing in the back yard. Mrs. O'Brien wondered how Annie could manage to make so much lovely bread in such cramped conditions.

"Well, what have you come all this way to tell me?' Annie said, as she poured the tea.

"Do you remember me friend, Sidney Levine?"

"Of course I do," Annie said.

"I told him about your delicious bread, and how you're making it for Bruno's Bakery," Mrs. O'Brien said. "Now, I'm thinking you could do better if you had more space and some help," Mrs. O'Brien said.

"To be sure," Annie said.

"Mr. Levine and I were thinking we could set you up in business," Mrs. O'Brien said.

"Away with you!" Annie laughed. "Me, having me own business? Have you lost your senses? What would I be doing with me family?"

"It can be worked out," Mrs. O'Brien said.

"Just how? Nels isn't happy about me baking at home, as it is. He'd go through the roof if I told him this," Annie said.

"You and your family can move back to New York City. We'll find you a place to live while we get the business started," Mrs. O'Brien said.

"I can't be doing that. All I know how to do is cook. I've got no head for business," Annie said.

"That's what Mr. Levine and I are for. We'll be your partners," Mrs. O'Brien said. "We'll find a shop and put up the money to get it fitted. Then, all we need is your talent."

"You make it sound so easy," Annie said.

"It *is* easy," Mrs. O'Brien said. "These are modern times. Women are working and running businesses now and doing very well."

"I don't know. Nels won't allow it," Annie said.

163

"Well, all you can do is talk to him. It's time you did something for yourself, deary. We can find something for him to do. He wouldn't be idle," Mrs. O'Brien said. "Think of the children. The schools are better in the city, and I can find a nice lady to care for them when you're working."

"It sounds lovely, but Nels will never agree," Annie said.

"Maybe he will. All you can do is ask. Let me know what you decide. I'll be going to Mass to say all me prayers," Mrs. O'Brien said. "There'll be a lot for Mr. Levine and me to be doing if you decide to come."

The ladies spent the rest of the afternoon catching up on the latest news. Mrs. O'Brien told Annie about the changes going on in the city and how wonderful her life would be if she moved back.

Mrs. O'Brien left as Annie collapsed into a chair. She couldn't believe this was happening! It sounded too good to be true. She wasn't afraid of the work, and it would be grand for the children. Nels would be home soon, so she practiced what she'd say to him. The more she thought about it, the more she wanted to do it.

Nels arrived home as sullen as usual. He washed up and ate his meal in silence. Annie knew he'd had a bad day, and she was a bit frightened to approach him about Mrs. O'Brien's offer. Nels sat down in the sitting room and opened the paper. Annie sat quietly for a few minutes, not knowing how to start.

"You got something to say?" Nels said.

"Yes, I do," Annie said.

"Tell me," Nels said as he put the paper down.

"Me friend, Mrs. O'Brien, came up from the city today," Annie said.

"Yah, so what did she want?"

"She wants to set me up in the bakery business in New York City," Annie said, then held her breath waiting for Nels to explode. Much to her surprise, he started to laugh.

"That's a good joke," Nels said.

"It's not a joke. She has a friend, and they both want to invest in it. It will be their money and my know-how," Annie said proudly.

"Your know-how?" Nels laughed. "Just because you can bake a couple of loaves of bread? Don't be crazy! You stay right here and do your job of taking care of me and children."

"They're good business people, and wouldn't ask me if they didn't think they could make money," Annie said. "I want to do it, Nels. They said you'd have a job, too."

That was the worst thing she could have said. She watched as his face turned red. He slammed his fist down on the side table, almost knocking the lamp over.

"Isn't that good of them! They'll give the old man a job!" Nels yelled. "Maybe I can sweep the floor or take out the trash!"

"They're not meaning that. They'd find something good for you to do," Annie said.

"No, no, no!" Nels roared. "We will *not* move to New York, and I don't want to hear another word about it."

Nels left the next morning without saying a word. Annie went to the kitchen to make the children's breakfast. After they left, she got busy baking her bread. She'd gotten so good at doing it she didn't have to even think about it. As she worked, her mind was a million miles away. She imagined what it would be like living in New York City again and running her own bakery. She wouldn't have to worry about the financial part of it as Mr. Levine would take care of that. Mrs. O'Brien trusted him, and Annie trusted Mrs. O'Brien, so she was sure it could be done. Now, if she could only convince Nels.

Days passed as Nels remained silent. This drove Ann crazy. She'd rather fight and get everything out in the open One evening, she heard the door slam. She knew it was Nel.

165

returning from work. He had a few days work at the coal company. He looked tired and was covered with soot. She felt sorry for him, and was sure a move to New York would benefit him as well as the children.

"Him and his damn pride!" Annie said, as she slammed a pot on the stove. "Nels, is that you?"

"Yah, who else could it be?" he grumbled.

Annie entered the sitting room. Nels was sitting on the sofa, dirty clothes and all. Annie was shocked to see him do this. Not that she cared, but it was so unlike Nels.

"Are you all right?" Annie asked.

"Yah," he said.

"Nels, I have to be writing to Mrs. O'Brien," Annie said softly.

"So, write!" Nels snapped. "Tell her I said you can't do it. We're not interested."

"I'm interested," Annie said.

"I don't want to hear any more about it. You're not going, and that's final. I'm the man in the family and my word is law!" Nels roared.

"Your word is law, me foot!" Annie roared back. "This is an opportunity of a lifetime. I'm tired of working hard and having nothing to show for it."

Once again, she'd said the wrong thing. He felt like a failure already without her reminding him. She could see the anger rise in him, then drain out of him as fast. She watched him leave the room and go upstairs. She felt sorry for him, seeing him so tired and looking so defeated. She knew in her heart the bakery was the thing to do. If only Nels would forget his pride and become part of it!

After the children went to bed, Annie sat at the kitchen table. The more she thought about having a bakery to run, the more excited she became. She would change Nels mind if it was the last thing she did. She made a plan in her mind as to what she'd say to him the next morning. She said an extra prayer that night before going to bed.

Annie woke up the next morning hearing the birds chirping. She put her hand out to touch Nels. Much to her surprise, he wasn't in bed. This was strange since she was always the first one up in the morning.

Annie dressed quickly and went to the kitchen. The coffee had been made, but Nels was nowhere in sight. On the table was a scrap of paper. It was in Nels handwriting. As Annie read it, tears ran down her face. All it said was, "Annie, going back to the farm." It was signed," Nels Peter Nielsen."

"Sweet Jesus, he's left us!" Annie sobbed. "How could he do such a thing?"

Annie sat at the table reading the few words over and over again. What farm did he mean? It must be his brother's farm in Racine. Surely he didn't mean the farm in Denmark! Maybe he was just mad and wanted to scare her, she thought. She was sure he'd be home at the end of the day.

That evening, Nels did not return. Annie was getting angry. If he was just trying to frighten her, it was a mean thing to do, but if he really left, it was a terrible thing to do.

A week went by with no word from Nels. Annie continued baking and tending the children. They wondered where Dad was, and Annie explained that he wasn't well and had to get away for a while. The older children knew there was more to it than that, but would say nothing.

Annie needed some things from the market. She went to the tea canister to get a few coins. Much to her surprise, it was empty. She couldn't believe her eyes. Annie knew there was six dollars and twenty-three cents in there at last count. She realized Nels had taken every cent they had. Annie was furious to think he'd do such a selfish thing. Luckily, the rent had been paid, and the few dollars she earned from her baking would feed them.

Annie was so angry she called Nels a few choice words when the children weren't around. It made her feel better.

"I can do very well without him," she said, as she kneaded the bread. "Signing his name 'Nels Peter Nielsen!" Who the bleeding hell does he think he is?'

Annie's anger gave her courage. She wrote to Mrs. O'Brien that day. She told her what had happened, and said that she'd be happy to come to New York. If Nels came back, she'd be gone.

Mrs. O'Brien was sorry for Annie's troubles, but glad in a way. She'd never understood what Annie had seen in Nels in the first place. Love is surely blind, she thought. Mrs. O'Brien preferred men that could tell a joke, give you a hug and maybe a playful slap on the backside. Nels was far too cold for her taste.

Mrs. O'Brien and Mr. Levine set about finding Annie a place to live. Mrs. O'Brien's boardinghouses were full, and besides, it was no place for all the children. She didn't want Annie to change her mind, or worse yet, not move before Nels returned.

Mr. Levine found a bakery shop in Gowanus that was for sale. There was a six-room flat over it. Mrs. O'Brien thought it was made to order. It was a working-class neighborhood, but not far from Park Slope, a section of New York where the Irish of means lived. The cooks that worked in the better homes often shopped in Gowanus. The baker that sold it to Mr. Levine was retiring. He opened his books to show that it was a good investment. Some of the workers wanted to stay, so Annie would have help right off.

Annie was sorry to tell Antoinette that she was leaving Balmville. Antoinette knew that Nels was gone and understood that she had to do what was best for her family. She said the customers would miss the soda bread, but knew better than to ask for the recipe.

CHAPTER 7

The move to New York City was exciting for Annie and her children. The little ones asked where Dad was, but Annie assured them he would join them later. She didn't like lying to them, but thought they were too young to understand. If he came back, she knew he'd be able to find them.

Annie and the children boarded the train. She was happy thinking this was a chance to have a better life, even though Nels didn't want any part of it. She knew she'd have to work hard, and was determined to make a go of it.

A truck had been sent to take their furniture to the new apartment. Mrs. O'Brien met them at the railroad station and took them out to lunch. It was a treat, as the children had only been in a restaurant once before. By the time they got to the apartment, their things had been delivered. On the floor was the box Annie had sent her prized geraniums in. She'd begged the movers to take good care of them saying,

"You can break the furniture, but you'd better not be breaking me sweet geraniums." She was sure the men thought she was a bit daft. The first thing she did was give them some water and put them on the window sills. Now, she felt at home.

The apartment was bigger than the house they'd had in Balmville. The ceilings were high and the rooms had hardwood floors. The place was spic and span, thanks to Mrs. O'Brien. Annie's few pieces of furniture looked shabby, but she hoped she could buy some new things once she started work.

Annie had a few days to get settled and register the children in school. It was a public school, but she hoped one day she could send them to a parochial school. She went to Mass and prayed that she would be able to make a go of her new adventure. She said an extra prayer for Nels, wherever he was.

Mrs. O'Brien brought an Irish girl to meet Annie. Her name was Laura Lynch, and she had just arrived from Ireland. She needed work, and Annie needed someone to tend the children while she was away at the bakery. Annie liked her right away, but wondered how she was going to pay her. Mrs. O'Brien said not to worry. She'd take care of it until Annie was on her feet.

After Annie had settled the children into school, Laura arrived. It was arranged that Laura would come first thing in the morning to see the children off. She'd then clean the apartment and stay until Annie returned in the evening. Mrs. O'Brien warned Annie that the hours would be long at first until they were established, but Annie wasn't afraid of hard work, and she loved to bake. She still wasn't keen on housework and was glad to have Laura do it.

Annie left the apartment at four o'clock in the morning and went down the flight of stairs to the bakery. The children were still asleep. Laura would arrive by six, so Annie knew she didn't have to worry about them, and besides, she was right downstairs.

The lights were already on when she entered. She was wearing a crisp blue cotton dress with her hair pinned neatly at the back of her head. Mrs. O'Brien told her that John Quinn, one of the bakers that worked for the previous owner, was staying on and would show her how things were run.

"Good morning," Annie called as she entered.

"Good morning," John said. "You're Mrs. Nielsen?"

"That I am," Annie said.

John was a short fellow and a bit overweight. Annie saw that he had a smile that lit up his face. She would learn that he had a good sense of humor and always had a joke to tell.

Annie saw stiff white aprons hanging on pegs, along with hats. She put one on and rolled up her sleeves.

"Well, where do we start?" Annie said.

John showed Annie around. The front of the shop had two large windows to show off the fresh-baked goods. There were shelves on the walls and display cases. The floor was made of little black and white tiles in a lovely design. On the counter was a cash register.

"Look at the size of that thing!" Annie laughed. "It certainly is a fancy machine."

"Yes, and the sound of the sales ringing up is beautiful," John laughed.

Annie liked John right off. He'd worked there for ten years, and would become a good friend to her. He was a take-charge kind of man, and it was decided that he would still make the same goods as he had previously. Annie would make the soda bread. Four other people worked in the shop as well. There were Kevin Mason and Joe Foley, baker's apprentices, Christine Ventola, who did the washing up, and her little sister, Amanda, who waited on the customers.

In the back where the baking was done, there ⸱⸱ ⸱⸱⸱ three large ovens and worktables the length of the room.

171

They were topped with marble, which kept the pastry dough at the right temperature. There was a large icebox that kept the eggs and milk cold. Huge sacks of flour and sugar sat in the corner. Annie marveled at the well-fitted kitchen.

She was a bit nervous, not knowing where to begin, but John helped her get started. He suggested she make a dozen loaves the first day so that she could get used to everything, especially the ovens.

"I used to make ten loaves at home in me little oven every morning, and thought nothing of it," Annie told John.

"Don't worry. By the looks of your bread, it will sell pretty fast and you'll be making a lot more," John laughed. "You'll wish you were back in your little kitchen."

"I doubt that,' Annie said.

John was right. Annie's soda bread was the hit of the bakery. Some of the Irish ladies would buy the bread just to compare it with the bread they baked at home. Most of them knew it was better than theirs, but would never admit it. They were sure Annie had some secret ingredient, and were determined to find out what it was. Annie would laugh, knowing the only difference was the eggs. No one knew she put eggs in it. The other workers in the bakery were sworn to secrecy.

Before long, Annie added whole wheat soda bread to her list, as well as oat meal bread. This was hearty country bread, and Annie was surprised how much city people liked it.

Many of the Irish cooks from Park Slope would frequent the bakery. Annie would pass the time of day with them when she had time. She found that the more she chatted, the more they bought.

The months flew, as the bakery did well. Mrs. O'Brien and Mr. Levine were pleased with the profit. Annie's share was growing as well. The first thing Annie did was open a savings account. She walked home from the bank with the little red account book clutched in her hand. She thought she'd burst with pride. She knew it was a sin to be prideful, but couldn't help it. Annie had a plan for the treasured savings account, a plan she dared tell no one—another dream.

Sunday and Monday were Annie's days off, and she was glad to have the rest. On Sunday morning Annie would line up the children for inspection and they would go off to Mass, just as her mother had done when she was a girl.

Annie prayed for Nels every night. At times, she missed him, but knew he'd never approve of what she was doing. She could only imagine what he'd say if, and when, he returned to Balmville and found her gone. She hoped he was well, but was still angry that he'd left her with seven children and no money. She compared him to Jack, who still hadn't gotten in touch with her. "Damn men!" Annie would say.

Once a month, Annie would go to the bank and make a deposit. She was delighted as the numbers rose. Laura was a great help, and the children loved her. She was a kind soul who had come from a big family, and was glad to be with Annie and her brood.

Mrs. O'Brien and Mr. Levine arrived one Sunday afternoon at Annie's apartment with another plan. They were welcomed in as Laura served tea. The older children were out, and the little ones were sent off to play.

"This is a nice surprise," Annie said. "What are you two up to?"

"What makes you think we're up to something?" Mrs. O'Brien said.

"I can tell by that silly look on your faces," Annie laughed.

"Tell her," Mr. Levine said.

"We're buying another bakery," Mrs. O'Brien said.

"Saints preserve us! Another bakery, is it?" Annie said.

"The one we have is doing so well, we've decided to buy another," Mr. Levine said.

"Don't worry, deary, you won't be moving. Joe and Kevin will stay with you, as well as Christen and Amanda. It would be hardship for them to travel so far, and I know you're fond of them. John will be going to the new bakery," Mrs. O'Brien said.

"Nothing will change for you, except you'll be making more money. You'd be liking that, wouldn't you?" Mr. Levine teased.

"That'd be lovely," Annie said.

Annie was a proper partner in the first bakery, thanks to hard work and Mrs. O'Brien. Mrs. O'Brien had put up the money for Annie, and Annie had paid it back with interest, a thing she was proud of.

"Are you wanting me to be a partner in the new one?" Annie said.

"To be sure," Mrs. O'Brien said.

"How much money will I be needing?" Annie asked.

"I'll have my lawyer draw up the papers and send them to you," Mr. Levine said.

"That will be fine," Annie said.

Within three months, the second shop opened. John made the soda bread which was the speciality of the second shop. Annie learned to take over his job at the first bakery. Mrs. O'Brien and Mr. Levine were delighted with the profits. Annie was becoming a good businesswoman and spent less time making bread, and more time running the shop. They'd hired another baker, who worked well with the others. Annie wouldn't allow bickering among her workers. Annie found ways to cut costs which pleased her partners.

Annie saved every nickel she could. The little red bank book was growing. She'd look at the numbers and couldn't believe her eyes. She'd never had so much money in her life!

Annie wore better clothes, now that she could afford it. She had to dress for her new position in life. She chose dark suits and lovely white blouses. Being practical, she still kept her old and tired housedresses. The family lived well, but there'd be no waste. The memory of hard times was still very clear in Annie's mind.

Annie referred to Laura as her "angel." She'd grown to depend on her, and could leave her in charge. Annie was putting on a few pounds, and worried that her brother's prediction would come true. When she was a girl, they teased her, saying she'd go to America, have seven babies and get fat. Annie would look at Laura and suffer a pang of envy. Laura was an attractive girl and very trim. She loved chocolate, and could eat more of it than anyone Annie had ever seen, and never gained an ounce.

"Someday, it's going to catch up with you," Annie teased.

"It might, but I'm enjoying meself in the meantime," Laura laughed.

Annie continued to work and her savings account grew. It was 1925, and the time had come to put her secret plan into action. One Sunday after Mass, she invited Mrs. O'Brien to tea. She wanted to discuss her plan with her.

"How have you been keeping, deary?" Mrs. O'Brien said.

"Just fine, to be sure," Annie replied.

"What is it you're wanting to talk to me about?" Mrs. O'Brien asked, as she settled down into a chair.

"I'm wanting to buy a house. A real house with grass and trees and everything," Annie said. "I'm wanting a home for me family. One with lots of rooms and a big front porch."

"That'd be lovely. Where would you like to be buying one, and do you have enough money?" Mrs. O'Brien asked.

"I'd like a house in Greenwich so I can be near me brother's family. I've been there, and it's a lovely place to be sure," Annie said. "As far as the money goes, I want you to tell me if I have enough."

Annie showed Mrs. O'Brien the prized account book. Mrs. O'Brien was impressed that Annie had saved so much.

"If you get a house in Greenwich, you'll still have to work," Mrs. O'Brien said. "How will you be getting to New York every day?"

"I've thought it all out. I made inquiries at the railroad station, and I can take a train into the city every day. A lot of gentlemen that live in Greenwich do it," Annie said.

"It'll be hard, but I can see you're determined," Mrs. O'Brien said.

"Do you think I have enough money?" Annie asked.

"You've done very well, and I'm sure it's enough for a down payment. We'll have to be asking Sidney. He's a lot smarted at these things than I am," Mrs. O'Brien said.

"Whatever you say," Annie said.

Mrs. O'Brien discussed it with Mr. Levine, who arranged to meet the ladies at the bank. Annie went to early Mass and prayed her plan would be realized. They arrived at the bank and were ushered in to see Mr. Wilson, the loan officer. Annie's heart was pounding so hard she was sure they could hear it.

Mr. Levine took over, telling Mr. Wilson how much money Annie had and what her earning potential would be for the next few years. Annie sat there, not understanding very much of the conversation. Mrs. O'Brien kept quiet as well, which was hard for her to do. After all, she'd been a property owner for years and knew how things worked. However, she was smart enough to let the man do the talking.

"Everything seems to be in order," Mr. Wilson said, as he turned to Annie. "Now, all you have to do is find a house. Of course, it has to be in your price range."

"Yes, I know," Annie said as she shook his hand.

When they go outside, Mrs. O'Brien was laughing.

"What's so funny?" Annie asked.

"I thought for sure you were going to kiss him by the look on your face," she giggled.

"Away with you! I wouldn't be doing that," Annie laughed.

That night, Annie told the children about buying a house. They seemed pleased, and looked forward to living in the country. Niel, Sis and Billy had finished school and had jobs. Niel was happy with his work in the city, and would move in with a fellow worker. However, he could visit Greenwich often. Sis worked in the office of a piano company in the city, and would travel with her mother every day. Annie would never allow Sis to live in New York alone. Billy's dream was to go into show business, a thing Annie wasn't happy about. He was a handsome boy, tall and blond, and she knew he had talent, but she was sure he'd starve to death.

It was agreed that Billy would stay in the city and rent a room at one of Mrs. O'Brien's boardinghouse. This way, she'd keep an eye on him. He'd get a job, and pursue his acting career in his spare time. Connie would have liked to be on his own too, but Annie said he was to stay in school, and there would be no further discussion. The younger children had no say in the matter.

Annie traveled to Greenwich on her day off and was met by William. He was pleased that she wanted to live in Greenwich. He'd already been house-hunting, and had three ready to be seen.

"I tried me best to find houses close to the railroad station since you're going to be traveling to the city every day," William said.

The first one was on Milbank Avenue. It was painted white and had a good-sized lawn. Annie didn't care for it, thinking it was too small. The next was on Field Point Road. The house was larger, but there was no front porch, a thing Annie wanted.

"Where will I be sitting in the summer evenings with me children?" Annie told William.

"I think you'll like the next one, Annie me darling," William said, as they rode out to Belle Haven. It was a lovely part of town, on the water. They drove under a railroad bridge and turned right onto Bush Avenue. William stopped at the second house. Annie knew at once this was the house she'd dreamed off. It had a big front porch with window boxes on the railings.

"It's lovely," Annie said. "Now, I can have as many sweet geraniums as I want. No more window sills!"

"Better be looking at more than the window boxes," William laughed.

The house was Victorian and painted gray. The gingerbread trim was pink, green and white. Much to Annie's delight, it had a stained glass window in the front door.

"Holy mother of God, will you be looking at that! Every color of a rainbow," Annie said, as she touched the glass.

William unlocked the door and watched Annie walk from room to room. There was a main stair that curved as it rose to the second floor. The rooms were large and bright. There were high ceilings with decorative cornice trim. At the end of the hall was a lovely bathroom that had a tub with claw feet. the walls and floor were tiled in white and decorated with a dark blue border that ran around the outer edge. The largest bedroom had a fireplace, and it was decided right off that this would be Annie's room.

On the first floor was a large sitting room with a bigger fireplace, and a dining room that had windows from ceiling to floor. In the back was the kitchen and a small pantry. There were cabinets with glass doors, a big black coal stove and a white porcelain sink. Annie stood there wide-eyed.

"Well, what do you think, little sister?" William laughed, seeing the expression of her face.

"It's lovely," Annie said. "I want this to be our home."

178

In the back was a small barn with a loft. Annie walked through it, enjoying the smell of the new hay. She thought about Nels and how much he was missing. Tears rolled down her cheek.

"You're not crying, are you?" William asked.

"A bit," Annie said. "I was thinking about Nels."

"Don't be saying his name in the same room as me!" William said. "To desert you and all those little ones was a terrible thing to do. What kind of man does that to his family?"

"Everything just got too much for him. He couldn't find a decent job, and felt like a failure," Annie said.

"Don't be making excuses for him. He should be horse-whipped!" William said.

"Let's not talk of past things. This is one of the happiest days of me life," Annie laughed through the tears.

Within a month, Annie signed the papers for the house. Mr. Levine agreed to be a co-signer, which was required. Annie's account book looked empty, but she knew she could start saving again.

She took a few days off from the bakery, leaving Kevin in charge. Laura decided to live with Annie since they'd become her family. The move was fairly easy, and it didn't take long to settle in.

Annie purchased some furniture for her house. Everything she'd ever owned was second-hand, and now she had the money to buy new. She selected a blue velvet settee and easy chair for the sitting room, as well as some small tables. In time, she would buy a lovely dining room set and long lace curtains for the windows. She remembered the curtains at the Thomsons' and wanted the same kind.

The two youngest children, Grace and Vincent, were enrolled in Saint Mary's Parochial School. Annie was delighted. It had the same name as the school she'd gone to Askeaton. There was a small fee, but this was something

Annie had wanted for a long time. Connie and Albert were too old, so they attended Mason Street School.

Annie enjoyed sitting on the porch in the evenings after a long day in the city. She managed very well taking the train to the city. "If all those men can do it, so can I," she'd tell Laura.

One evening, Annie was rocking back and forth on the porch swing when Laura appeared carrying two cups of tea and a plate of chocolate biscuits.

"Thought you could use this," Laura said.

"Thank you, that's lovely," Annie said. "Come sit with me."

"Don't mind if I do," Laura said.

Laura was more of a friend than a servant. The ladies sat there for a long time enjoying the evening breeze until Laura finally broke the silence.

"What are you going to be doing if the Mister shows up."

"Sweet Jesus, whatever made you think of that?" Annie said, a bit shocked.

"I know it's none of me business, but he could show up."

"That he could," Annie said.

"You never talk about him. Why is that?" Laura said.

"The hurt is too deep. The younger children don't even remember him, and the older ones know the truth, so there's no need talking," Annie said.

"Do you think he'll come back?" Laura said.

"God only knows. If he does, I'll be surprised, and *he'll* be in for a bigger surprise."

They'd been living in the house for a few months when Annie told the children she had something to show them. She told them to come to the barn, and much to their delight, they saw a big brown and white cow staring at them.

"Gee, I thought we were going to get a beating, you taking us out to the barn," Connie said.

"Since when do I beat you?" Annie laughed. "How do you like me surprise?"

"Is it ours?" Grace asked.

"Yes, it is," Annie said.

"Who's going to milk it?" Albert asked.

"You and your brother," Annie said.

"I ain't going to milk any smelly old cow," Connie said.

"Yes, you are, and I'm just the lady to teach you," Annie laughed.

"Moms can't milk cows," Grace said.

"Oh, yes they can. What do you think I did on the farm in Ireland?"

"What's her name?" Vincent said.

"Her name is Miss Emdella," Annie said.

"That's a stupid name," Connie said.

"What would you be calling it?" Annie asked.

"I'd call it Sport," Connie said.

"Now, who's being stupid. That's a dog's name, and this is a girl," Albert said, as he ran from the barn knowing Connie would smack him for saying he was stupid.

Annie thought buying a cow was a grand thing to do, knowing her family now could have fresh milk and butter. However, she found that poor old Emdella caused more trouble than she was worth The boys constantly fought over who was going to milk her.

There was a small field in back of the barn where Emdella grazed. Annie enjoyed watching the cow come in for milking in the evening. Emdella would stand and look at the gate, letting them know it was time.

Albert and Connie were in the field one afternoon tormenting poor Emdella, a thing they'd been warned not to do. It was Sunday afternoon, and Annie was relaxing in the sitting room when she heard a terrible noise. Running to the

181

front door, she saw Emdella trying to climb the porch stairs, and mooing as if in terrible pain. The animal's eyes were wild with fright and had a glazed look. Albert and Connie came running as Vincent, who was sitting on the porch, took off over the railing.

"Good Lord, what's wrong with Emdella?" Annie said, as she grabbed the halter and backed the cow down the stairs.

"Look out Mom, she might bite you!" Vincent yelled.

"Cows don't bite. She's eaten something she shouldn't have, or she's been frightened," Annie said. "Albert, what's happened to her?" Annie said.

"I don't know," Albert said.

"He fed her green apples," Connie said.

"You told me too!" Albert said.

"Did not!" Connie said.

"Cornelius, tell me the truth!" Annie demanded.

"We only gave her a few. She liked them," Connie confessed.

"Are you out of your minds! The poor thing is drunk," Annie said. "Cows get drunk from eating green apples."

"We didn't know that," Albert said.

"Well, you know now. The milk will be bad tonight," Annie said. "Put her in the barn so she doesn't hurt herself."

Sometimes, Annie thought, it was easier to travel to the city and go to work than to stay home with "the wild bunch," as she called them. Laura seemed to handle the boys better than she did. The bakeries did so well, a third was added to what Mrs. O'Brien laughingly called "the empire." This one was in Bay Ridge. Annie invested again.

The first Christmas in Belle Haven was grand. It had snowed for days. The boys complained about having to shovel the drive. The railroad station was less than a mile away, but even in the cold, Annie enjoyed the early morning walk to get there.

182

That Christmas they had a big tree in the living room. It had popcorn and garland strung as well as lovely store-bought decorations. Annie had kept the homemade decorations in a box in the attic. She didn't want to forget the lean days when the children had made them. Annie thought of Nels, and remembered that Christmas was his favorite holiday. She wondered what kind of Christmas he was having.

Putting up the tree was a special event as everyone helped. Niel and Billy came home to be with the family.

Annie had been commuting for a long time and was used to it. One morning, she made the acquaintance of a gentleman that took the same train. They sat in the same car every day, and one morning he offered her his newspaper. Annie took it, and as time passed, they became friends. They would chat on the way to work. His name was Henry Parker, and he was a widower. He was a good-looking man, well over six feet. His hair was gray, and he had a lovely smile. Annie noticed how well-dressed he was. Henry didn't have any family, and loved the stories Annie told him about hers. He assumed she was a widow since she never mentioned a husband. Annie never told people that she was a deserted wife, and besides, it was nobody's business. Henry lived alone in a house on Round Hill Road, which was a very posh part of Greenwich. He ran an investment firm in New York City.

As time passed, their friendship grew. One afternoon when they'd returned to Greenwich, Henry invited Annie to tea. She accepted. He directed his driver to take them to a lovely restaurant on Greenwich Avenue. Annie enjoyed the tea and conversation.

"I hope you don't think me forward, Mrs. Nielsen, but my company is having a dinner dance. It's next month, and I was wondering if you'd do me the honor of attending with me?" Henry said. "It's nothing special. Just a little celebration for having a profitable year."

"Oh, I don't know. I have a very full calender," Annie lied, not knowing what to say.

"I'm sure you'd have a nice time. You can let me know," Henry said.

Henry took Annie home in the longest automobile she'd ever seen. The driver got out and opened the door. She could see the boys peeking out from behind the curtains. Henry walked her to the door and shook her hand.

"I'll look forward to seeing you in the morning," He said.

"To be sure," Annie said.

Annie closed the door behind her and leaned against it. Her heart was pounding so hard she couldn't breath. Laura came running and helped her off with her coat.

"Who was that?" Laura asked.

"That's me friend from the train. I told you about him," Annie said. "A lovely man."

"Why are you so late? Could it be you were with him all this time?" Laura teased.

"Sweet Jesus, Laura, you sound like me keeper!" Annie laughed. "He only took me to tea."

"Really?" Laura laughed.

"Yes, that's all, but he did invite me to a dinner dance," Annie said.

"Holy mother, he's asked you out?" Laura said.

"Well, it's not like a date. It's a function his company has every year."

"Are you going to go?" Laura said.

"I don't know, me being married and all," Annie said.

"Married! That's a good one! I don't see any husband around here," Laura said.

"Well, I have one, whether you like it or not," Annie said.

"Excuse me," Laura said. "A servant shouldn't be speaking out of turn."

"You're not a servant, and I don't want you to ever say that again," Annie said.

"Well, are you going to go?"

"I'll think about it," Annie said.

The next morning, Henry asked her again, and he asked every day until Annie finally agreed to go. She thought it would be proper since they were only friends. Annie told Laura that she'd accepted the invitation, but asked her not to tell the children. They might not understand.

Annie made an appointment with the dressmaker. She chose a pale blue chiffon. The color made her eyes look even bluer. It would have a scoop neck and a long full skirt.

The night of the dinner dance arrived. Annie went home early so she would have plenty of time to dress. She was as excited as a schoolgirl. Laura did her hair for her, using small pearl combs. She did it the usual way, pinning it up in the back, but she curled the wisps of hair that always seemed to fall down around Annie's face. Annie put on a lacy corset as Laura told her to hold onto the door jamb so she could pull it tight.

"Jesus, Joseph and Mary, are you trying to kill me?" Annie screamed. "It's too tight!"

"It's never too tight. Ladies always have a small waist. Now, stop your complaining," Laura ordered.

"I can hardly breath," Annie said. "How am I supposed to eat?"

"You're not supposed to eat. Ladies don't eat. It just isn't done," Laura laughed. "You and your farmgirl appetite. Shame on you!"

Annie had shoes to match, and carried a small evening bag.

Just as she was finishing, Sis appeared.

"Where are you going all dressed up?" Sis asked.

"Just a business dinner in New York," Annie said.

"It must be some fancy dinner," Sis said.

185

Before Annie could say another word, Sis was off and returned with some lip rouge.

"Wear a little of this, Mother. It'll give you some color. And put some jewelry on. If you're going to wear a fancy dress, you have to have all the extra touches," Sis said.

Annie protested, but did what Sis suggested. She slipped on long white gloves that went the full length of her arms. She had to admit, she did look nice. Can this be the little Irish girl from the Craggs who used to run barefoot through the field? Could this be the girl who used to pick up dried cow dung and fling it at her brothers, she thought, as she stood there admiring herself?

Henry picked her up in his lovely black automobile and drove to the city. They went to the Waldorf Astoria, the grandest hotel in all of New York. Henry took her arm as they entered the ballroom. They were seated at a table near French doors that opened onto a terrace. Annie sat there in silence trying to take it all in.

"You're very quiet. Is this the lady that loves to talk on the train?" Henry teased.

"To be sure," Annie said, as she watched couples waltzing around the floor.

The waiter poured champagne as Henry chatted on. Dinner was served, but Annie wasn't sure what it was. She could hardly say the names of the dishes.

Annie was glad that they were seated alone. She knew she was dressed properly, but she felt she didn't belong there. For the first time, she was ashamed of her Irish accent. The less she had to talk, the better.

Henry was a good man, and Annie was beginning to have feelings for him, feelings she knew she shouldn't have. As they sat there, Henry took Annie's hand. She pulled it back immediately.

"I'm sorry. I shouldn't be so bold, but I'm very fond of you," Henry said. "I've been hoping you might feel the same."

"You're a dear sweet man, and I consider you me friend, but that's all," Annie said.

"I'm sorry, but I was hoping you might care for me."

"That can't be," Annie said.

"Why not?" Henry asked.

"Because I'm a married woman," Annie blurted out, knowing she shouldn't have accepted his invitation.

"Married? Why didn't you tell me? In all these months you never mentioned a husband!" Henry said. "Where is he?"

"God only knows! He deserted me years ago,' Annie said. "Just packed a bag and left. I've been too ashamed to tell anyone."

"That's terrible. What an awful thing to do. He must be out of his mind leaving a lovely lady like you," Henry said. "When did this happen?"

"Almost seven years ago."

"You're telling me, you've never heard from him in all that time?" Henry said.

"Not a word," Annie said.

"Do you know why he left?" Henry asked.

"Yes. A wife, seven children and no work. That's why," Annie said.

"That's a cowardly thing to do," Henry said, shaking his head.

"In a way, it was good. That's when me baking business started. He wouldn't have allowed it if he'd stayed. So, everything is for the best," Annie said.

"Why don't you divorce him?"

"I couldn't be doing that."

"Why not?" Henry asked.

"I'm a Catholic, and that means I'm married forever," Annie said.

"He could be dead for all you know," Henry said.

"Yes, but until I do know, I'm a married woman," Annie said.

When the dinner dance was over, they got into the automobile and drove home in silence. Henry walked her to the door and shook her hand.

"Even if you're an old married lady, we can still be friends, can't we?" Henry laughed.

"Of course we can," Annie said.

"I think it'd be all right if we see each other," Henry said. "I'll be a perfect gentleman. I promise you that."

"I'd like that," Annie said. "There's no reason we can't enjoy each other's company."

Henry continued to meet Annie on the train every morning. She really cared for him and wished it could be more, but that could never be. On occasion, Annie would meet Henry in the city and go to the theater with him. He enjoyed her company, and especially her sense of humor.

After Annie had known Henry for a long time, she decided to invite him to dinner. She warned him to be prepared for a noisy time. All seven children would be there.

Sis had been the angriest at her father for leaving, and thought it grand that her mother had a gentleman friend. The older boys weren't too sure about it.

The night of the dinner went well. Laura prepared a delicious meal and served it family-style. This was something Henry wasn't used to, but he did enjoy it. Grace took a liking to him, and chatted away to him the whole time. This surprised Annie, since Grace was so shy. Perhaps she missed having a father, Annie thought.

Henry became a fixture in Annie's house. He'd spend Sunday with the family, having dinner and sitting on the front porch. He had a sailboat tied up at Grass Island and would take the boys sailing on occasion. This made him a grand fellow in their eyes. He'd try to get Annie to go, but she'd refuse, saying she liked land under her feet.

Henry was a generous man and took great pleasure in buying Annie's children gifts. She'd scold him, saying he was spoiling them.

She was happy living in Belle Haven and working in New York. She had a fine gentleman friend, lovely clothes to wear and a grand house to live in.

Annie still took care of her geraniums. They were in full bloom in the summer, and put away in the winter. She was still teased about her love of geraniums, but she didn't care.

William and Alexandra visited often, and Michael and Nora would make the trip from New York when they could. They were happy for Annie's success. When they all came at the same time, it was like one great party.

Annie introduced her brothers to Henry. She could see the difference in them. Henry was a gentleman, while her brothers could be rather crude at times. Annie laughed at herself thinking she was becoming a snob.

As happy as Annie was, she thought about Nels and worried that he might be ill or, worse yet, dead. How would she know? She missed her father as well, but at least she knew where he was.

Then there was Jack. She still didn't know where he was. She hadn't seen him since she'd left Mrs. O'Brien's boardinghouse, and Michael and William swore they hadn't heard from him either. She was sure something terrible had happened to him. She prayed for them all every night.

Annie was kept busy with her work. She didn't bake anymore, but directed the running of the three bakeries with the assistance of John. Mr. Levine and Mrs. O'Brien left them to it. There would be no more stiff white aprons for Annie.

It was 1927 spring and summer passed, and Annie was looking forward to the cool weather of October. The leaves turned a lovely red, and fell from the trees covering the lawn. In the evening, she'd sit on the porch and think of the October nights back home in the Craggs. She remembered the full moon being bigger in Ireland than it was in America. It must be because I was smaller, a lot smaller, she thought.

Halloween arrived. It was a bright night, perfect for ghosts and goblins. Connie and Albert were raring to go. They were too old to wear costumes, but not too old to get into mischief. They wore dark clothes and blackened their faces with coal soot. Annie warned them to behave.

Sis was in charge of the little ones. She dressed Grace in a witch's costume, and Vincent went as a ghost. They each took a pillow case, hoping to fill it before they got home.

"Don't be eating too much candy, or you'll be getting sick!" Annie called after them.

Connie and Albert returned at eleven o'clock. Annie scolded them for staying out so late.

"What have you two been up to?" Annie asked.

"Nothing," Connie said, as she winked at Albert.

"I hope you behaved yourself. I don't want to be getting any bad reports," Annie said.

"Yeah, we were good little boys," Connie said sarcastically.

"Don't be a wise guy, Cornelius!" Annie said. "Now, get up the stairs and take a bath. You look like a pair of coal miners. And wash out the tub when you're finished."

The next morning was Sunday, and Annie was getting ready to go to Mass when she heard a knock on the door. Opening it, there stood a policeman.

"Are you Mrs. Nielsen?"

"Yes, I am," Annie said.

"Do you have two sons by the name of Albert and Connie?" the police officer asked.

"Yes. They're still asleep," Annie said.

"Get them down here!" the policeman demanded.

"There's been some vandalism on Bush Avenue, and we think your boys are the culprits. I'm here to take them down to the station."

The boys appeared and were told by the policemen to go with him. Annie stood there in shock, not knowing what

190

to do. The officer took the boys and put them into the police car. Annie could see Albert on the verge of tears as Connie sat next to him with his chin stuck out in defiance.

Luckily, Niel was home for the weekend and would take charge.

"I'll go and find Uncle William. He'll know what to do. He's got a lot of friends on the force," Niel said, as he grabbed his hat and was out the door.

As it was Sunday morning he knew that his uncle would be at early Mass. The police station wasn't far from the church. It didn't take long to locate William and tell him what had happened.

"I don't know what they did, but I'm sure it isn't too bad. The cops pull kids in all the time. They just want to scare them," William said.

The men entered the police station and were greeted by Paddy Gillespie, the desk sergeant.

"Top of the morning, William. How've you been?" Paddy said.

"Can't complain," William said. "We're here to see about me nephews, Albert and Cornelius Nielsen. They were brought in this morning."

Officer Gillespie started to laugh. He said that the boys had switched porch furniture at some of the houses on Bush Avenue, and the people were mad as hell about it. It was all lightweight wicker, and nothing was damaged. It seemed the boys thought it would be a great prank to pull on Halloween. When Mr. Pate came out and found Mrs. Bonte's furniture on his porch, he was furious. Niel was relieved that it wasn't anything more serious. Just then, a door opened as another officer brought the boys out. Both of them looked scared out of their wits, even tough guy Connie.

"Do you want to take these criminals home, or should I keep them locked up?" Officer Gillespie said as he winked at Niel.

"I'll take them, but they'll wish they were in jail when my mother gets ahold of them," Niel said, as he grabbed them by the scruff of the neck and dragged them out the door.

William thanked Paddy and was on his way. Niel took the boys home in utter silence. They knew they'd disgraced the family.

"I wouldn't want to be you when Mom hears what you did," Niel said. "It will probably be in the paper tomorrow, then she's really going to kill you."

Niel was right. Annie was furious. She'd have to punish them severely.

"This is terrible! What am I raising?" Annie said. "Next thing, they'll be robbing banks!"

"Don't worry. The police scared the wits out of them. I think they learned a good lesson," Niel whispered.

Annie made the boys go to Mr. Pate and Mrs. Bonte and apologize. This was the worst punishment she could have given them.

"Mr. Pate's an old crab," Connie said. "He'll yell at us."

"Good! I hope he does," Annie said. "If he gives you a good smack, that will be all right with me, too."

Listening to Mr. Pate was nothing compared to what their mother had to say to them. She told her sons she was ashamed of them, and from now on she'd think of them as criminals. Every morning when she woke them up, she'd say, "Get up, jailbirds!" Albert didn't like it one bit, but Connie started calling himself Jesse James. The rest of the family thought it was all pretty funny. Annie couldn't see the humor in it, and would give Connie a swat on the head when he said it.

In the evenings, Annie would sit by the fire telling stories about Ireland and singing silly songs. Grace loved the skating song, and would ask her to sing it.

"I went out to skate one night, the ice was very stony," Annie would sing. "The ice it bent and down I went and I broke my tanglee-oony."

Vincent would pretend to skate around and crash to the floor breaking his tanglee-oony.

Annie adored Billy, who rarely came home. She missed him, but he'd assure her he was so busy he didn't have time to visit. He was different than the other children, and reminded her of her grandfather, Austin Fitzgerald, who had been in show business in Ireland. When Billy did come home, the house would burst with excitement. Sometimes he'd try to get his mother to be more stylish. Annie was forty-four, and her hair was beginning to turn white. He suggested she use a blue rinse. She'd scream with laughter and chase him away.

Even though Annie could support her family, she insisted her children have jobs. She believed it built character.

Albert got a job doing yard work for a woman named Wills. She took a special interest in him. He would arrive home from his job filled with stories to tell his mother. Sometimes Mrs. Wills would buy him a present. One day, he was raking leaves when she noticed he wasn't wearing gloves.

"Get the dear boy some gloves," Mrs. Wills told the houseman. "He'll get blisters on his poor hands."

Albert only wore the gloves when she was around. He'd put them in his pocket, thinking they were too good to wear while raking leaves.

Grace was eight year old and did well in school, as did six-year-old Vincent. He seemed to be the one interested in sports. He was forever throwing a ball against the porch steps, driving his mother crazy.

Late one afternoon, Albert returned from his work. Annie could hear him taking the porch steps two at a time.

"Look what Mrs. Wills gave me!" Albert called to his mother, as he came flying through the door.

"Sweet Jesus, calm yourself. What did she give you?"

"She gave me a tennis racket," Albert said.

"That was nice of her, but won't her daughter be needing it?"

"Naw, she's got a roomful. She's always playing tennis. I think she won some medals or something," Albert said.

Just then, Sis arrived home from work and heard the conversation.

"What's all this about a tennis racket?" Sis said.

"Mrs. Wills gave me one," Albert said. "Her daughter plays tennis and has a million of them."

"Don't you know who their daughter is?" Sis said.

"Of course I do. She's their daughter."

"Boy, are you a dope! Helen Wills is a gold medal champion in the Olympics. Don't you read the papers?"

"Not really," Albert said. "I guess she's really important."

"She sure is. She's won more gold medals than any other tennis player in the world."

"So that's why she's never home," Albert said. "Ain't that something?"

"What are you going to do with the racket?" Sis said. "Are you going to learn how to play?"

"Naw, I'm going to give it to Vincent. He likes to play ball. Maybe he can be a champion, too," Albert said.

Albert presented the old tennis racket to little Vincent with great fanfare. He warned him to take good care of it, and went on at length about the Olympics, pretending to know more about it than he did. Vincent was thrilled with the gift and slept with it every night until Annie put a stop to it.

Annie and Laura would sit after dinner and talk over the events of the day. She'd think about Nels and wonder where he was.

Laura saw a look on Annie's face, one that she'd seen often.

"Thinking about the Mister again?" Laura asked.

"Yes, and me brother, and me father, too," Annie said.

194

"You don't do too well with the men in your life," Laura said.

"All except Henry. He's a dear man," Annie sighed.

A few weeks later, William and Alexandra arrived. Annie had had a busy week running from one bakery to the next. They were adding new baked goods, and she supervised the making of them. Annie was tired, but she was happy to see them.

Everyone sat around the dining room table as Annie poured tea and sliced soda bread. William said he had sad news, and it was best that Annie sit down. He told them that he'd gotten a letter from young Cornelius in Ireland that their father wasn't long for this world. He was seventy-eight and had been ill for a time. The doctor said he had only a few months to live. Annie started to cry as William put his arm around her.

"Young Cornelius said he's calling for you," William said.

"Calling for me? I thought he hated me," Annie sobbed.

"He doesn't hate you. He's just so thick he wouldn't give in. You know how he is," William said.

"Couldn't he write to me?" Annie said.

"He's too ill for that now. He knows he's dying, and wants to see you. He's not wanting us, only you," William said.

"I'm three thousand miles away," Annie said. "What could he be thinking?"

William and Alexandra didn't stay long. They'd delivered the sad news and went on their way. Laura joined Annie at the table and poured another cup of tea.

"I wish I could go and see me poor Old Da one more time," Annie said.

"What's stopping you?" Laura said.

"I couldn't be leaving you in charge of me hooligans. It'd be too much to ask," Annie said.

"Nonsense, I can manage them better than you can," Laura said. "They're not babies anymore, and Sis will help."

"Do you think it'd be all right?"

"Of course it's all right. Now, make your plans before you change your mind. Besides, I can always call on that darling Mr. Parker if the boys get out of hand," Laura laughed.

"You'd better not be making eyes at him while I'm away," Annie teased.

Monday morning, Annie rode the train to New York with Henry. She told him about her father. He thought it best that she go. Annie went straight to see Mrs. O'Brien, who'd bought a small brownstone not far from Mr. Levine's shop. Mr. Levine was getting on in years, but he kept his shop open. Mrs. O'Brien thought it nonsense, but Mr. Levine said he'd go mad if he couldn't work.

Mrs. O'Brien was glad to see Annie, and welcomed her in. Annie hardly had her hat off before Mrs. O'Brien was pouring tea. It seemed as if they couldn't talk without a cup in their hand.

"What brings you here, deary," Mrs. O'Brien said.

"I've gotten word that me poor Old Da is dying and wants me with him," Annie said, as a tear ran down her face.

"I'm sorry to hear that. Are you wanting to go there?" Mrs. O'Brien said.

"Yes, but I wanted to get your approval first," Annie said.

"Approval! What are you talking about? You don't need to be asking me. You seem to forget, you're a full partner. You're one of the bosses, you know," Mrs. O'Brien laughed.

"I'd be gone two months. Do you think you can manage without me?" Annie said.

"Of course we can. I know Sidney will go along with it," Mrs. O'Brien said. "John can take over for you. Don't be worrying. We'll take care of everything while you're gone."

Annie left Mrs. O'Brien's and took the trolley to the booking agent. It didn't take long to purchase passage on a ship to Ireland. She clutched the ticket in her hand, not believing it was real. It was for second class. She could have gone first class, but knew she wouldn't feel comfortable, and she certainly wouldn't go steerage. It had been an unpleasant experience on the way over.

Annie went to the bakery in Park Slope, knowing that John would be there. She told him about going to Ireland, and he assured her all would run smoothly without her.

"I don't know if I like the sound of that!" Annie said.

"It'll be hard, but we'll manage," John laughed. "I've just tried a new recipe. It's a chocolate cake. Take one home and let me know what the family thinks of it."

John boxed the cake and off she went. She took a taxi to the railroad station and got the next train to Greenwich. She laughed at herself, being so wasteful spending money on a taxi! This was something she never did.

Annie told Laura the minute she got home that she'd purchased her passage, but decided to wait until the evening meal to tell the children. She handed the cake to Laura and asked her to serve it for dessert. Annie was seated at the table when Albert and Connie came racing through the door.

"You sound like a herd of elephants," Annie scolded. "Now sit down and behave."

Sis, Grace and Vincent entered and took their places. Annie looked at the two empty chairs and wished that Niel and Billy were home to hear the news. She saw Connie trying to sneak a piece of chicken off the platter and slapped his hand.

"Cornelius, shame on you!" Annie said. "Wait until we thank the good Lord for this lovely meal."

Annie said grace, then passed the bowl of potatoes to Sis. Sis served the younger ones, then passed it on to Albert and Connie, who were always served last since they'd empty the bowl without thinking. When their plates were cleaned, Laura cleared them away and placed the chocolate cake on the table. Annie could see that half of it was missing.

"What happened to the cake?" Annie asked.

"I took a taste to see if it was good," Laura said.

"It was more than a taste by the looks of it," Annie laughed.

"Oh, you know me and chocolate. I crave the damn stuff! Sometimes I lose me head," Laura said.

After the meal, the children asked to be excused. Annie told them to wait as she had something important to tell them.

"What is it?" Sis asked.

"I've had very bad news. Your dear old grandfather is dying and is calling me home," Annie said.

"Are you going to Ireland?" Albert said.

"Yes, I've booked me passage and will be leaving in two weeks," Annie said.

"Do you have to go?" Albert said.

"Yes, he needs me," Annie said. "You'll be fine with Laura and Sis, and you can always call on Mr. Parker."

"What if the ship sinks?" Connie said.

"It's not going to sink, but if it does, I'll just swim home," Annie laughed.

"You better learn how to swim first," Connie laughed.

Sis knew it was her mother's duty to go. Albert worried something might happen to her, but Connie was delighted thinking he'd get away with murder while she was gone. Niel and Billy would be on hand in case they were needed.

Annie was surprised that it would only take a week to get to Ireland. She remembered it taking twelve days to come to America so many years ago. She wrote to her father and told him to hang on as she was coming home. She also wrote to young Cornelius, giving him the date of her arrival.

Annie's packing began, with Sis telling her what to take. Annie couldn't have cared less. Just going home was enough. Clothes didn't seem important at a time like this.

"You must dress well," Sis said. "After all, you're an American businesswoman, and you should look like one."

"Silly girl, I'm not trying to impress anyone," Annie said.

"Leave it to me. I'll do it for you," Sis said.

"Whatever you say, deary," Annie laughed.

Sis went on a shopping spree for her mother. She bought hats and gloves to go with every outfit, as well as a fox scarf to wear around her neck.

"I'll be the most stylish lady in Askeaton. They'll all be thinking I'm rich and wanting to be getting a loan," Annie laughed.

CHAPTER 8

The time flew as Annie got ready for the trip. The children were as excited as she. Albert was the only one that worried. Annie assured him everything would be fine and she'd be back before she knew it.

"You're almost sixteen, practically a man. I'll be depending on you to help Laura," Annie said.

"I don't want anything to happen to you," Albert said.

"Nothing's going to happen to me," Annie said.

One Saturday afternoon, Annie made an appointment with a photographer to have the family's picture taken. She was proud of them, and wanted to show them off when she got back to Ireland. Each one had some excuse why he couldn't go, but Annie held her ground and insisted they be there. They all managed to arrive on time, wearing their Sunday best. Annie lined them up, with her in the middle, then nodded to the photographer to go ahead.

The photos were ready the next week. Annie was pleased with the results and knew her family in Ireland would be impressed by the handsome group.

Annie left on April 1, 1928. Henry offered to drive her to New York City. The children all wanted to go, but there wasn't enough room in his automobile. Annie cried saying goodbye to her family, and in one moment almost changed her mind. Sis kissed her and made her promise to write the minute she got there. Down the road they drove, Annie waving out the window. She looked back and saw her children standing on the porch. The tears came again.

She composed herself and settled back in the automobile. With that, Henry handed her a small velvet box.

"What's this you're giving me?" Annie asked.

"Open it and find out," Henry said.

Annie opened it carefully, folding the bit of wrapping paper, a thing she always did. Henry laughed, knowing she never wasted a thing. Annie's breath was taken away when she saw a beautiful diamond brooch in the shape of a heart.

"Henry, it's lovely, but you shouldn't have," Annie said.

"Yes, I should have. I want you to think of me when you wear it," Henry said, as he pinned it on her coat.

"I don't need a brooch to help me think of you. I'll be thinking of you every minute," Annie said. "You're a dear sweet man."

"You just remember that. I don't want some big Irishman stealing my lady," Henry said.

"Your lady, is it?" Annie laughed, but knew he meant it.

They arrived at the seaport in plenty of time. Henry took her bag and carried it on board. He handed the steward the passage, and was directed to second class. Down a flight of stairs they went. At the end of the passageway they found her cabin. She thought it rather nice, and she'd be sharing it with three other ladies.

The ship's whistle blew, letting the guests know it was time to leave. Much to Annie's surprise, Henry put his arms around her and kissed her full on the lips.

"Glory be!" Annie said.

"You come back. I'll be waiting," he said.

Henry left the ship, leaving Annie standing there. She could feel herself blush. She was very fond of Henry. Maybe it was *more* than fond, she thought.

Annie pulled herself together and chose a lower berth. She sat down, not knowing what would happen next. Within minutes, three young ladies entered the cabin. They were giggling as they put their bags down.

"Don't mind us. We're so excited about going home we don't know what we're doing," one woman said.

"I know how you feel," Annie said.

"Me name's Peggy. This is Ruthie, and the silly one is Beanie. After you get to know her, you'll know why she's called that," Peggy said.

"How do you do. Me name's Annie."

"Nice to meet you," Beanie said.

"Let's go on deck," Ruthie said.

The three ladies started to leave when Beanie called to Annie to come along. Annie didn't want to intrude, but they said she was most welcome to join them. Annie felt better having made friends so fast.

The deck was crowded as people waved good-bye. The ship sailed down the Hudson River passing the Statue of Liberty and then out to sea. Annie remembered standing at a rail much like this one when Robert died. It had been a sad time for her, and yet if he hadn't died, she'd never have met Nels and had all those wonderful children. It was strange how one sad thing could change your whole life. If Nels hadn't left, she'd never have met Henry. She wondered what

Nels would say if he knew what she was doing. She said a prayer for safe passage and returned to the cabin.

The trip was pleasant, and with the company of the three ladies the time passed quickly. They ate their meals together and sat in the salon evenings listening to Irish music.

Seven days later, the ship entered the Shannon River. Annie and her cabin mates went on deck. She could see the outline of Ireland, and tears came to her eyes. As they got closer, she could see the very dock she'd left from. When she saw the road leading to Askeaton, she felt like she was really home.

Their papers were checked as they left the ship. Annie carried her own bag when they disembarked. Her case was heavy since she'd packed everything she'd need for two months. She stood on the dock and looked around. She had a great desire to get on her knees and kiss the ground, but knew that wouldn't be proper.

She wondered what her family would think of her. She'd put on a few pounds, and her hair was streaked with white. After all, she was forty-five years old, not the young girl they remembered. She was wearing a new print dress and lovely black coat and hat. The hat had little violets surrounding the brim, matching the violets in her dress. Sis had selected the outfit. Annie put on her white gloves. Sis had insisted she wear them, saying she had to look like a proper lady from America. She pictured Old Da and Rose, and wondered how much they'd changed.

Just then, she heard someone calling her name. Annie looked around and saw young Cornelius running towards her. When he reached her, he hugged her so hard she lost her breath. They were both crying and talking at the same time.

"Me darling Annie, you've come home!" young Cornelius cried. "I never thought I'd see the day!"

"I can't believe it meself!" Annie sobbed. "I've missed you so much."

Cornelius took her bag and led her to his automobile. As they drove towards Askeaton, Annie looked at her older brother. She couldn't believe how he'd changed. She remembered him as the young man she left so many years before.

"How's Old Da?" Annie said. "He knows I'm coming, doesn't he?"

"To be sure. Talks of nothing else," young Cornelius said. "He realizes what a stubborn old jackass he's been."

"They drove through Foynes and passed the inn where her father and Rose had their wedding reception so many years before. Annie remembered it like it was yesterday. As they entered Askeaton, Annie was surprised to see that nothing had changed. In the square, the Kendall Tea Room, Saint Mary's School, and O'Toole's Boarding House looked the same. They passed the ruins of Desmond's Castle, then drove by Corbett's Pub, which was still doing business. Many a night she had waited for her father to come home from that very same pub. Up through the Craggs they drove. The road was still as bumpy as ever. Young Cornelius slowed as they got to the cottage that they'd grown up in.

It looked the same to Annie. She could picture her mother standing at the door calling them for the evening meal. The fields were as green as ever. Roses still grew on the wall in front. She started to cry, thinking of the past and wishing the children could be here to see it.

"Don't cry. I'll be taking you to the cottage tomorrow. I thought you should be seeing Old Da first," young Cornelius said.

"Yes, I think that would be best," Annie said.

They pulled up in front of Rose's big cottage. This, too, was the same. Young Cornelius blew the horn to let everyone know they'd arrived. The big red door with the brass door knocker was opened by Rose. Out came young Cornelius's wife, Nellie, and their daughter, Jessica. Nora, the housemaid, came next. Annie was surprised, thinking Nora had left years ago. Everyone was crying as they hugged

204

and kissed Annie. Rose looked much the same. She was still overweight, and her eyes were as blue as ever. Her hair was pure white, but the style hadn't changed. Annie was sure she was still curling it with the old hot iron. Rose had on a red dress, a color she loved.

"Annie me darling, you've come home!" Rose sobbed, as she gave her a big wet kiss.

"This is a dream come true," Annie said.

"Your Old Da's waiting for you. Been talking of nothing else."

"Where is he?" Annie said.

"He's in the sitting room. The doctor wants him to stay in bed, but you know how stubborn he is," Rose said. "He said he'd not be greeting his daughter in his nightshirt."

Annie entered the room and saw her father sitting in the big leather chair. He looked so old and frail. It was hard for Annie to believe this was the tall, strong man she'd left. She walked over and knelt down in front of him.

"Old Da, it's me, Annie."

"Annie, you've come home!" Old Da cried. "Is it really you, or am I dreaming?"

"It's really me," Annie said as she hugged him.

"God bless you! I never thought I'd see you again," Old Da sobbed.

"Don't be crying, or I'll be crying."

"Can you ever forgive me?" Old Da said. "I've wasted so many years being angry."

"Let's not be talking of the past. I'm here now, and that's all that counts," Annie said.

"You've changed, Annie me darling," Old Da said.

"It's been a long time, and I've had seven babies," Annie said.

"They tell me that husband of yours deserted you," Old Da said.

Annie had hoped he didn't know, but deep down she had been quite sure that Jack had written and told him. William and Michael had promised that they wouldn't, and she knew they would have kept their word. Annie was angry and thought about telling her father about Jack's behavior in America, but Old Da was dying. What purpose would it serve?

"Yes, he did desert me, but I've done very well on me own," Annie said.

"You know I never changed me mind about you not being married in the Catholic Church. I knew it'd turn bad," Old Da said.

"I don't want to be talking about it," Annie said.

"If that's the way you want it, okay for now, but we will be talking about it later," Old Da said.

Annie dug in her purse and pulled out the pictures of her children. She handed them to her father, telling him who they were and what they were doing.

"This one is Cornelius," she said. "I named him for you."

"That's lovely. He's a fine-looking young man," Old Da said. "You always said you were going to have a whole parcel of babies."

"Yes, and they're all perfect!" Annie said proudly.

"Rosie, get the whiskey! This calls for a celebration!" Cornelius roared.

"The doctor said you shouldn't be drinking," Rose scolded.

"You can tell that old flannel mouth of a doctor to go straight to hell! Now get me the damn whiskey!" Cornelius roared back.

"Don't be getting yourself in an uproar, you old devil!" Rose yelled.

Rose did as he asked and poured a drop for everyone. She then excused herself and went to see about the evening meal. Annie could see the dining room from where she was, and saw that the table was set for at least ten people. She wondered who else was coming. The aroma of the food cooking brought back memories of the lovely meals she'd had when she lived there. Rose loved to eat, and only served the best.

Rose returned and showed Annie to her room, thinking she'd like to freshen up after the long trip. Annie entered the bedroom, her old room. It was the one that looked down on the little cottage, which was why Rose had chosen it for her.

Annie changed her dress and combed her hair. She took the brooch that Henry had given her and pinned it on her dress. She'd promised to wear it, and wear it she would. Annie heard the houseman ring the dinner bell, and went downstairs. Everyone was in the dining room.

"Who else is coming?" Annie asked.

"That's a surprise. Just wait and see," Rose said. "Everyone sit down."

Just then, the door burst open and there stood Jack. Annie turned white and almost fainted. She stared at him, not believing her eyes. He came running and gave her a big hug and kiss. She pushed him away in shock and anger.

"Sweet Jesus, are you trying to give me a heart attack?" Annie yelled. "Where did you come from? I thought you were dead."

"Well, I'm here, and I'm not dead," Jack laughed.

"When I get through with you, you'll wish you were," Annie screamed.

Annie could see a big change in Jack. His red hair was graying at the temples and his face was weathered and deeply lined. He was thinner than she remembered him.

Jack tried to explain that he had been so mad at her for marrying Nels, he never wanted to see her again. Then he got in so much trouble drinking and fighting he couldn't keep a job. He thought it best to go back to Ireland. Annie didn't care what the reasons were. All she could think of was how worried she'd been.

"I'll never forgive you!" Annie said. "You should be ashamed of yourself!"

Jack had never told anyone he was leaving. He had worked on the docks for a time, and had gambled away every cent. He had owed some money to some very rough men, and they had threatened to beat him senseless, so he borrowed the price of passage and was on the next boat back to Ireland. Annie was furious that Old Da and Rose knew where he was all along, and let them know how angry she felt. Rose the peacemaker tried to calm Annie down, saying the past was the past.

Annie was so shaken she hardly noticed the woman that had arrived with Jack. The woman walked over to Annie and put her arm around her.

"You don't remember me, do you?"

"You look familiar," Annie said.

"I'm Ellen, Ellen Hart. You used to call me your best friend in the whole world," she laughed.

"Of course I remember, but what are you doing with that black-hearted devil," Annie said, pointing to Jack.

"I married him, that's what I'm doing with him," Ellen said.

"Sweet Jesus, Joseph and Mary!" Annie said. "You call yourself me best friend, and never wrote to me?"

Jack wouldn't let me," Ellen said. "Please forgive me."

"I'll not be forgiving anyone! All it would've taken was one letter. What about poor Michael and William? They searched all over New York City looking for him. How many times they went to the police hoping to find him!" Annie screamed.

Annie was crying. She got up from the table and went to her room. She slammed the door behind her and stood at the window that looked down on the little cottage. She was so angry she wanted to smash something or, better still, smash Jack. There were lights flickering in the windows of the cottage and smoke coming from the chimney. She remembered all the good times, as well as the bad times, living there.

She heard a rap on the door and opened it. There stood Rose—and Ellen—carrying two cups of tea.

"Thought you'd like a cup," Rose said. "May I come in and have a little talk?"

"I suppose so," Annie said.

"I know how hurt you are now, but maybe you can understand how hurt your Old Da and Jack felt," Rose explained. "Being married outside the church was the worst thing you could have done," in their eyes.

"Well, now they know that Nels abandoned me, I suppose they're happy," Annie said.

"You know your father and Jack. Sometimes their mouths run away with them. They overlook their own shortcomings and criticize others," Rose said.

"I'm forty-five years old and haven't heard from me Old Da, and haven't known where Jack was, for over twenty years. How do you think I feel? Am I supposed to forget that in one minute.

"Annie dear, please come down to dinner," Ellen said. "You've come all this way to see your father. There's no sense staying up here."

"I'll not be coming down," Annie said. "You must've known we were out of our minds with worry."

"We were afraid your father or Jack would find out if we told you," Rose said.

"There's no excuse," Annie said angrily.

"We're sorry. Please come down. Old Da needs to see you," Ellen said.

"I'll not be coming down," Annie said. "Just leave me alone."

Rose and Ellen left the room, leaving Annie staring out the window. She was very angry, angrier than she'd ever been. "I have a mind to leave right now," Annie thought, as she twisted the ribbon on her dress.

She wanted to leave, but knew she couldn't. She took out her rosary beads and sat near the window praying. She got into bed and fell asleep.

Annie woke up with the sun coming through the window. She heard a rooster crow and a clock strike five. The house was quiet as she dressed and went downstairs. Annie went to the kitchen and made a pot of tea. She filled a cup and sat at the kitchen table sipping the hot tea. When she finished, she went outside. Annie was still angry and thought the morning air would clear her head. She went out the front door and admired the lovely roses just beginning to bloom. Annie opened the gate and walked down through the Craggs as far as the little cottage. Young Cornelius and Nellie still lived there with their daughter Jessica. She stood near the stone wall for a long time and looked at the place she'd grown up in. She could see the cows grazing in the pasture. Nothing had changed, but everything seemed smaller. Annie wanted to go inside the cottage, but no one would be up yet, and she didn't want to disturb the family.

She turned and walked up through the Craggs. She could see the outline of Robertstown Church at the top of the hill. She remembered her mother saying the church was built on the hill so it would be closer to God. The road hadn't changed, she thought, as she walked in the dried wheel tracks. She'd forgotten how many stone walls lined the roads and divided the farmland. They were truly works of art. The memories flooded back as she remembered Jack racing home after Mass hoping to get the first slice of the Sunday soda bread.

Annie went to the cemetery in the back of the church. She was surprised to see how overgrown and unkempt it was. She went straight to her mother's grave, and knelt down saying a prayer. Tears ran down her face. Annie talked to her mother as if her mother could hear her. She told her about her children.

"I named me first girl after you. Remember, I promised to when I was little?" Annie said.

Annie pulled the weeds away from the stone and was upset that it hadn't been taken care of. She walked around reading the old headstones. She recognized many of the names. There was Constable Kevin Dooley's grave. She was sure that he had been buried in his well-worn uniform. No man was prouder of a uniform than old Dooley. Dr. O'Hara and old Mr. Corbett, the pub owner, were there, too. In the next row were Paddy O'Niel and his long-suffering wife. Many a night Old Da and Paddy had to be carried home from Corbett's Pub. Annie giggled to herself, thinking how her mother would put the fear of God into Old Da the next morning and drag him off to Mass.

Annie peered over the stone wall at the graves of Mary O'Connell and her husband, Ryan. Not far away was the grave of Sam Casey. Ryan had murdered Sam and Mary in a jealous rage when he found them together one night, so many years ago. Annie shivered, thinking of that terrible time. She understood that they couldn't be buried in consecrated ground, so were buried outside the church walls like outcasts.

She walked to the far corner of the cemetery and saw two new stones. One said "Edward Enright, born 1914, died 1916." The other was "Cornelius Enright, 1917, died 1918." On the stones, was written that they were the sons of Jack and Ellen Enright. Annie couldn't believe her eyes. Jack had two boys that had died as babies, and he'd never even let her know. She was angry again.

As she stood by the gate of the cemetery, she heard music coming from the church. A shiver ran up her spine, thinking old Bessie, the organist, was playing. She knew this couldn't be, since Bessie had died years ago, but it sounded so much like Bessie's playing she could have sworn it must be her ghost.

Annie walked around to the front of the church and up the stairs. The door creaked as she opened it, and she noticed the paint was peeling off. Sitting at the organ pumping away was an old priest. It was eerie looking as a shaft of light came from the window directly over the organ. She

211

could see a few candles lit at the alter, and could smell the wax. At first, she thought it was Father O'Leary, but knew he, too, was long gone. She cleared her throat, hoping to get the priest's attention.

"Excuse me," Annie said.

The priest stopped playing and turned around. He adjusted his spectacles so he could see who it was. Annie realized it was Father Donald. He'd come to Askeaton to assist Father O'Leary, who was getting old, just before Annie had left for America. She remembered when he'd arrived, and how his being Scottish had worried the parishioners. It took time for them to get used to him. They would have preferred an Irish priest, but grew to love Father Donald in time.

"I'm sorry to bother you, Father," Annie said.

"No bother. No bother at all," the priest said. "Come closer so I can see you."

"You won't remember me, Father Donald. I met you many years ago when you first came here. I'm Annie Enright."

"You're Cornelius' girl. Of course I remember you! Didn't you marry Rose's nephew?"

"Yes, I did. I'm sad to say that the poor boy died on the ship before we reached America," Annie said.

"Yes, I remember it now. God rest his soul," Father Donald said, as he made the sign of the cross. "That was a terrible thing to happen."

"Yes, he was so young, and full of hope going to America," Annie said.

"From what I hear, you married again."

"That I did," Annie said.

"I've been told you married outside the church the second time," Father Donald said, giving her a stern look.

"Yes, I did," Annie said defiantly.

"Well, you know how I feel about such things, but it's too late now. You know you'll be suffering the consequences when you face the good Lord. I'll keep you in me prayers and hope you're forgiven," the old priest said.

Father Donald invited Annie into his rooms for a cup of tea and a chat. He wanted to know all about her life in America, and she was only to pleased to tell him about her children. She didn't mention Nels, or that she was a working woman. She didn't know how much he knew, but knowing her father, she was sure the priest had been told. She could just picture her Old Da going to confession and telling the priest about his fallen daughter.

Annie sipped the hot tea as Father Donald told her about the changes that had taken place in Askeaton. He was very much like Father O'Leary, who took his morning walks in the square and heard all the town gossip. He knew who was doing what, and used it as ammunition in his Sunday sermon, just as Father O'Leary had done.

"Looks as if you've done pretty well in America," Father Donald said.

"Yes, I have," Annie said as she fingered the brooch.

"You're lucky. Our poor old church hasn't fared too well in the past few years. We've been building the new one for a long time, but keep running out of money. If it wasn't for your dear step-mother, we'd be lost," Father Donald said.

The new Robertstown Church was being built on the main road near Corbett's Pub. The old one was in need of so much repair that it wasn't worth the cost. This was sad news for Annie, but she knew the cemetery would be undisturbed.

Father Donald kept chatting on about needing money to finish the new one. Annie knew he was hinting for a donation from her. She decided she would make a generous contribution before she returned to America.

She enjoyed the visit, and left saying she'd see him at Mass on Sunday. As she walked back to Rose's, she could hear Father Donald playing the organ again. It echoed down through the Craggs like music from heaven. She thought about the two graves of Jack's boys, and was again upset that no one had told her. After all, they were of her blood and she had a right to know.

Rose greeted Annie at the door. She had been worried when she found Annie gone. Rose motioned her into the sitting room and offered her a chair.

"Where have you been, deary?" Rose said.

"I took a walk up to the church and saw Father Donald," Annie said.

"I guess you saw a big change in him after all these years," Rose said.

"Yes, indeed," Annie laughed.

"It's good to hear you laugh. That's one thing that hasn't changed. I hope you've had a good rest," Rose said.

Nora entered the sitting room and said that breakfast was being served. Old Da was already there slurping his tea from the saucer. Annie laughed to herself thinking, some things never change. He'd been doing that for years and always being scolded for it. He said it tasted better that way.

"Cornelius, do you have to be doing that?" Rose said.

"Yes, me love, I do," Cornelius said. "Annie, come sit by me."

Annie did as he asked. The aroma of breakfast cooking brought back memories of the lovely meals they all had had together at this very same table. Annie was hungry, since she hadn't eaten the night before, and the walk to church had only added to her hunger. Nora served the food as everyone piled their plates. Annie had two fried eggs, some bacon and hot rolls. She dipped the roll into the egg yoke and cleaned her plate. It was nice being waited on. She wondered what her children would think about her being treated like a grand lady. Rose insisted that Nora wear a black uniform and white apron when they had guests. Annie would never ask Laura to wear one. After all, Laura was one of the family.

"William wrote and told us you're running a bakery," Rose said. "Tell us about it."

"I own and run three bakeries," Annie said proudly.

214

"Sweet Jesus, you're an American millionaire!" Rose laughed.

"Not quite," Annie said, knowing she was laying it on a bit thick.

"Look at her, she's covered in diamonds," Rose cackled, pointing to Annie's brooch.

Annie told them how the businesses got started and how well she'd done. She knew it wasn't nice to brag, but she got carried away. Since they thought she was a failure in marriage, she would show them she was a success in business. She described her home, and made it sound like a mansion. Old Da sat there smiling and taking it all in.

"I can't tell you how happy I am that you've come home," Old Da said. "I missed you, me darling, and I'm glad for your good fortune."

"I'm glad to be back, too," Annie said.

"I hope you'll forgive an old man and his stubborn ways, but you must understand how I felt," Old Da said. "When you married outside the church, I nearly died. All I could think of was your sainted mother, God rest her soul, and how her heart would've been broken."

"I know, but you never gave me a chance," Annie said.

"It was a terrible shock to us all. Father O'Leary was still around. He spread the story from one end of the Craggs to the other. Everyone was talking about the Enright girl living in sin. It was hard to take, the shame of it all," Old Da said as he rolled his eyes. "Then to top it off, that no good husband leaves you! What did you expect, marrying outside the church? It was your punishment."

That may well be, but I haven't failed in everything," Annie snapped. "Why did God give me seven healthy children if I'm such a sinner?"

"I guess you're right, but me cousin in Boston married outside the church and the wrath of God was on her. She had three babies, and they all died. Then her husband left her for another woman, so you can understand us worrying," Rose explained. "She was truly punished."

Rose or Old Da always had a story to prove what they were saying was true, but Annie didn't believe most of them.

"You shouldn't blame God for her troubles," Annie said.

"I suppose, but what about your soul?" Rose asked.

"Don't be worrying about me soul," Annie said. "I'll find out when the time comes."

"Young Cornelius is expecting us for tea this afternoon," Rose said, trying to change the subject. "Will you be going?"

"Yes, I want to see the cottage," Annie said.

That afternoon, Rose and Annie walked down the road to the little cottage. Old Da wanted to go, but was put back to bed and threatened by Rose to stay there. She told Nora to keep a close eye on him. It had taken a lot out of him just coming down for breakfast.

As they walked along, Rose began to sing. Annie remembered the day she discovered that her stepmother had such a lovely voice. Rose bragged that she'd been on the stage. Of course, Annie knew it had been only once, but it was Rose's moment of fame and she loved to tell the story.

As they got closer to the cottage, Annie could see it was newly painted. The gate was in good repair, and she laughed thinking about the times Jack had torn it off the hinges during one of his temper tantrums. Roses were growing over the stone wall that curved around the cottage. She wondered if they were the same rose bushes her mother had planted so many years ago. She laughed when she saw one window box filled with red geraniums. Rose saw the expression on her face, and giggled.

"Young Cornelius put them there to welcome you home. It's his little joke. Nellie will be making him pull them out when you leave," Rose laughed.

"He didn't forget. That was nice of him," Annie said.

Just then the cottage door opened. Jessica came out to welcome her "American Aunt," as she called Annie. They entered the little cottage. Time seemed to have stood still. Over the mantle was her mother's picture, just as it had been for so many years. Her mother's cherished blue vase sat in the same place. The very same cupboard was against the wall, as was the ladder that went to the lofts above. She noticed a coal stove and a sink had been added, as well as an icebox.

Nellie hugged Annie and offered her a chair, as Rose sat down in the rocker. Young Cornelius came in from the field and washed up before sitting at the table.

"Hasn't changed much, has it?" Cornelius said.

"No, not much. It's like going back to me past," Annie said, as a tear rolled down her face.

"We did make a few improvements since you left. We've added a fine toilet and a sitting room at the back. We don't need any more room than that since we only have Jessica, and she'll be going off on her own one of these days," young Cornelius said. "As you can see, we've made a nice kitchen out of this room."

"The place looks lovely," Annie said.

"Would you prefer to be having tea in our new sitting room?" Nellie said.

"No, I'd rather be here in the kitchen, thank you," Annie said.

"Have we changed much?" young Cornelius asked.

"Not at all," Annie said.

"You're not a very good liar, little sister," he laughed.

"Can't be calling me little sister anymore. I've put on a few pounds, and me hair is turning white," Annie said. "You used to tease me when I was little that someday I'd get fat."

"You're not fat," Nellie said. "Look at me, I'm twice the size."

"No one can say *I've* gotten fat. I've always been that way," Rose giggled.

Nellie served tea and sweet rolls, the kind Annie had loved as a child. She couldn't believe she was home, really home, in the Craggs.

"Jack and Ellen were supposed to come, but he had to work," young Cornelius said.

"Well, he won't be missed!" Annie snapped.

Young Cornelius thought it best not to mention Jack again, knowing how Annie felt. He wanted it to be a pleasant visit. Rose reminded Annie that it was getting late and they should get back to Cornelius. Annie'd been angry with young Cornelius, too, not letting her know where Jack was, but understood the control her father had over him. The anger she had had for young Cornelius, however, couldn't compare with her anger towards Jack. He was the one she'd always taken care of and loved the best.

"I went to visit mother's grave, and saw two wee graves of an Edward and Cornelius buried there. The headstones say they're Jack's sons," Annie said. "What happened to them?"

"Both lads died of pneumonia as infants. It was a terrible time. Jack was near out of his mind," young Cornelius said. "Ellen handled it better."

"How very sad," Annie said, "having such a tragedy and not even letting me know, what with me sending letters about me healthy babies."

"When the second boy died, Jack wouldn't speak of it, and wouldn't let anyone else bring up the subject," Rose added. "He doesn't know I see him walking to the cemetery every evening at dusk to pray for the babies. He's been doing it for years. It's a sad sight to see him standing there all alone as the sun goes."

Annie and Rose walked back to the big cottage. She noticed another cottage had been built across the road. It seemed like an intruder sitting there.

Old Da was still in bed when they returned. Nora told them that he'd had a bad afternoon and she was glad they were back. Rose and Annie went to his room. He smiled weakly as they entered. Annie could see how ill he was. Rose took command as usual and gave him his medicine. He coughed and sputtered all the while.

"Bejesus, Rose, are you trying to kill me?" Old Da moaned.

"Now just be me sweet old darling boy and take the damn stuff," Rose ordered.

"Shut your face, Rosie, or I'll be shutting it for you," Old Da yelled.

"Now, that's more like it, you old reprobate. If you think you can shut me face, then I guess you're feeling better," Rose laughed.

"You're still good at bossing him around," Annie giggled. "Nobody but you could get away with it."

"Well, somebody has to, the old devil."

"Come closer, Annie," Old Da said. "Get the hell out of here, Rosie. I want to be talking to me daughter. Damn old woman drives me crazy!"

"I'm leaving, but I'll be back," Rose said.

Annie sat down close to his bed and took his hand. She couldn't believe these had been the strong calloused hands she remembered. His bright red hair had turned white, but his green eyes had the same sparkle. He told her how sorry he was for being a damned old fool, and hoped she'd forgive him. Annie looked at his thin wrinkled face and knew she couldn't let him die without her forgiveness. She kissed him and said she did. He fell asleep with a smile on his face. She turned off the light and went downstairs.

Rose was in the sitting room crying. Annie went to her and put her arms around her, hoping to comfort her.

"What will I be doing without me darling man?" Rose sobbed.

"I don't know. I just don't know," Annie said.

Rose pulled herself together and took Annie's hand. She told her that Jack was on his way to see her, and asked her for father's sake, that she please talk to him.

"When he gets here, I'll be civil," Annie said.

"That's all I ask," Rose said.

Annie left Rose and wandered into the kitchen. Nora was busy peeling potatoes as she entered.

"Would you be liking a cup of tea?" Nora asked.

"That'd be lovely," Annie said. "I can't believe you're still working here. I thought for sure you'd be married and be long gone."

"Never met the right man, and besides, I've been happy here. The Missus has been very good to me. I have no regrets," Nora said. "I have a lovely room and plenty of time to meself."

"That's good to hear," Annie said. "I best be getting back to Rose."

Annie went back to join Rose. They were having a chat when a hat came flying through the air into the room. The ladies were startled and looked at each other. With that, Jack appeared. Annie's first instinct was to hit him, a thing she'd done many times as a girl.

"Thought I'd better throw me hat in before you throw me out," Jack laughed.

"You're not funny," Annie snapped.

"Annie me darling, please forgive me," Jack said.

"Don't think you can charm me, you black-hearted devil," Annie said.

Jack sat down and tried to explain again. Annie said she would call a truce for the sake of their father, but she made it clear that was the only reason.

"Why didn't you tell me about your boys dying?" Annie asked.

"I don't want to talk about it," Jack said. "I have to be leaving."

Jack retrieved his hat and was out the door. Rose sat there just shaking her head.

"He never talks about it. Guess the pain is too great," Rose said.

"That's to be understood. I shouldn't have said anything," Annie said.

"Cheer up, deary. Let's not talk of sad things," Rose said.

Annie wanted to tell Rose about Henry and what a good friend he'd been, but thought better of it. The first thing Rose would ask would be if he was Catholic, and since he wasn't, Rose would never approve.

The next morning, Rose asked Annie if she'd like to go into Askeaton and visit the old shops. Annie was delighted, and said she'd like to buy something for the children. She laughed to herself saying "the children." Her oldest was twenty-three and wouldn't appreciate being called a child.

Annie was just putting on her hat when she heard a horn blow. Looking out the front door, there was Rose behind the wheel of a big black automobile. She was waving to Annie to hurry up. Annie grabbed her coat and was out the door.

"Sweet Jesus, do you know how to drive?" Annie asked.

"Of course, deary. Your father won't get behind the wheel, so I had to learn. He won't even ride in one if he can help it. Nothing to it," Rose giggled.

"Will wonders ever cease?" Annie laughed.

Rose hit the gas as she let out the clutch. The automobile lurched forward a few times before Rose got it in gear. Off they flew down through the Craggs. Annie tried to close her eyes as Rose sped along, leaving a cloud of dust behind them. As they turned onto the main road to Askeaton, Corbett's Pub was a blur of white stucco as they raced by.

Rose came to a quick stop in the square, and Annie finally caught her breath. Rose was well into her seventies, but she was as sharp as a twenty-year-old. "No grass grows under me feet," Rose was known to say.

Annie stood in the square and looked around. Saint Mary's School looked the same, as did the shops. The cobblestone was still there, and the flowers that surrounded it were well tended. Towering over the square were the ruins of Desmond's Castle. It still looked like a great monster. She remembered the nights she and her friends had climbed the winding stairs to the tower at midnight to tell ghost stories.

"Let's have a cup of tea before we start," Rose said. "Shall we go to the Kendall Tea Room, or that other one?"

Annie laughed, knowing the Kendall Tea Room was for the people of class while the other was for the farmers and the servants that worked in the big houses. The "other one," as Rose called it, was where Annie used to go when she was a girl, but Annie knew it was beneath Rose's station in life. Annie told Rose the Kendall would be fine.

After tea and a fine selection of cakes, the ladies went on to the shops. Annie found that her money went a lot farther in Ireland than it did in America. For one dollar, she got five pounds worth of goods. She decided to buy all the children woolen scarves: navy blue for the boys, pale green for the girls, and yellow for Laura. Annie laughed at herself for being so careful with money. She had plenty, but couldn't bring herself to be a spendthrift.

It was getting late, so Rose said they'd have to be getting back. Annie knew Rose was worried about Old Da. Rose left Askeaton the way she had entered—on two wheels. Annie hung on for dear life as they rounded the corners.

The automobile came to a sudden halt, throwing Annie forward and knocking her packages to the floor.

"Rose, are you trying to kill us?" Annie screamed.

"Don't worry, deary, I'm a very good driver," Rose said.

When they entered the big cottage, Nora came running. Her face was white and strained.

"I'm glad you're back, Mrs. Enright! The Mister has taken a turn for the worse! I've called Dr. Malone. He's up there now," Nora said.

Annie and Rose raced up the stairs to the bedroom. Dr. Malone put his finger to his lips, letting them know to be quiet. He motioned them out of the room and down the hall.

"How is he?" Rose asked.

"I'm afraid he's very bad," Dr. Malone said softly. "I doubt if he'll last the night."

Rose started to cry as Annie led her downstairs. Tears welled up in Annie's eyes, too, but she held them back, trying to be strong. Rose sat in the sitting room with Dr. Malone as Annie went to the kitchen to ask Nora to bring a pot of strong tea.

Within minutes, Nora arrived carrying a tray. Tears ran down her face as she put it down. Annie remembered how Old Da would roar at Nora for crying so easily. He'd yell that she was watering his soup with her tears.

"Nora, get one of the farmhands to fetch Father Donald, and go to town and spread the word. Then send for young Cornelius and Nellie. Jack and Ellen are probably there, too." As upset as Rose was, she still took charge.

It didn't take long for Father Donald to arrive. He spoke to Rose and Annie, then went to Old Da's room. Annie could see that her father's breathing was shallow and he could barely open his eyes. Rose sat on one side of the bed holding his hand, as Annie took a seat on the other side. Rose was sobbing loudly, but Annie tried to contain herself. Young Cornelius and Nellie arrived, along with Jack and Ellen. They stood quietly at the back of the room. Father Donald gave the last rites as they all bowed their heads. Nora arrived, setting out chairs for the family. Mrs. O'Hara, young Maureen Tobin and Mrs. Kelly were next to arrive. They were known to wail louder than any other women in town. They were always invited for the death watch. The minute the poor soul died, they'd start in. It was considered an old-fashioned custom, but Rose was an old-fashioned lady and insisted on having wailers. She knew Cornelius would want them, too.

Downstairs, more people began to arrive, most of them having stopped their work or closed their shops. Cornelius Enright was well thought of in the community and deserved this show of respect. However, Corbett's Pub would remain open in case the mourners needed a little libation before going on to the Enright cottage.

Candles were lit as the rest of the guests took seats in the sitting room waiting for the passing of Cornelius. Everyone owned a black outfit for such an occasion. A wake or a funeral was a big affair in Askeaton, and everyone knew to be dressed properly. Tea was poured by Nora as the mourners helped themselves to whiskey.

In the bedroom, mumbled prayers were said. Annie took her father's hand and whispered that she loved him. She was sure he heard her. The evening passed as they waited. Dr. Malone checked on Old Da's condition and shook his head, knowing he would die at any minute.

By one o'clock in the morning, Cornelius Enright had left this world. Father Donald said a final prayer and left the room. Rose let out a scream that could be heard in Askeaton. Annie cried quietly as the wailers began. It sent shivers through her, remembering the sounds from when she was a girl.

Annie kissed her father and went downstairs. She was in need of a good strong cup of tea. She knew this was only the beginning, and dreaded the days to come. The cottage was filled with Cornelius's friends. Annie felt warm, so she went outside for a breath of air. It was starting to rain as she stood there looking down through the Craggs. She cried for her father, and missed her children. The night seemed to last forever.

Paddy O'Niel's son was there, and he was very much like his father, who had died years ago and had been Cornelius's drinking chum. Annie laughed as Paddy's wife tried to get him to go home. Old Paddy was always the last to leave a party, and his son was the same.

Annie was glad when the door closed on the last guest. She went to bed, prayed for her father and fell asleep.

The next morning, the wake began. Annie rose early and dressed in the black dress she'd brought with her. She had come well prepared.

Cornelius was laid out in the sitting room. Rose had selected a fine coffin for him. It was mahogany, and had brass handles. He wouldn't be buried in a pine box like the common folk, Rose would say. The drapes were pulled and candles lit as the ladies continued their wailing. Food and drink were ordered by Rose, so no one would go home hungry.

Three sisters arrived from Saint Mary's School to extend their sympathy. Annie had loved the Sisters when she was a girl, and she was happy to see them. They, of course, were not the ones that had taught her as a girl, but they still brought back fond memories. Father Donald stayed with Rose the entire time. During the afternoon, he would say the rosary and everyone would kneel and pray.

The windows were steamed up from the heat. Annie wiped a spot so she could see out. It was raining hard and the wind blew, whipping the trees into a frenzy. The black clouds overhead reminded Annie of the day her mother died.

Jack was in the dining room pouring drinks for his pals. The more they drank, the rowdier they got. Annie didn't like it, but she had been to enough wakes to know that this was the way it was. The ladies sat in little groups talking quietly. The wake was beginning to get on Annie's nerves, and she knew it would go on for some time to come.

At last the three-day wake was over. Annie knew that the funeral would be a grand affair. Askeaton's only undertaker now had a fine hearse to carry the dearly departed to church, but Rose would have none of it. Cornelius had hated automobiles and wouldn't ride in one if he could help it. He had made Rose promise to have him carried to church by six pallbearers, just as his father before him, and he had given Rose a list of the men he'd like to do it. They were honored to be asked. He wanted Mike Corbett, his old friend's son, Pat McGlynn, and Charlie Broody, who was near eighty. Rose worried Charlie would have a heart attack while doing it, but he wouldn't be deterred from the honor. Colin Ryan, Ian Duffy and Danny Casey accepted without hesitation. They were all the sons of Cornelius's long-gone chums from the pub.

Everyone lined up in front of the big cottage. The six men started up the road with the coffin as Father Donald followed saying prayers. Rose walked with Jack, and Annie took young Cornelius's arm. Nellie, Jessica and Ellen filed in behind them. The rest of the mourners came next. It was a long procession, with the entire town taking part.

Up the stone steps of the old church they went carrying the coffin, and then down the aisle to the altar. The family took the front pew as the town's people filled the church. Annie turned and saw the church was overflowing with her father's weeping friends.

Father Donald said the Mass. His voice rose and fell, reminding Annie of Father O'Leary. Father Donald had been taught well by the old priest. There was a young man playing the organ whom Annie didn't recognize. The music echoed through the church.

After Mass, the coffin was carried to the cemetery and placed next to Anne Fitzgerald Enright's grave, his first wife and the mother of his five children. When the time came, Rose would be buried with her first husband, Timothy Maloney. Rose would have preferred to be laid to rest with Cornelius, but knew it wouldn't be proper, and she was a stickler for the rules.

When the service was over, the final prayers were said. Everyone left the cemetery. Rose stayed behind for a few minutes, then joined the rest of the family for the walk home.

The big cottage was crammed with visitors. Annie took charge and ordered Rose to sit down. Nora had done a good job preparing the food and drink. Everything was laid out on the dining room table. Rose invited the fiddler from Corbett's Pub to play for them. She knew it would please Cornelius. Rose clapped her hands to get her guests' attention. Everyone quieted down and waited for her to speak. She lifted a glass to make a toast.

"Here's to me darling Cornelius, God rest his soul," Rose said. "Cornelius said that when this day came he wanted all his family and friends to have a grand time. He wanted music, drink and no tears. He told me he had a good life, and not to be sad."

It didn't take long for the party to get into full swing. Cornelius had been a great toast-maker when the occasion called for it, and now Jack would take over. Annie watched him, and thought how much he looked like their father. He could charm anyone. It was hard to stay mad at him.

The fiddler played as everyone sang. Annie watched as Rose sang her father's favorite songs. Young Cornelius sat quietly next to her. She'd always looked up to her older brother, but she didn't seem to know him anymore. It had been over twenty years, and she realized she'd spent more years in America than here in the Craggs.

The funeral went on for hours. Annie was so tired, every bone in her body ached. She longed to go to bed, but knew she'd have to stay to the end.

By two o'clock in the morning, the last guest left. Rose closed the door and collapsed into a big chair.

"Can I be getting you anything, Annie dear?" Rose asked.

"No, not a thing. It's me bed I'm wanting," Annie said.

"Let's be off," Rose said, as she started up the stairs.

Rose would sleep in the little sewing room for some time to come. It had a small bed, and was most comfortable.

She couldn't bring herself to climb into the big bed in the room that she'd shared with Cornelius for so many years. It would be too empty without him.

Annie woke up early the next morning and felt good, considering the late hour she'd kept the night before. Rose was already seated at the table when Annie entered the dining room. She watched as Rose put five teaspoons of sugar in her tea. Rose's sweet tooth had not changed. Annie saw her eyes were red and swollen from crying, and she felt sorry for her. Rose would be alone now, even though young Cornelius and Nellie lived close by. Jack lived closer to town and only visited when he needed something. Rose was as generous as ever, and denied him nothing. "I can spoil the boy if I want to," Rose would say.

Rose's brother, Martin, and her nephew, Robert, had died long ago, and Annie would be going back to America soon. Rose still had many friends, and there was always Robertstown Church to keep her busy. With the new church being built, Annie knew Rose would run the show. Nora would stay and look after her. Annie wouldn't worry about Rose, knowing she'd be well cared for.

Days passed. Rose pulled herself together and tried to keep Annie entertained. Rose put away her bright colored dresses and wore black. She would wear black until the day she died. Annie knew how much Rose loved clothes, and the gaudier the better. This was a true sacrifice for her.

Rose invited everyone for afternoon teas so that Annie was sure to see all the people she'd known as a girl. Her cousins, the McNulty family, arrived and spent a day of reminiscing. When Annie had left Askeaton, their children, Steven, Thomas and Erin, were only babies. Now, they were grown and had families of their own. As much as Annie enjoyed seeing them, however, she longed to go back to America. She ached to see the children and Henry.

Annie had written to Sis and received two letters in return. They were doing fine and hoped she was well. There was a little tug at her heart, thinking they could do without her.

Jack stopped in often and tried to make up with Annie. She had to admit, it was hard to stay angry, but however hard she tried, deep down she would never really forgive him.

Rose kept Annie busy. She arranged a trip to Dublin, planning to stay in the Ennis Hotel where they had attended Rose's brother's wedding many years before. Annie was delighted to go, but found out that Rose would be driving.

"Do you think you should be driving all that way?" Annie said.

"Of course, deary. I'm an excellent driver," Rose said, as she gave out one of her cackles.

Annie laughed, thinking Rose still sounded like a chicken about to lay an egg. She agreed to have Rose drive, knowing she was taking her life in her hands. She didn't want to hurt her feelings. The morning they left, Annie said ten Hail Mary's. Off they flew, down through the Craggs. When they got to the main road, Rose took the corner on two wheels, causing the automobile to squeal. Annie said ten more Hail Mary's.

"Holy mother of God, Rose! Do you have to go so fast?" Annie said.

"I'm not going fast. I know what I'm doing."

At last, they arrived in Dublin. It hadn't changed one bit in Annie's eyes. All the painted doors and lovely wrought iron fences were the same. She could see the brass name plates gleaming in the sun. Rose drove down a street that looked familiar to Annie. Rose hit the brakes, causing the automobile to come to a screeching halt.

"Rose, take it easy," Annie said.

"When you were a girl, you would have loved it," Rose giggled.

"Well, I'm not a girl, and I'd like to live long enough to get back to America."

The hotel managed greeted Rose, saying he was glad to see her again. She'd been going to the same hotel for forty years, and was well known. Rose introduced Annie, saying she was sure he'd remember her darling stepdaughter. He said certainly he did, and welcomed her. Up the stairs they went as he showed them to their room.

"He remembers me, me foot," Annie laughed.

She had a grand time in Dublin. They went to the best restaurants and saw a show. Rose dragged her off to visit all their old friends. Annie didn't remember many of them, since it was so long ago.

One afternoon, Rose took Annie to see her old friend, Bertha Sweeney. Annie remembered her well. She was a wealthy woman and the leader of Dublin's society. As a girl, Annie had been a bit intimidated by her.

Her front door was still painted purple, a thing Annie remembered since only Mrs. Sweeney had the nerve to have a purple door. Rose pulled the bell handle, all the while peeking in the side window. A houseman opened the door, and Rose informed him that they were expected. He ushered them into a large sitting room. Annie remembered this room and how impressed she'd been as a young farm girl the first time she saw it. Bertha pulled herself up from an easy chair when she saw them enter. Annie could see a big difference in Mrs. Sweeney. She'd been about fifty when Annie left for America, and was now in her seventies. She still put a rinse in her hair, but her face and hands were very wrinkled. She'd lost her girlish figure and was overweight. Annie could see she was wearing a corset, hoping to keep the extra pounds out of sight.

"How lovely to see you, my dear," Bertha said.

"It's grand to be seeing you, too," Rose said. "You remember me stepdaughter, don't you?"

"Of course. How are you, Annie?" Bertha said.

230

"I've been very well, thank you."

The three ladies sat down as the houseman served tea. The room was just the same as it had been when Annie had first visited. The long lace curtains and heavy drapes were new, but the same style. The carpet was thick and the floors shined. The chandelier sparkled, but was now electrified.

"Has Ireland changed much?" Bertha asked.

"A few changes, but still much the same," Annie said.

"I hear you married again after poor Robert passed on, and have a house full of children," Bertha said.

"Yes, I did. And I have seven of the most beautiful children you've ever seen," Annie bragged.

"That's lovely," Bertha said. "I've been admiring your lovely suit. Was it designed for you?"

"Yes, it was," Annie lied. "I have to look nice going to business every day."

"You go to business? My, you are a modern woman," Bertha said.

"Yes, I guess I am," Annie said.

"She has a beautiful home in a very posh town," Rose bragged.

Rose went on and on about Annie's life in America, describing her home as if it were a castle. She told Bertha about Annie's staff, and the stables she owned. Annie couldn't believe the story Rose was concocting. She laughed to herself thinking about her "stables," a cow barn.

Rose knew old Bertha was impressed. Rose knew she'd spread the story, and was glad, now she'd have something to tell the ladies of her "inner circle," as she called them. It was really a circle of gossips.

When Annie first met Bertha, she had a companion living with her. Being young, she hadn't quite understood the relationship. She thought he was a nice young man and asked about him.

"I've been wondering about Richard, your companion. He was a lovely boy. Is he well?" Annie said.

"My goodness, I got rid of him years ago. He got too old for me," Bertha laughed. "Got me a new one. You should see him. He's adorable. Cost me a fortune, but he's worth it."

"That's nice," Annie said, not knowing what else to say.

The afternoon flew as the ladies caught up on the latest gossip. Finally, Rose noticed it was getting late and said they'd have to be on their way. They thanked Bertha for the lovely visit, then left.

"That was a nice visit," Rose said.

"Yes, but I'm wondering what Mrs. Sweeney meant about Richard getting too old?" Annie said. "He was half her age, if he was a day."

"She's been a widow for years, and enjoys the company of younger men. Nothing wrong with that," Rose said. "When they get near thirty, she gets rid of them and gets a new one. She pays them well."

"That's terrible!" Annie said.

"No, it's not. She's got a lot of money and can afford it. You should see her latest," Rose laughed. "He's about twenty, but looks twelve. I think he's Italian. Dark and handsome. I've met him a couple of times, but for the life of me I can't understand a word he says."

"God love her! Isn't she too old for that?" Annie said.

"You're only as old as you feel," Rose giggled.

"Maybe you'll be buying a young man for yourself, too," Annie teased.

"Not me. I couldn't be bothered. Besides, I'm going to give my money to the church. I'm no fool. I want a place in heaven," Rose cackled.

Rose and Annie climbed into the automobile and sped off. As they flew down the street, Annie saw a gentleman's clothing shop. She screamed to Rose to stop. Rose did as she was told and slammed on the breaks.

"What is it?" Rose said.

"I want to go into the men's shop," Annie said.

"You scared the living daylights out of me!" Rose said.

"If you didn't drive so fast, I wouldn't have to be screaming at you."

The ladies entered the shop. Rose engaged a sales clerk in conversation as Annie looked around. She wanted to get Henry something, and she wanted it to be special. She'd tell Rose it was for her oldest son. God forbid she tell her about Henry! Annie saw a pair of gold cuff links that had a small Gaelic design in the center. They were plain, but he was very conservative in his manner of dress and she knew he'd like them.

The next day, Rose and Annie returned to Askeaton. It had been a nice trip, but they were glad to be home. There was a letter from Henry saying he missed her, and one from Sis telling her that all was well. Sis said Albert was counting the days of her return. She had decided to give Laura a rest, and had taken over the cooking. That didn't go over very well with Connie, who said she was trying to poison him. Annie hoped they were taking good care of her precious geraniums.

Jack and Ellen arrived that evening. Jack told stories and jokes, trying to get Annie to laugh. He invited her to their home for a meal, but Annie refused, saying she would be too busy getting ready to go back to America.

Annie knew it was best that Jack had returned to Ireland. The way he had been going, she was sure he would've ended up in jail. Annie marrying Nels was just what he needed for an excuse to go home. Old Da had straightened him out in short order, and marrying Ellen was the best thing that could have happened to him. Losing the children was very sad, however, and there would be no more.

CHAPTER 9

The time for Annie to return to America was nearing.

She went to Mass with Rose every Sunday. She sat in the front pew with Rose and listened to the organ. All the ladies were dressed to the teeth, each trying to outdo the other. Rose had always been the best dressed, but now she'd have to be content with her black, widow's weeds.

Annie made a handsome donation to the building fund of the new church. Father Donald was overwhelmed with her generosity. Deep down, Annie knew she was only trying to impress him. She also knew he'd tell everyone in the parish.

Annie enjoyed the family meals with everyone around the big table. No one sat in Old Da's place at the head of the table. Rose would put a bottle of Irish whiskey and a glass in his place, saying it made her feel like he was still with them. Annie thought it a bit bizarre, but it made Rose happy, and that was what counted.

The night before Annie was to leave, she packed her case and put it near the bedroom door. She kept out her traveling outfit, wanting to look nice when she left. As she was finishing, Rose stuck her head in the door.

"How are you doing, deary?" Rose asked.

"I've just finished packing," Annie said.

As Rose entered the room, Annie could see she was carrying a bottle of Irish whiskey and some lovely wrapped packages.

"Put these in your case. You and the boys can have a drink when you get home," Rose laughed. "I'll bet William and Michael haven't had the good stuff since they left. The packages are just some sweets for the children."

"That's very nice of you, but I don't know if I can be bringing whiskey into the country. I think you have to tell the authorities what you have," Annie said. "There's a law called prohibition that says you can't make or buy spirits."

"That's a stupid law! What idiot thought that up?" Rose said. "Just don't tell them. They're not going to search you, are they?"

"No, I don't think so, but it is against the law," Annie said.

"To hell with them!" Rose cackled loudly. "Tell them it's for medicinal purposes."

Annie spent her last evening with Rose and the family, telling stories of the past. Annie had two glasses of wine, a thing she wasn't used to, but it made her feel good. Young Cornelius was quiet, as usual, and left the limelight to Jack, who was entertaining them with his wild stories.

Annie gave Rose the picture of her family, and accepted photos of her Craggs family to take home. Annie looked at all the faces and knew, this time, she would never see them again. When she left so many years ago with Robert, she thought perhaps she'd return one day, but after she married Nels she had little hope. They all stayed up late that night, not wanting it to end. Annie finally got to bed around three in the morning. She couldn't sleep for thinking about going home.

Annie got up at five o'clock in the morning. The sun was just coming up, and she could hear the birds starting to chirp. She looked out the window and could see her old cottage. She wanted to fix every detail in her mind, knowing she'd never be back. A light could be seen coming from the kitchen. She knew that young Cornelius would be getting ready to join the other men in the daily chore of milking the cows. The cows were Holstein's, black and white, while Emdella at home was a Guernsey, brown and white. She could see them lining up at the meadow gate waiting to be taken in for milking.

Annie dressed in her traveling suit and went downstairs. The cottage was quiet as she made herself a cup of tea. She could hear Nora stirring in her room, and knew she'd be soon starting the morning meal. Annie was hungry, but decided to go for a walk. She went down through the Craggs, singing a song that she'd always loved. She remembered doing this when she was a girl. She walked as far as Corbett's Pub, then back past the little cottage and on up to the church. Annie walked around to the cemetery for one last prayer. She stood in front of her parents' grave and said good-bye as a tear ran down her face.

When she returned to the big cottage, she got a whiff of bacon frying in the kitchen. Rose was busy checking on Nora, making sure the table was set properly.

"Mrs. Enright, I've been setting the table for thirty-five years. I should know what I'm doing by now," Nora said.

"I know, deary, but I want everything to be perfect," Rose said.

Annie laughed, watching the two women. They'd snap at each other, and yet they'd be lost without each other. Rose turned and saw Annie standing there.

"Where have you been?" Rose asked.

236

"Went for a little walk," Annie replied.

"The whole family is coming for breakfast. They should be here very soon," Rose said.

"Good, I'm fair starving," Annie said.

Before long, the family arrived. Rose hadn't mentioned that she'd invited Father Donald, too. Annie liked him well enough, but he did make her uncomfortable. He had a way of looking at her that made her feel guilty, and she knew why.

Everyone took their place, leaving Old Da's chair empty. Father Donald stood and said grace. It lasted a long time, and Annie felt he was giving a sermon, rather than a simple prayer of thanks. He went on and on about people straying from the church and the consequences of such an act. Annie knew he meant her. She thanked the good Lord he didn't say anything about Nels deserting her. She guessed that giving a fine donation to the church still didn't absolve her of her sins, in the priest's eyes.

When the prayer was over, Nora served breakfast. Rose had Nora serve each person individually, rather than family-style. Rose *would* do things properly, or know the reason why. Annie piled her plate and enjoyed the meal.

"This is very tasty, Rose," young Cornelius said.

"Glad you're enjoying it," Rose replied.

Jack was the first to finish, and motioned to Nora to bring more.

"Just leave the platter here," Jack said.

Nora put the platter down, but looked at Rose to get her reaction. Rose nodded, giving her approval. Nora went back to the kitchen, then returned with a basket of hot biscuits and blackberry jam.

"I'll take some of them," Jack called from across the table.

"Jack, don't be so rude," Ellen scolded.

"Aw, come on, old Rosie don't care," Jack laughed.

237

"That's right, me darling boy. You can have anything you want, but don't be calling me 'old Rosie'."

"You're still spoiling him, aren't you?" Annie said.

"That's right. Look at him. He's just like me darling Cornelius, God rest his soul," Rose laughed.

"Did you ever learn to make geranium jelly?" Jack said, trying to be funny.

"No, but if I do, I'll be sending you a big jar,"Annie said.

"She still wants to poison me," Jack laughed.

After breakfast, everyone got ready to leave. The ship was sailing at eleven o'clock, and they wanted to get there in plenty of time. The men was anxious to go on board and see what the new ships were like.

Rose's big black automobile was brought around to the front door. Young Cornelius insisted on driving although Rose wanted to.

"I don't know why you don't want me to drive," Rose said.

"I'm too young to die," young Cornelius laughed.

Nora came from the kitchen, took one look at Annie and started to cry.

"Why are you crying?" Annie said. "I've come home and laid me father to rest and seen all my family. It's time to be going back."

"I know, but I'll be missing you. It's as if the years never passed. You're still the girl I went to school with," Nora sobbed.

"I wouldn't want to be holding me breath since I was a girl," Annie laughed. "Here take me hanky and wipe away the tears."

Nora hugged Annie and disappeared into the kitchen. Jack put Annie's case in the trunk of the automobile as they all piled in. Young Cornelius, Rose and Nellie sat in front, as Ellen, Jack and Annie squeezed into the back. Off they drove down through the Craggs. Annie sat near a window

238

and watched the scenery pass by. Rose started to sing, and the rest joined in.

They arrived in Shannon in plenty of time. Jack carried Annie's bag as they boarded the ship. Young Cornelius helped Rose up the gangplank, as Ellen and Nellie followed. Annie gave the steward her ticket and was directed to her cabin. It looked much the same as the one she'd come over in. She hoped she'd have nice cabin mates again.

"This is pretty nice," Jack said. "A lot better than the one I had."

"Sure is," young Cornelius said. "I remember it well."

"This wouldn't suit me," Rose said. "I should have gotten you better accommodations for the way home."

"This is fine," Annie said. "Let's go on deck. I want to fill me eyes with dear old Ireland before we sail."

The family left the cabin and climbed the stairs. The ladies stood at the rail as Jack and young Cornelius went off to explore the ship. Rose was holding Annie's hand, and tears rolled down her face.

"You're not going to cry again, are you?" Annie said.

"I'm trying me best not to," Rose said. "I wish you could be staying."

"I know, but me family's waiting on me," Annie said.

"You must promise to write," Rose said.

"I will," Annie said, but thought of all the years she would have done anything to hear from her family. Deep down, she was still hurt. Rose was an old lady, so Annie would keep her promise.

A gong sounded, letting the guests know that it was time to leave the ship. Jack and young Cornelius returned.

"I guess this is it, Annie me darling," Jack said.

"It's been grand seeing you again," young Cornelius said. "I never thought I'd see the day."

"It's too bad it took your father's death to bring you home," Rose said.

"I'm glad I was here when his time came," Annie said.

"I am, too," Rose said, as she started to cry.

"Pull yourself together, Rose dear," Nellie said. "We've had a grand time with Annie being home."

"That's right," Ellen said. "Think of all the lovely memories you'll have."

"I guess you're right," Rose said.

The gong sounded again as the farewells began. Jack hugged her, but Annie pulled back. She could see the hurt look in his eyes, but she'd never feel the same towards him, and he knew it.

Young Cornelius kissed her, as did Nellie and Ellen. Rose was the last and clung to Annie, sobbing loudly. At last, young Cornelius pulled her away and led her down the gangplank.

Annie stood at the rail as the ship began to move. She waved to her family until they were out of sight. She remembered the day she'd left with Robert, and was glad there was no rainbow peeking through the clouds. She'd seen one that day so many years ago and thought it to be good luck, but it brought no luck to Robert.

Annie waited until Ireland was out of sight, knowing she'd never see it again. She returned to her cabin, wondering who would be her cabin mates. As she opened the door, she found three nuns.

"Sweet Jesus!" Annie mumbled to herself.

The nuns turned as if they had one body. They smiled and welcomed her in.

"How do you do. I'm Sister Mary Victoria Mitchell."

"How do you do. I'm Annie Nielsen."

"This is Sister Mary Helen Hennesey and Sister Mary Patrick Garrity."

"Nice to meet you," Annie said.

Annie could see that Sister Mary Victoria was young, while the other two were a good age. She also saw that the two older Sisters had taken the bottom bunks, leaving the uppers to Sister Mary Victoria and her. Annie wondered how in the world she'd be able to sleep in the upper, let alone climb up there. Jack had left her case in the middle of the floor, so she moved it out of the way for fear one of the ladies would trip over it. All she needed on this trip was to kill a nun! Annie quickly made the sign of the cross. Maybe it would be the good Lord's way of punishing her or maybe they would find out about her. She hoped not. She'd be very careful not to say much and to watch her language. Deep down, Annie had great guilt about not being married in the Catholic Church, but would never admit it to anyone.

There was only one small chair in the corner, and Annie sat down. She felt very uncomfortable as the three Sisters said a prayer for safe journey. She bowed her head and pretended to pray with them. She was hoping the floor would swallow her up.

The minute they stopped praying, Annie excused herself and left. She walked down the corridor to the second-class salon. It was a large room, with wooden tables and chairs placed around the walls. There was a young man dressed in white behind a counter serving tea. Annie went to the counter and asked for a cup. She carried it back to a corner table and took a seat. The tea was piping hot. Annie blew on it to cool it a bit, and took a sip. She was surprised that it was so good. The tables were filling up as the other passengers arrived. A young woman and man stopped and asked Annie if they could share her table. She agreed, and was glad for the company. They introduced themselves as Hugh and Sally Mullen. They said they were going to live with relatives in Lowell, Massachusetts. Annie told them of the wonders of America, and warned them of the pitfalls. She felt like an expert on the subject.

The days flew as Annie walked the decks and chatted with her new friends, Hugh and Sally. She took her meals with the Sisters, as they were assigned to the same table. They were lovely ladies and very gentle in manner, but she still felt uncomfortable. She had a feeling they knew her secret. It reminded her of the old priest, Father O'Leary, who always knew what you'd done just by looking at you.

At last, they arrived in New York. Annie has been away for two months. She admired the Statue of Liberty and the skyline of the great city. Seeing the Lady this time was under happier circumstances than it had been the first time. Her younger children would be getting out of school for the summer break, and she would glad to be home with them.

Annie said good-bye to the Sisters, who blessed her and wished her well. Down the gangplank she went. There would be no Ellis Island for her this time. She was a resident of the United States of America, and had produced seven American citizens. That was something to be proud of.

Henry was there to meet her. He hugged and kissed her, lifting her right off the ground. Annie compared him to Nels, who acted as if it were a crime to kiss in public.

"How was the trip?" Henry asked.

"Just grand," Annie said. "I have so much to tell you."

"Everyone is at the house waiting for you—your brothers and their wives, and of course, that big brood of yours. Laura has been making the kids clean the house for your coming home, even Connie, who says its girls' work," Henry laughed. "I kept an eye on them. Hope you don't mind."

"Of course not. How's Albert?" Annie asked. "He's the only one I worry about."

"He's fine. Can't wait to see you," Henry said, as he waved for his driver to bring the automobile around.

Henry helped Annie in. Once she was settled, she handed Henry the gift she'd gotten for him.

"What's this? A present for me?" Henry said.

"You're the only one I see around here. Must be," Annie laughed.

Henry was pleased with the gift, and thanked her. Annie explained that the Gaelic sign on the cuff links was for friendship. Henry hoped for more than friendship.

The driver stepped on the gas, and away they went. Annie didn't complain about driving too fast this time. At last, they turned into Bush Avenue. Laura and the children were on the porch waiting for her.

Annie got out of the automobile and was surrounded by her children all screaming questions at the same time. She was pleased to see that Niel and Billy had come from the city for the homecoming.

"Glad you're home," Vincent said. "I sure missed you!"

"I'm glad to be home, me darling," Annie laughed.

The homecoming turned into a grand party. Laura had a lovely baked ham ready to be served, along with hot rolls and cheese. The men drank the Irish whiskey that she'd smuggled into the country, while the children made short work of the sweets.

Michael and William were feeling no pain, and teased Annie about being Mrs. Al Capone, the bootlegger's wife.

"Better watch out! They'll be sending you up the river," Michael laughed.

Annie told the family all about her trip. She went into great detail about the family and her father's death. Hearing about the wake and funeral made Michael cry. He sobbed loudly, saying what a fine old gent his father was. Annie really shocked them when she said she'd found Jack. She told them the whole story. Henry sat there quietly taking it all in. Annie had told him everything about her family since he'd become such a good friend.

"You're telling us Jack's been home all these years?" William asked.

"Yes, and he's married to Ellen Hart and lives right in Askeaton," Annie said. "How do you like that? He's been there since we moved to Balmville."

"I was asking just last week about him! I ran into one of his cronies, and thought he might have some news of him!" Michael roared.

"I can't believe it!" Alexandra said. "Poor William has been worried about him for years. That's some brother you have!"

"Well, he's no brother of mine!" William yelled.

"You can imagine how I felt when he walked in bigger than life? I'll tell you, I had all I could do to keep from smacking him!" Annie said.

"Too bad you didn't. I would have killed him!" Michael said.

"He'll be getting a piece of me mind," William said. "I'll be writing and tell him just what I think of him. Then he'll not be hearing from me again."

"In other words, the whole bleeding family knew where he was and never wrote to tell us?"Michael said.

"I'm afraid so, and it's all me fault," Annie said.

"What are you meaning?" William said.

"If he hadn't gotten so mad at me, this would have never happened."

"Don't be thinking that," Michael said. "He was in trouble, and that's the reason he went back. He's just using you as an excuse. He would have ended up in jail, to be sure.

"Don't you be feeling guilty, Annie. If you didn't go back, we still wouldn't know," William said.

"I'm glad I went. Old Da has been put to rest, and we know where Jack is. That's a lot to be thankful for," Annie said. "Now all I need to know is, what has happened to Nels?"

"To hell with him! You've done better without him," William yelled. "Good riddance!"

"Yeah, he's as bad as Jack," Michael added.

"He's still the children's father," Annie said. "Don't be saying anything in front of them."

Annie's brothers and their wives left, as did Henry. Annie thanked them for coming and told Henry she'd see him at the railroad station come Monday. The children

244

climbed the stair to bed, as Annie followed. It was good to be in her own bed again. From the darkness, she heard a voice.

"Glad you're home, Mom." She knew it was Albert.

The next morning was Sunday. Annie got up early and put a couple of loaves of soda bread in the oven. She always brought it home every weekend from the bakery, but the children thought it tasted better if Annie made it at home. It didn't take long for the aroma to drift up stairs. Within minutes, all seven children were in the kitchen waiting for the bread to bake. Laura appeared and offered to help, but was chased away by Annie saying she had the day off.

"We haven't had any good soda bread since you left," Connie said. "Laura let Sis make some, and it near killed us. Boy, is she a rotten cook!"

"Yeah, and you're a rotten kid!" Sis said, as she smacked him on the head.

"Now, stop that! Sis, you'll be scrambling his brains, and Cornelius, you should be glad having a sister taking good care of you," Annie scolded.

"How can I scramble his brains? He doesn't have any," Sis said, as she hit him again.

"Now finish up! We're all going to Mass," Annie said.

Everyone had an excuse why he couldn't go, but Annie held her ground. Niel had gotten his driver's license and would drive them to church. Annie was proud that he'd brought an automobile on his own. She wanted all her children to be self-sufficient. Annie laughed as Niel walked around the automobile with a soft cloth, polishing every little smudge. Annie counted heads as her family climbed in. Niel warned them not to put their feet on the seats. Annie counted six, and saw one was missing. It was Connie, who'd rather cut off his arm than go to Mass.

"Cornelius, get out here!" Annie demanded.

"Aw, Mom! I got a date," Connie said, sticking his head out the window.

"The only date you'll be having is with the good Lord! Now get your backside out here!" Annie said.

Connie did as he was told and got into the back seat, but not before giving Albert a smack.

"Don't be hitting your brother, Cornelius!" Annie said.

"He was laughing at me," Connie complained.

"It's a free country. I can laugh if I want to," Albert said, as he stuck out his tongue.

Annie always felt good going to Mass, and even better when she could get the whole family to go. She always made sure she sat between Connie and Albert, just in case they decided to poke each other. Saint Mary's needed a priest like Father O'Leary. He could say Mass and still managed to glare at any child who wasn't behaving. "He could put the fear of God into you," Annie would say.

The day flew by as Annie settled in. By five o'clock, she started the evening meal. She had missed cooking for her gang, as she called them. The icebox was well stocked. There were two large chickens ready for roasting. Annie put them and some potatoes in the oven at the same time. There were spring carrots and baby asparagus to go with it. Fresh butter and rolls would add to the meal. Laura kept insisting it was her job, but Annie said she was enjoying herself.

"Best meal we've had since you left, not that Laura's and Sis's weren't good," Albert said, not wanting to hurt their feelings.

"Boy, are you a liar," Connie said.

"Shut up!" Billy said, giving Connie another smack on the head.

Laura did the dinner dishes as everyone else gathered on the front porch. It was a lovely evening, and the last hint of apple blossoms gave off a sweet aroma. The white flowers lay on the ground like snow.

Annie returned to work the next day. Mrs. O'Brien and Mr. Levine were happy to have her back. Annie was glad that everything had gone well under the supervision of John. She hadn't realized how much she'd missed it. They were enlarging the bakery in Park Slope because it was doing so well.

Annie didn't worry about money anymore, and had put aside a tidy sum. She'd always been thrifty, and would never change. The hard days of Balmville were still fresh in her mind. She still kept a tea canister on the top shelf in the pantry, where she saved money at home. There was a great deal of money in it, and Laura warned Annie they could be robbed. Annie said not to worry. It made her feel good knowing there was money close at hand.

CHAPTER 10

Fall arrived with all its color. Annie liked the crisp air and the smell of burning leaves. One cold night in November, Annie was sitting by the fire knitting mittens for Grace and Vincent. It would be Christmas before she knew it, and she wanted to finish them. She could well afford store-bought mittens, but enjoyed making them. It was a sweet reminder of the poor, but happy, Christmases when all her children were babies.

The house was quiet, and Annie dozed off. She woke with a start, thinking she heard someone knocking on the front door. She waited, and heard it again. Annie got up and opened it, thinking one of the children had forgotten his key. She could see someone standing there in the half light. She could tell it wasn't any of her children, so she switched on the porch light. When she saw who it was, she gasped and reeled back. She put her hand to her mouth to stifle a scream.

"Holy mother of God!" Annie cried, as she made the sign of the cross. "I must be seeing things!"

"Yah, it's me. I've come back."

Annie couldn't believe her eyes. It was like a ghost returning from the grave. There stood Nels. Her first thought was to slam the door, but she couldn't move. As Nels stepped forward, she stepped back. She thought she must be dreaming. Her heart was pounding so hard she thought it would burst.

"Can I come in?" Nels said. "It's pretty cold out there."

Annie didn't say a word as she opened the door wider. The light was on in the foyer, giving Annie a better look at him. He was very thin and his hair was white. His face looked like leather being dried in the hot sun. His eyes were the same clear blue. Annie could see he hadn't aged well. She stopped and counted. He was fifty-seven years old. He was wearing a well-worn suit, but his shoes were highly polished. Some things never change, Annie thought. He was carrying a small leather suitcase.

Nels walked into the sitting room and warmed his hands at the fire. Laura appeared, having heard the door close.

"Who the bleeding hell is that?" Laura whispered.

"I'll tell you later," Annie said. "Would you be a dear and make some coffee?"

"Yes, madam! Right away, madam!" Laura said sarcastically.

Laura went off as Nels sat down in a chair close to the fire. Annie stood there, not knowing what to do or say. She was still in a state of shock.

"I guess you're surprised," Nels said.

" 'Surprised' is putting it mildly. Who the hell do you think you are showing up in the middle of the night and scaring me half to death!" Annie said.

"I wanted to come back," Nels said.

"Oh, just like that!" Annie said. "You walk out, leaving me with seven babies and not a cent to feed them, and you want to come back. Well, isn't that lovely!"

Laura returned, carrying a tray. She poured two cups of coffee slowly. Annie knew she was dying to know who the man was, but gave her a look sending her away.

"I see you're doing pretty well," Nels said.

"No thanks to you," Annie said. "By the look of you, I can't be saying the same for you."

Annie realized how cruel she sounded, but she couldn't help it.

"I'm sorry, Annie," Nels said in a small voice.

"Sorry, are you? Well, isn't that just grand!"

"I know what I did was wrong, but I couldn't stand being a failure. I was tired, tired of working and having nothing."

"Nothing, you say? What about our babies? Do you call them nothing? How was I to manage alone?" Annie said.

Nels didn't answer. He sat there sipping the hot coffee. She could see his hands shake as he held the cup. Nels started to cough. His whole body convulsed as he tried to stop. Annie got him a glass of water, hoping it would help.

"That's a terrible cough you have," Annie said.

"Yah. I've had it for months. Can't seem to shake it," Nels said.

"Are you still smoking those stinking cigars?" Annie asked.

"Yah, one a week, like always."

Annie was tired, and could see that Nels wasn't well. She told him he could spend the night. Niel was in the city, so she put him in his room. Annie wished she hadn't opened the door, and thought she'd wake up from a dream at any minute. She went to bed without another word and said her prayers, but she didn't sleep.

250

The next morning, Annie sat at the table with the children having breakfast. She knew she had to tell them that their father had come home. She could hear him coughing all night, and was sure they'd heard him as well. She hoped he'd stay in bed until she had a chance to prepare the children. She wished Niel and Billy were home. She'd need her big boys at a time like this.

Laura served breakfast, then started to leave the dining room, but Annie called her back and asked her to stay. Laura was like one of the family. She had a right to know.

"Mom, you look worried," Sis said.

"I have something very important to tell you," Annie said.

"What's going on?"Connie said.

"There's no easy way to tell you, so I'll come straight out with it," Annie said.

"Don't keep us waiting. I've got work to do," Laura said impatiently.

"What is it?" Sis asked.

"Your father's come home," Annie said, as she looked at the children.

"Dad came back?" Albert said.

"What does he want?" Connie said sarcastically.

"Cornelius, I'll have no disrespect!" Annie warned.

"Sweet Jesus! How long has it been?" Laura said.

"Over seven years," Annie said.

"Aren't you supposed to be declared dead after seven years?" Laura asked.

"That's enough, Laura!" Annie said.

"I don't want to see him," Sis said.

"I do, I do!" Grace yelled.

"Yeah, me too," Vincent added.

"You don't even remember him," Albert said.

"I do, and I remember when he left. We could have all been dead, and he didn't even care," Connie said.

"Yeah, he walked right out on us," Albert added.

251

"Now, children, doesn't the good Lord teach us to be forgiving and kind to one another?"Annie said.

"Let the Lord forgive him and be kind to him! I ain't going to!" Connie said, as he left the room, knocking over his chair.

"Albert, go after him," Annie said.

Annie asked Sis to get the children off to school before she went on to work. She explained that they could see their father when they got home. She knew Nels would be up soon and wanted to talk to him before they saw him. Laura walked away shaking her head. Annie knew she'd hear plenty from *her* later.

Annie sat there not knowing what to do. The older children were full of resentment, while the little ones didn't even remember him. She'd have to tell Henry that very morning. Annie sat there stirring her tea, making a clicking sound on the side of the cup. What was she to do? She couldn't turn her back on Nels. He still was her husband. He seemed to be ill. She'd nurse him back to health, then tell him to be on his way, she thought. What would people say? Everyone assumed she was a widow, something she didn't correct them on. Now they would know she was a deserted woman. The shame of it all! What would her brothers say? The thought of that sent shivers through her. They'd probably get drunk and try to kill Nels. As she sat there, she heard him coming down the stairs.

"Good morning," Nels said.

"Good morning," Annie said coldly. "Will you be having breakfast?"

"Just coffee," Nels said.

Laura entered and poured Nels a cup of coffee. She'd never met him, but knew the story. She glared at him. Annie cleared her throat, letting Laura know to leave the room.

"Well, don't you think you owe me an explanation?" Annie said.

252

"I just couldn't do it anymore. I had no job and no future. I should have never come to this country," Nels said.

"Well, wasn't that just too bad! Poor Nels couldn't take it any more!" Annie said. "So you just leave? Maybe I shouldn't have come to this country either."

"I knew you wouldn't understand," Nels said.

"You're damn right I don't understand! All you thought about was yourself! To blazes with me and the children!" Annie yelled.

"No need to raise your voice," Nels said.

"I'll be raising me voice all I want! This is my house and I can do anything I damn well please!" Annie said.

Nels sat there in silence as Annie went into a tirade. She went on and on about him leaving her and taking the last few dollars.

"If it hadn't been for me friends, we would've starved to death!" Annie roared.

"Yah, yah, your friends! They put bad ideas in your head. Made me look bad," Nels said. "They're the ones that started all the trouble."

"Don't be blaming me friends. You made yourself look bad. Well, I've done pretty well without you. I've made a good life for me and the children," Annie said, sticking the knife in deeper.

Nels started to cough. He shook from head to foot making an awful noise. Annie thought he'd choke to death as he gasped for air. She gave him some water and waited until he composed himself.

"You sound terrible. Have you seen a doctor?" Annie asked.

"No, it'll go away," Nels said. "Can I stay here until I get better?"

"I suppose so," Annie said, knowing she couldn't send him away in his condition. "Niel and Billy will be home tonight. I don't know what they'll be saying. You're going to have to do a lot of explaining. They're young men now."

"They're my sons. A father doesn't have to explain anything," Nels said.

"You haven't been a father to them in years, and you're as arrogant as ever," Annie said.

Annie couldn't believe Nels's attitude. He acted as if he'd been away only for a few days, and expected everyone to forget what he'd done. It was getting late, and Annie still had to go into the city. She told Laura what was going on, and that Nels would be staying.

"Staying?" Laura said. "Are you our of your mind?"

"Don't start," Laura said. "He's ill. I wouldn't send a dog away like that."

Annie left to catch the train as Nels went back to bed. She sat with Henry as usual and told him of Nels's return.

"What are you going to do?" Henry asked. "Are you going to let him stay?"

"I'll have to. He's ill, and he's still me husband, like it or not," Annie said.

"You do what you think best," Henry said. "You know you can count on me."

"You're a dear sweet man, and a good friend," Annie said.

"I best not come to the house for a while," Henry said. "I'll miss seeing the boys, but I'll see you on the train every day."

Annie had a lot of work to do that day, but couldn't keep her mind on it. John noticed she was upset and asked if he could help. She thanked him, but told him everything was fine.

Annie left work early and stopped off to see Mrs. O'Brien. Mrs. O'Brien knew the whole story, but she held her tongue, knowing Annie would do what she thought best. Mr. Levine would be told, but that was as far as it would go. There was no need for any of the workers at the bakeries to know her business.

When she got home that evening, Niel and Billy were already there. Sis and the four younger ones were home as well. When she entered, she could hear Nels talking to them. She was surprised how quiet they were. She looked into the dining room and saw that the table was set. She could hear Laura slamming pots in the kitchen. As she entered the kitchen, Laura looked up.

"I'm glad you're home," Laura said. "I feel very uncomfortable with that old man around," Laura said.

"Whatever do you mean?" Annie said.

"He's been poking around and telling me how to be doing me job. The nerve of him!" Laura said. "If he stays, I'll be leaving."

"You don't mean that. What would I be doing without you?" Annie said. "As soon as he's well, he'll be gone."

"I ate a five-pound box of chocolates today. That's how upset I am!" Laura said.

Annie calmed Laura down and went to the sitting room. Nels was going on at great length telling the children where he'd been. He told them he'd gone back to his brother's farm in Racine, Wisconsin, and how wonderful it was. Annie couldn't believe what she was hearing! He truly thought what he'd done was all right. Grace and Vincent seemed to be warming up to him, but the older ones were distant.

"So, did you make a lot of money while you were away?" Connie said sarcastically.

"No. No money," Nels said.

"Mom did. She bought us this house," Connie boasted. "She buys us anything we want."

"Stop lying. She doesn't buy everything we want," Billy said.

"Yah, your mother did good. I can see that," Nels said.

"Yeah, and she worked like a dog, too," Albert added, being proud of his mother.

Laura entered and said that dinner was ready. Everyone filed out and took their seats. The children's eyes widened as Nels took the chair at the head of the table.

"That's Mom's chair. You're not supposed to sit there," Vincent said.

"That's all right. He can sit there," Annie said.

Laura walked in carrying a soup tureen, and almost dropped it seeing Nels at the head of the table. Annie thought she'd drop it *on* him by the look on her face.

It didn't take long for Nels to come back into their lives. Annie said he did it as fast as he'd left it. She had no feelings for Nels, and would never really forgive him, but he was her husband and she felt sorry for him.

Annie finally got up the nerve to tell her brothers. Michael and Nora were visiting William and Alexandra for the weekend. She knew she'd see them after Mass on Sunday. She purposely waited until Mass was over to tell them. She hoped they wouldn't yell too loud standing there in front of the church. They were furious, and thought Annie was out of her mind taking him back. She explained that he was ill.

"Good! Serves him right!" William said.

"Don't say that," Alexandra scolded.

"I'd like to be giving him a piece of me mind!" Michael yelled.

"Be quiet! We're in front of the church. You can yell all you want when we get home," Nora said.

Annie asked her family not to visit for a while. She had enough to worry about without her brothers starting trouble. They agreed, but didn't like it.

Three months passed as Nels settled in. He acted as if he'd never been away. He spent his days in bed or sitting in front of the fire. Annie would make him hot cups of tea with honey or lemon, which seemed to ease the coughing. When spring arrived, he'd sit on the front porch in the sun. His cough was getting worse, and Annie insisted he see a doctor.

She called Doctor Shaw, who said he would come to the house.

The doctor arrived and entered Nels' bedroom. Annie waited outside, thinking good strong cough syrup would do the trick. She listened at the door and could hear the doctor talking and Nels coughing. In a short time, the doctor came out.

"How is he?" Annie asked.

"It's very bad, Mrs. Nielsen," Doctor Shaw said. "He has consumption in the advanced stage."

"Can you be treating it?" Annie asked.

"I'm afraid it's too far gone," Doctor Shaw said. "He should have seen a doctor a year ago."

"What can I be doing for him?" Annie said.

"He'll have to stay in bed a good part of the time. He won't want to eat, but make him take light meals. Beef broth is good. He'll lose weight, and might have a fever at times. so give him aspirin to bring it down," the doctor said. "I want you to keep the children away from him. They can visit from the door, and you must scrub your hands when you leave him. We wouldn't want to spread the sickness."

"Sweet Jesus, he's dying, isn't he?" Annie said.

"I'm afraid so. It won't be long, but he doesn't know. If you think you should tell him, it's up to you. Call me if I'm needed," Doctor Shaw said as he left.

Annie entered the bedroom and saw Nels lying there. He seemed to white and frail. So this is how it's going to be! He's come home to die, she thought.

It was hard on Annie as she went to work each day. She raced from bakery to bakery making sure everything was running well, then hop on the train to Greenwich. Annie enjoyed the restful train ride, and was glad to be with Henry. He was very understanding and a good listener. When she'd arrive home at night, she'd tend Nels and spend time with the children. They knew how ill their father was, and were on their best behavior. Even Connie and Albert stopped fighting.

257

Annie didn't get much rest, either. She was up and down, seeing to Nels. His coughing kept her awake most of the night.

A few weeks later, Nels got a high fever. Annie called Dr. Shaw, who arrived and examined him. There was little he could do.

"Give him aspirin and a hot toddy," Dr. Shaw said. "Put cool cloths on his head to bring down the fever."

The doctor left, and Annie went to the kitchen and heated some whiskey and sugar. Stirring the toddy, she returned to Nels and spoon-fed him the warm mixture. It seemed to sooth him.

"You're so good to me," Nels said in a weak voice.

Annie wanted to lash out and give him a piece of her mind, but knew it would be too cruel. As Nels's condition worsened, Annie would spend the night on the settee in his room. It was easier than running from her room to his when he needed her.

Annie told Mrs. O'Brien how ill Nels was, and that she'd be taking time off. Her good friend told her not to worry.

One night, Annie was fast asleep when she woke with a start. The house was so quiet, she wondered what was wrong? She listened and realized she didn't hear Nels's coughing. The sun was just filtering through the lace curtains, and she could see him lying there not moving. She went to the bed and called his name. She put her ear to his chest and couldn't hear his heart beating. Annie knew he was dead. She sat there for a long time looking at him and remembering the day she met him. It seemed so long ago. She remembered the good times and how much she once loved him.

Annie always carried her rosary beads in her pocket. She got down on her knees at the side of the bed and prayed for Nels. She wondered what the old Lutheran would say if he knew he was being sent off with "her Catholic prayers,"

258

as he called them. She pulled the sheet up over his face and closed the drapes. When she left the room, she locked the door, not wanting the children to enter.

Annie scrubbed her hands, remembering what Doctor Shaw had told her, and went downstairs to the waiting children. She told them as gently as she could that Dad had died. Annie then sent for the doctor, knowing it wouldn't be official until he arrived.

There were mixed reactions from the children. The older ones offered their help, while Grace and Vincent cried.

"Is Dad going to heaven?" Vincent asked through tears.

"Yes, he is, and I expect he'll be with his mother," Annie said softly.

"Will she take care of him?" Grace asked.

"To be sure, me darling. She'll take good care of him," Annie said.

Connie, who always had something to say, didn't say a word. He went out to the barn saying he had to milk Emdella. Annie knew he was on the verge of tears, but would never admit it. Albert didn't say anything. He went to his room, wanting to be alone.

Doctor Shaw arrived and pronounced Nels dead. Mr. Knapp, the funeral director, was called and spoke to Annie. She included the older children in making the arrangements. It had always been Nels's wish to be cremated, and his ashes to be sent home to Denmark. He wanted to be buried with his mother, a thing Annie had teased him about. At the time, she thought it could never be, but now she had the money to carry out Nels's last wish.

It was arranged that there would be a private memorial service at the funeral home, and Mr. Knapp would take care of returning Nels to Denmark. As Niel drove the family home, not a word was spoken. A lovely arrangement of flowers was waiting for them when they got there. It was from Henry.

259

Laura had made a light lunch and laid it out in the dining room. The children were very quiet.

"How come you didn't cry?" Billy asked, as he took his mother's hand. "You were married to him for a long time."

"I cried an ocean of tears over that man for years. I have none left," Annie said.

Annie cleaned Niel's room. She scrubbed it from floor to ceiling. Doctor Shaw said it had to be disinfected so the sickness wouldn't spread. Neil complained about the terrible smell of pine for weeks after.

While Annie was cleaning, she came across Nels's suitcase in the closet. She opened it and found a few shabby shirts, along with socks and underwear. In the bottom, wrapped in a cloth, was the little wooden cross that Nels had brought from Denmark. Annie had forgotten about it. There was a letter from his mother folded neatly. It was so old, the paper had turned yellow and the writing was practically worn off. It wasn't much to show for a life, Annie thought.

That evening, Annie sat on the front porch in her favorite wicker chair and admired her family. It was sad that Nels had missed so much. Niel was sitting on the wicker settee next to her with his long legs outstretched. Sis was next to him with her legs crossed, her skirt neatly pulled down. Sis was Annie's young lady, to be sure. Grace was hanging by her knees at the end of the porch. Annie didn't worry about her. Grace was her tomboy and was always hanging from something. She was a skinny little girl, but as tough as the boys. Albert, Connie and Billy sat on the front steps being very quiet for a change. Vincent was almost eight and still liked to sit on his mother's lap. His big brothers would tease him and call him a baby, but he'd stick his chin out, smack whoever was closest to him and announce to the world that he was a big boy.

Annie sat there rocking Vincent and looking up at the stars. She thought about Nels, and hoped he was at peace.

She was sure her parents were together again in heaven. It was good that she'd gone back to Ireland, said good-bye to her father and found Jack. At least that was settled in her mind. Annie would say many prayers, trying to find forgiveness in her heart for Jack and Nels, but it would take a long time.

Annie thought back over her life and decided she wouldn't have changed a thing. Her dream of coming to America and having seven children had come true. She'd been poor at times, but being poor wasn't all that bad, especially when you don't know your poor. "Food on the table, a roof over your head and a pair of shoes are all we need," Annie would say. She was happy she'd prospered, and proud that she had done it on her own. Henry would be a good friend and companion to her for many years. He would have liked to be more than a friend, but Annie was happy just the way it was. "Two husbands is more than enough for any woman," she'd laugh.

Annie continued to work for many years, taking the train every day to the city. They would lose two bakeries during the Great Depression, but they managed to survive with just one. Mrs. O'Brien and Mr. Levine retired. John Quinn stayed and continued to work for Annie. She considered him her right arm. Laura, who had started out as a servant, became Annie's best friend and stayed with her. Annie never did find the recipe for sweet geranium jelly.

As time went on, each child would marry and leave home. They would present her with many grandchildren. Annie taught them the same silly songs she'd taught her own children. They loved to hear about the fairy folk and the ghosts that roamed the halls of Desmond's Castle. Nobody could tell a story better. She acted out the parts as her tale unfolded, making it real to the children.

Annie continued to bake soda bread on Sunday for her grandchildren. They would gather around the kitchen table waiting for the first loaf to come out of the oven. She could have brought it home from the bakery, but it was always better made at home in the old coal stove. She'd stand back, wipe her hands on her apron and decide she'd done a good job raising her children, and now she would enjoy her grandchildren. "God love them," Annie would say.

ANNIE'S SODA BREAD

4 cups sifted flour	1 cup raisins
3/4 cup sugar	1/4 cup butter
1 tsp. salt	1 1/3 cup buttermilk
1 tsp. baking powder	1 egg
3 tbs. caraway seeds	1 tsp. baking soda

Sift and mix dry ingredients, except baking soda. Stir in caraway seeds and raisins. Cut in butter. Combine buttermilk, egg and soda in small bowl. Mix with dry ingredients. Turn onto floured surface and knead. Put in greased pans and bake at 350° for 40 minutes. Makes 2 small loaves.